That Printer Of Udell's
A Story Of The Middle West

by
Harold Bell Wright

That Printer Of Udell's
A Story Of The Middle West
by Harold Bell Wright

Copyright © 2024

All Rights reserved.

No part of this publication may be reproduced, stored in a retrieval system, or transmitted in any form or by any means, electronic, mechanical, photocopying or Otherwise, without the written permission of the publisher.
The author/editor asserts the moral right to be identified as the author/editor of this work.

ISBN: 978-93-63056-42-8

Published by

DOUBLE 9 BOOKS
2/13-B, Ansari Road
Daryaganj, New Delhi – 110002
info@double9books.com
www.double9books.com
Tel. 011-40042856

This book is under public domain

ABOUT THE AUTHOR

Harold Bell Wright, a well-known American author, speaker, and clergyman who lived from May 4, 1872, to May 24, 1944, is most remembered for his widely read books from the early 20th century. Wright was raised in a pious Baptist household and was raised in Rome, New York. His early upbringing was heavily influenced by religion, which laid the groundwork for his future work as a writer and clergyman. Before focusing on the ministry, Wright attended Boston University College of Oratory to further his studies in music. Although he was a pastor in many places, he gained widespread notoriety for his literary works. Wright pursued his writing career in addition to his ministry work, giving sermons and discussing social and theological concerns. He rose to prominence as a speaker and was well-liked outside of the literary community. Wright's ability to entwine moral teachings into compelling stories has had a significant influence on American literature. This talent enables his writings to be both thought-provoking and entertaining.

CONTENTS

DEDICATION 7
CHAPTER I 8
CHAPTER II 18
CHAPTER III 23
CHAPTER IV 29
CHAPTER V 37
CHAPTER VI 41
CHAPTER VII 48
CHAPTER VIII 55
CHAPTER IX 61
CHAPTER X 68
CHAPTER XI 75
CHAPTER XII 84
CHAPTER XIII 91
CHAPTER XIV 99
CHAPTER XV 105
CHAPTER XVI 112
CHAPTER XVII 119
CHAPTER XVIII 124
CHAPTER XIX 130
CHAPTER XX 139
CHAPTER XXI 148
CHAPTER XXII 156
CHAPTER XXIII 167

CHAPTER XXIV 175
CHAPTER XXV 182
CHAPTER XXVI 192
CHAPTER XXVII 199
CHAPTER XXVIII 204
CHAPTER XXIX 211

DEDICATION

TO THAT FRIEND WHOSE LIFE HAS TAUGHT ME MANY BEAUTIFUL TRUTHS; WHOSE WORDS HAVE STRENGTHENED AND ENCOURAGED ME TO LIVE MORE TRUE TO MY GOD, MY FELLOWS AND MYSELF; WHO HOPED FOR ME WHEN OTHERS LOST HOPE; WHO BELIEVED IN ME WHEN OTHERS COULD NOT; WHO SAW GOOD WHEN OTHERS LOOKED FOR EVIL; TO THAT FRIEND, WHOEVER HE IS, WHEREVER HE MAY BE, I AFFECTIONATELY DEDICATE THIS STORY.

H. B. W.

"And the King shall answer and say unto them, Verily I say unto you, Inasmuch as ye did it unto one of these my brethren, even these least, ye did it unto me."

CHAPTER I

"O God, take ker' o' Dick!—He'll sure have a tough time when I'm gone,—an' I'm er' goin'—mighty fast I reckon.—I know I aint done much ter brag on,—Lord,—but I aint had nary show.—I allus 'low'd ter do ye better,—but hit's jes' kept me scratchin'—ter do fer me an' Dick,—an' somehow I aint had time—ter sarve—ye like I ought.—An' my man he's most ways—no 'count an' triflin',—Lord,—'cepten when he likers up,—an' then,—you know how he uses me an' Dick.—But Dick, he aint no ways ter blame—fer what his dad an' mammy is,—an' I ax ye—fair,—o Lord,—take ker o' him—fer—Jesus' sake—Amen."

"Dick!—O Dick,—whar are ye honey?"

A hollow-cheeked wisp of a boy arose from the dark corner where he had been crouching like a frightened animal, and with cautious steps drew near the bed. Timidly he touched the wasted hand that lay upon the dirty coverlid.

"What ye want, maw?"

The woman hushed her moaning and turned her face, upon which the shadow was already fallen, toward the boy. "I'm er goin'—mighty fast,—Dicky," she said, in a voice that was scarcely audible. "Whar's yer paw?"

Bending closer to the face upon the pillow, the lad pointed with trembling finger toward the other end of the cabin and whispered, while his eyes grew big with fear, "Sh—, he's full ergin. Bin down ter th' stillhouse all evenin'—Don't stir him, maw, er we'll git licked some more. Tell me what ye want."

But his only answer was that broken prayer as the sufferer turned to the wail again. "O Lord, take ker o'—"

A stick of wood in the fire-place burned in two and fell with a soft thud on the ashes; a lean hound crept stealthily to the boy's side and thrust a cold muzzle against his ragged jacket; in the cupboard a mouse rustled over the rude dishes and among the scanty handful of provisions.

Then, cursing foully in his sleep, the drunkard stirred uneasily and the dog slunk beneath the bed, while the boy stood shaking with fear until all was still again. Reaching out, he touched once more that clammy hand upon the dirty coverlid. No movement answered to his touch. Reaching farther, he cautiously laid his fingers upon the ashy-colored temple, awkwardly brushing back a thin lock of the tangled hair. The face, like the hand, was cold. With a look of awe and horror in his eyes, the child caught his parent by the shoulder and shook the lifeless form while he tried again and again to make her hear his whispered words.

"Maw! Maw! Wake up; hit'l be day purty soon an' we can go and git some greens; an' I'll take the gig an' kill some fish fer you; the's a big channel cat in the hole jes' above the riffles; I seed 'im ter day when I crost in the john boat. Say Maw, I done set a dead fall yester'd', d' reckon I'll ketch anythin'? Wish't it 'ud be a coon, don't you?—Maw! O Maw, the meal's most gone. I only made a little pone las' night; thar's some left fer you. Shant I fix ye some 'fore dad wakes up?"

But there was no answer to his pleading, and, ceasing his efforts, the lad sank on his knees by the rude bed, not daring even to give open expression to his grief lest he arouse the drunken sleeper by the fireplace. For a long time he knelt there, clasping the cold hand of his lifeless mother, until the lean hound crept again to his side, and thrusting that cold muzzle against his cheek, licked the salt tears, that fell so hot.

At last, just as the first flush of day stained the eastern sky, and the light tipped the old pine tree on the hill with glory, the boy rose to his feet. Placing his hand on the head of his only comforter, he whispered, "Come on, Smoke, we've gotter go now." And together boy and dog crept softly across the room and stole out of the cabin door—out of the cabin door, into the beautiful light of the new day. And the drunken brute still slept on the floor by the open fire-place, but the fire was dead upon the hearth.

"He can't hurt maw any more, Smoke," said the lad, when the two were at a safe distance. "No, he sure can't lick her agin, an' me an' you kin rustle fer ourselves, I reckon."

Sixteen years later, in the early gray of another morning, a young man crawled from beneath a stack of straw on the outskirts of Boyd City, a busy, bustling mining town of some fifteen thousand people, in one of the middle western states, many miles from the rude cabin that stood beneath the hill.

The night before, he had approached the town from the east, along the road that leads past Mount Olive, and hungry, cold and weary, had sought shelter of the friendly stack, much preferring a bed of straw and the companionship of cattle to any lodging place he might find in the city, less clean and among a ruder company.

It was early March and the smoke from a nearby block of smelters was lost in a chilling mist, while a raw wind made the young man shiver as he stood picking the bits of straw from his clothing. When he had brushed his garments as best he could and had stretched his numb and stiffened limbs, he looked long and thoughtfully at the city lying half hidden in its shroud of gray.

"I wonder"—he began, talking to himself and thinking grimly of the fifteen cents in his right-hand pants pocket—"I wonder if—"

"Mornin' pard," said a voice at his elbow. "Ruther late when ye got in las' night, warn't it?"

The young man jumped, and turning faced a genuine specimen of the genus hobo. "Did you sleep in this straw-stack last night?" he ejaculated, after carefully taking the ragged fellow's measure with a practiced eye.

"Sure; this here's the hotel whar I put up—slept in the room jes' acrost the hall from your'n.—Whar ye goin' ter eat?"—with a hungry look.

"Don't know. Did you have any supper last night?"

"Nope, supper was done et when I got in."

"Same here."

"I didn't have nothin' fer dinner neither," continued the tramp, "an' I'm er gettin' powerful weak."

The other thought of his fifteen cents. "Where are you going?" he said shortly.

The ragged one jerked his thumb toward the city. "Hear'd as how thar's a right smart o' work yonder and I'm on the hunt fer a job."

"What do you do?"

"Tendin' mason's my strong-holt. I've done most ever'thing though; used ter work on a farm, and puttered round a saw-mill some in the Arkansaw pineries. Aim ter strike a job at somethin' and go back thar where I know folks. Nobody won't give a feller nuthin' in this yer God-fer-saken country; haint asked me ter set down fer a month. Back home they're allus glad ter have a man eat with 'em. I'll sure be all right thar."

The fellow's voice dropped to the pitiful, pleading, insinuating whine of the professional tramp.

The young man stood looking at him. Good-for-nothing was written in every line of the shiftless, shambling figure, and pictured in every rag of the fluttering raiment, and yet—the fellow really was hungry,—and again came the thought of that fifteen cents. The young man was hungry himself; had been hungry many a time in the past, and downright, gnawing, helpless hunger is a great leveler of mankind; in fact, it is just about the only real bond of fellowship between men. "Come on," he said at last, "I've got fifteen cents; I reckon we can find something to eat." And the two set out toward the city together.

Passing a deserted mining shaft and crossing the railroad, they entered the southern portion of the town, and continued west until they reached the main street, where they stopped at a little grocery store on the corner. The one with the fifteen cents invested two-thirds of his capital in crackers and cheese, his companion reminding the grocer meanwhile that he might throw in a little extra, "seein' as how they were the first customers that mornin'." The merchant, good-naturedly did so, and then turned to answer the other's question about work.

"What can you do?"

"I'm a printer by trade, but will do anything."

"How does it happen you are out of work?"

"I was thrown out by the Kansas City strike and have been unable to find a place since."

"Is he looking for work too?" with a glance that made his customer's face flush, and a nod toward the fellow from Arkansas, who sat on a box near the stove rapidly making away with more than his half of the breakfast.

The other shrugged his shoulders, "We woke up in the same straw-stack this morning and he was hungry, that's all."

"Well," returned the store-keeper, as he dropped the lid of the cracker box with a bang, "You'll not be bothered with him long if you are really hunting a job."

"You put me on the track of a job and I'll show you whether I mean business or not," was the quick reply. To which the grocer made answer as he turned to his task of dusting the shelves: "There's lots of work in Boyd City and lots of men to do it."

The stranger had walked but a little way down the street when a voice close behind him said, "I'm erbliged ter ye for the feed, pard; reckon I'll shove erlong now."

He stopped and the other continued: "Don't much like the looks of this yer' place no how, an' a feller w'at jes' come by, he said as how thar war heaps o' work in Jonesville, forty miles below. Reckon I'll shove erlong.

Aint got the price of er drink hev' ye? Can't ye set 'em up jest fer old times' sake ye know?" and a cunning gleam crept into the bloodshot eyes of the vagabond.

The other started as he looked keenly at the bloated features of the creature before him, and there was a note of mingled fear and defiance in his voice as he said, "What do you mean? What do you know about old times?"

The tramp shuffled uneasily, but replied with a knowing leer, "Aint ye Dicky Falkner what used ter live cross the river from Jimpson's still-house?"

"Well, what of it?" The note of defiance was stronger.

"Oh nuthin, only I'm Jake Tompkins, that used ter work fer Jimpson at the still. Me 'n yer daddy war pards; I used ter set 'em up ter him heap o' times."

"Yes," replied Dick bitterly, "I know you now. You gave my father whiskey and then laughed when he went home drunk and drove my mother from the cabin to spend the night in the brush. You know it killed her."

"Yer maw allus was weakly-like," faltered the other; "she'd no call ter hitch up with Bill Falkner no how; she ort ter took a man with book larnin' like her daddy, ole Jedge White. It allus made yer paw mad 'cause she knowed more'n him. But Bill lowed he'd tame her an' he shor' tried hit on. Too bad she went an' died, but she ort ter knowed a man o' Bill's spirit would a took his licker when he wanted hit. I recollect ye used ter take a right smart lot yerself fer a kid."

The defiance in the young man's voice gave way to a note of hopeless despair. "Yes," he said, "you and dad made me drink the stuff before I was old enough to know what it would do for me." Then, with a bitter oath, he continued, half to himself, "What difference does it make anyway. Every time I try to break loose something reaches out and pulls me down again. I thought I was free this time sure and here comes this thing. I might as well go to the devil and done with it. Why shouldn't I drink if I want to; whose business is it but my own?" He looked around for the familiar sign of a saloon.

"That's the talk," exclaimed the other with a swagger. "That's how yer paw used ter put it. Your maw warn't much good no how, with her finicky notions 'bout eddicati'n an' sech. A little pone and baken with plenty good ol' red eye's good 'nough fer us. Yer maw she—"

But he never finished, for Dick caught him by the throat with his left hand, the other clenched ready to strike. The tramp shrank back in a frightened, cowering heap.

"You beast," cried the young man with another oath. "If you dare to take my mother's name in your foul mouth again I'll kill you with my bare hands."

"I didn't go fer to do hit. 'Fore God I didn't go ter. Lemme go Dicky; me'n yer daddy war pards. Lemme go. Yer paw an' me won't bother ye no more Dicky; he can't; he's dead."

"Dead!" Dick released his grasp and the other sprang to a safe distance.—"Dead!" He gazed at the quaking wretch before him in amazement.

The tramp nodded sullenly, feeling at his throat. "Yep, dead," he said hoarsely. "Me an' him war bummin' a freight out o' St. Louie, an' he slipped. I know he war killed 'cause I saw 'em pick him up; six cars went over him an' they kept me in hock fer two months."

Dick sat down on the curbing and buried his face in his hands. "Dead—Dead"—he softly repeated to himself. "Dad is dead—killed by the cars in St. Louis.—Dead—Dead—"

Then all the past life came back to him with a rush: the cabin home across the river from the distillery; the still-house itself, with the rough men who gathered there; the neighboring shanties with their sickly, sad-faced women, and dirty, quarreling children; the store and blacksmith shop at the crossroads in the pinery seven miles away. He saw the river flowing sluggishly at times between banks of drooping willows and tall marsh grass, as though smitten with the fatal spirit of the place, then breaking into hurried movement over pebbly shoals as though trying to escape to some healthier climate; the hill where stood the old pine tree; the cave beneath the great rock by the spring; and the persimmon grove in the bottoms. Then once more he suffered with his mother, from his drunken father's rage and every detail of that awful night in the brush, with the long days and nights of sickness that followed before her death, came back so vividly that he wept again with his face in his hands as he had cried by the rude bedside in the cabin sixteen years ago. Then came the years when he had wandered from his early home and had learned to know life in the great cities. What a life he had found it. He shuddered as it all came back to him now. The many times when inspired by the memory of his mother, he had tried to break away from the evil, degrading things that were in and about him, and the many times he had been dragged back by the training and memory of his father; the gambling, the fighting, the drinking, the periods of hard work, the struggle to master his trade, and the reckless wasting of wages in times of wild despair again. And now his father was dead—dead—he shuddered. There was nothing to bind him to the past now; he was free.

"Can't ye give me that drink, Dicky? Jest one little horn. It'll do us both good, an' then I'll shove erlong; jes fer old times' sake, ye know."

The voice of the tramp broke in upon his thoughts. For a moment longer he sat there; then started to his feet, a new light in his eye; a new ring in his voice.

"No, Jake," he said slowly; "I wouldn't if I could now. I'm done with the old times forever." He threw up his head and stood proudly erect while the tramp gazed in awe at something in his face he had never seen before.

"I have only five cents in the world," continued Dick. "Here, take it. You'll be hungry again soon and—and—Good bye, Jake—Good bye—" He turned and walked swiftly away while the other stood staring in astonishment and wonder, first at the coin in his hand, then at the retreating figure. Then with an exclamation, the ragged fellow wheeled and started in the opposite direction toward the railroad yards, to catch a south-bound freight.

Dick had walked scarcely a block when a lean hound came trotting across the street. "Dear old Smoke," he said to himself, his mind going back to the companion of his early struggle—"Dear old Smoke." Then as the half-starved creature came timidly to his side and looked up at him with pleading eyes, he remembered his share of the breakfast, still untouched, in his pocket. "You look like an old friend of mine," he continued, as he stooped to pat the bony head, "a friend who is never hungry now—, but you're hungry aren't you?" A low whine answered him. "Yes, you're hungry all right." And the next moment a wagging tail was eloquently giving thanks for the rest of the crackers and cheese.

The factories and mills of the city gave forth their early greeting, while the sun tried in vain to drive away the chilly mist. Men with dinner buckets on their arms went hurrying along at call of the whistles, shop-keepers were sweeping, dusting and arranging their goods, a street-car full of miners passed, with clanging gong; and the fire department horses, out for their morning exercise, clattered down the street. Amid the busy scene walked Dick, without work, without money, without friends, but with a new purpose in his heart that was more than meat or drink. A new feeling of freedom and power made him lift his head and move with a firm and steady step.

All that morning he sought for employment, inquiring at the stores and shops, but receiving little or no encouragement. Toward noon, while waiting for an opportunity to interview the proprietor of a store, he picked up a daily paper that was lying on the counter, and turning to the "want" column, read an advertisement for a man to do general work about the barn and yard. When he had received the usual answer to his request for work, he went at once to the address given in the paper.

"Is Mr. Goodrich in?" he asked of the young man who came forward with a look of inquiry on his face.

"What do you want?" was the curt reply.

"I want to see Mr. Goodrich," came the answer in tones even sharper, and the young man conducted him to the door of the office.

"Well," said a portly middle-aged gentleman, when he had finished dictating a letter to the young lady seated at the typewriter, "What do you want?"

"I came in answer to your ad in this morning's Whistler," answered Dick.

"Umph—Where did you work last?"

"At Kansas City. I'm a printer by trade, but willing to do anything until I get a start."

"Why aren't you working at your trade?"

"I was thrown out by the strike and have been unable to find anything since."

A look of anger and scorn swept over the merchant's face. "So you're one of that lot, are you? Why don't you fellows learn to take what you can get? Look there." He pointed to a pile of pamphlets lying on the table. "Just came in to-day; they cost me fifty per cent more than I ever paid before, just because you cattle can't be satisfied; and now you want me to give you a place. If I had my way, I'd give you, and such as you, work on the rock pile." And he wheeled his chair toward his desk again.

"But," said Dick, "I'm hungry—I must do something—I'm not a beggar—I'll earn every cent you pay me."

"I tell you no," shouted the other. "I won't have men about me who look above their position," and he picked up his pen.

"But, Sir," said Dick again, "what am I to do?"

"I don't care what you do," returned the other. "There is a stone-yard here for such as you."

"Sir," answered Dick, standing very straight, his face as pale as death. "Sir, you will yet learn that it does matter very much what such fellows as I do, and some day you will be glad to apologize for your words this morning. I am no more worthy to work on the rock pile than yourself. As a man, I am every bit your equal, and will live to prove it. Good morning, Sir." And he marched out of the office like a soldier on parade, leaving the young lady at the typewriter motionless with amazement, and her employer dumb with rage.

What induced him to utter such words Dick could not say; he only knew that they were true, and they seemed somehow to be forced from him; though in spite of his just anger he laughed at the ridiculousness of the situation before he was fairly away from the building.

The factory whistles blew for dinner, but there was no dinner for Dick; they blew again for work at one o'clock, but still there was nothing for Dick to do. All that afternoon he continued his search with the same result— We don't need you. Some, it is true, were kind in their answers. One old gentleman, a real estate man, Dick felt sure was about to help him, but he was called away on business, and the poor fellow went on his weary search again.

Then the whistles blew for six o'clock, and the workmen, their faces stained with the marks of toil, hurried along the streets toward home; clerks and business men crowded the restaurants and lunch counters, the street cars were filled with shoppers going to their evening meal. Through hungry eyes, Dick watched the throng, wondering what each worked at during the day and what they would have for supper.

The sun went behind a bank of dull, lead-colored clouds and the wind sprang up again, so sharp and cold that the citizens turned up the collars of their coats and drew their wraps about them, while Dick sought shelter from the chilly blast in an open hallway. Suddenly a policeman appeared before him.

"What are you doing here?"

"Nothing," answered Dick.

"Wal, ye'd better be doing something. I've had my eye on you all the afternoon. I'll run ye in if I ketch ye hanging round any more. Get a move on now." And Dick stepped out on the sidewalk once more to face the bitter wind.

Walking as rapidly as possible, he made his way north on Broadway, past the big hotel, all aglow with light and warmth, past the vacant lots and the bicycle factory, until he reached the ruins of an old smelter just beyond the Missouri Pacific tracks. He had noticed the place earlier in the day as he passed it on his way to the brickyard. Groping about over the fallen walls of the furnace, stumbling over scraps of iron and broken timbers in the dusk, he searched for a corner that would in some measure protect him from the wind. It grew dark very fast, and soon he tripped and fell against an old boiler lying upturned in the ruin. Throwing out his hand to save himself, by chance, he caught the door of the firebox, and in a moment more was inside, crouching in the accumulated dirt, iron rust and ashes. At least the wind could not get at him here; and leaning his back against the iron wall of his strange bed-room, tired and hungry, he fell asleep.

CHAPTER II

The next morning Dick crawled from his rude lodging place stiff and sore, and after making his toilet as best he could, started again on his search for employment. It was nearly noon when he met a man who in answer to his inquiry said: "I'm out of a job myself, stranger, but I've got a little money left; you look hungry."

Dick admitted that he had had no breakfast.

"Tell you what I'll do," said the other. "I ain't got much, but we can go to a joint I know of where they set up a big free lunch. I'll pay for the beer and you can wade into the lunch."

Poor Dick, weak from hunger, chilled with the March winds, tired and discouraged, he forgot his resolve of the day before and followed his would-be benefactor. It was not far and they soon stood in a well-warmed saloon. The grateful heat, the polished furniture, the rows of bottles and glasses, the clean-looking, white-jacketed and aproned bar-tender, and the merry air of those whom he served, were all wonderfully attractive to the poor shivering wanderer from out in the cold. And then there was the long table well loaded with strong, hot food. The starving fellow started toward it eagerly, with outstretched hand. "Two beers here," cried his companion.

Then Dick remembered his purpose. The hand reaching out to grasp the food was withdrawn; his pale face grew more haggard. "My God!" he thought, "what can I do. I must have food."

He saw the bartender take two large glasses from the shelf. His whole physical being plead with him, demanding food and drink, and shaking like a leaf he gazed about him with the air of a hunted thing.

He saw one of the glasses in the hand of the man in the white jacket and apron filling with the amber liquid. A moment more and—"Stop!" he cried, rushing toward the one who held the glasses. "Stop! it's a mistake. I don't drink."

The man paused and looked around with an evil leer, one glass still unfilled in his hand. Then with a brutal oath, "What are ye in here for then?"

Dick trembled. "I—I—was cold and hungry—" his eyes sought the food on the table—"and—and—this gentleman asked me to come. He's not to blame; he thought I wanted a drink."

His new-found friend looked at him with a puzzled expression. "Oh take a glass, stranger. You need it; and then help yourself to the lunch."

Dick shook his head; he could not speak.

"Look here!" broke in the bartender, with another string of vile language, as he quickly filled the empty glass and set it on the counter before Dick. "You drink this er git out. That there lunch is fer our customers and we aint got no room fer temperance cranks er bums. Which'll it be? Talk quick."

Dick's eyes went from the food to the liquor; then to the saloon man's hard face, while a strange hush fell over those who witnessed the scene. Slowly the stranger swept the room with a pleading glance, but met only curious indifference on every side. Again he turned to the food and liquor, and put out his hand. A light of triumph flashed in the eyes of the man behind the bar, but the hand was withdrawn and Dick backed slowly toward the door. "I won't," he said, between his clenched teeth, then to his would-be friend, "Thank you for your good intention."

The silence in the room was broken by a shout of harsh laughter as the bartender raised the glass of beer he had drawn for Dick and mockingly drank him good luck as the poor fellow stepped through the doorway leaving warmth and food behind.

All that day Dick continued his search for work. Night came on again and he found himself wandering, half dazed, in the more aristocratic portion of the city. He was too tired to go to the old smelter again. He could not think clearly and muttered and mumbled to himself as he stumbled aimlessly along.

The door of a cottage opened, letting out a flood of light, and a woman's voice called, "Dick, Oh Dick, come home now; supper is waiting." And a lad of ten, playing in the neighboring yard with his young companion, answered with a shout as he bounded across the lawn. Through the windows our Dick caught a glimpse of the cosy home: father, mother, two sisters, bright pictures, books, and a table set with snowy linen, shining silver and sparkling glass.

Later, strange voices seemed to call him, and several times he paused to listen. Then someone in the distance seemed to say, "Move on; Move on." The words echoed and re-echoed through his tired brain. "Move on; Move on," the weary, monotonous strain continued as he dragged his heavy feet along the pavement. "Move on; Move on;" the words seemed repeated just ahead. Who was it? What did they want, and why couldn't they let him rest? He drew near a large building with beautiful stained glass windows, through which the light streamed brilliantly. In the center was a picture of the Christ, holding in his arms a lamb, and beneath, the inscription, "I came to seek and to save that which was lost."

"Move on; Move on;" the words seemed shrieked in his ears now, and looking up he saw a steeple in the form of a giant hand, pointing toward the stormy sky. "Why of course,"—he laughed with mirthless lips,—"of course,—it's a church. What a fool—I ought to have come here long ago.— This is Thursday night and that voice is the bell calling people to Prayer Meeting."

"I'll be all right now," he continued to himself as he leaned against a tree near the building. "I ought to have remembered the church before.— I've set up their notices many a time; they always say 'Everybody welcome.' Christians won't let me starve—they'll help me earn something to eat.—I'm not a beggar—not me," and he tried to straighten his tired figure. "All I want is a chance."

By this time, well-dressed people were passing where Dick stood muttering to himself, and entering the open door of the church. Then the organ began to play, and arousing himself by a supreme effort of his will, Dick followed them into the building.

The organ now filled the air with its sweetly solemn tones. The bell with its harsh command to move on was forgotten; and as Dick sank on a cushioned seat near the door, his heart was filled with restful thoughts. He saw visions of a Gracious Being who cared for all mankind, and who had been all this time waiting to help him. Had he not heard his mother pray, years ago in the cabin, "O Lord take care o' Dick!—" How foolish he had been to forget—he ought to have remembered,—but he would never forget again,—never.

The music and the singing stopped. The pastor arose and read the lesson, calling particular attention to the words recorded in the twenty-fifth chapter of Matthew: "Inasmuch as ye have done it unto one of the least of these, my brethren, ye have done it unto me." Then after a long prayer and another song, the man of God spoke a few words about the Christian's joy and duty in helping the needy; that the least of these, meant those who needed help, no matter what their positions in life; and that whosoever gave aid to one in the name of Christ, glorified the Master's name and helped to enthrone him in the hearts of men.

"The least of these," whispered Dick to himself, then unconsciously uttering his thoughts in the dialect of his childhood—"that's me shor'; I don't reckon I kin be much less'n I am right now." And as one after another of the Christians arose and testified to the joy they found in doing Christ's work, and told of experiences where they had been blessed by being permitted to help some poor one, his heart warmed within him, and, in his own way, he thanked God that he had been led to such a place and to such people.

With another song, "Praise God from whom all blessings flow," the congregation was dismissed and began slowly passing from the building, exchanging greetings, with more or less warmth, and remarking what a helpful meeting they had had, and how much it had been enjoyed.

Dick stood near the door, hat in hand, patiently waiting. One by one the members passed him; two or three said "Good Evening;" one shook him by the hand; but something in their faces as they looked at his clothing checked the words that rose to his lips, and the poor fellow waited, his story untold. At last the minister came down the aisle, and greeting Dick, was about to pass out with the others; this was too much, and in a choked voice the young man said, "Sir, may I speak to you a moment?"

"If you'll be brief," replied the preacher, glancing at his watch. "I have an engagement soon."

Dick told his story in a few words. "I'm not begging, Sir," he added. "I thought some of the church members might have work that I could do, or might know where I could find employment."

The minister seemed a little embarrassed; then beckoning to a few who still remained, "Brother Godfrey, here's a man who wants work; do you know of anything?"

"Um, I'm sorry, but I do not," promptly replied the good deacon. "What can you do?" turning to Dick. He made the usual answer and the officer of the church said again, "Find it rather hard to strike anything in Boyd City I fear; so many tramps, you know. Been out of work long?"

"Yes sir, and out of food too."

"Too bad; too bad," said the deacon. And "Too bad; too bad," echoed the preacher, and the other followers of the meek and lowly Jesus. "If we hear of anything we'll let you know. Where are you stopping?"

"On the street," replied Dick, "when I am not moved on by the police."

"Um—Well—we'll leave word here at the church with the janitor if we learn of anything."

"Are you a Christian?" asked one good old mother in Israel.

"No," stammered poor confused Dick; "I guess not."

"Do you drink?"

"No mam."

"Well, don't get discouraged; look to God; he can help you; and we'll all pray for you. Come and hear our Brother French preach; I am sure you will find the light. He is the best preacher in the city. Everybody says so. Good-night."

The others had already gone. The sexton was turning out the lights, and a moment later Dick found himself once more on the street, looking with a grim smile on his hunger-pinched features, at the figure of the Christ, wrought in the costly stained glass window. "One of the least of these," he muttered hoarsely to himself. Then the figure and the inscription slowly faded, as one by one the lights went out, until at last it vanished and he seemed to hear his mother's voice: "I ax ye fair—O Lord—take ker o' Dick—fer Jesus sake—Amen."

The door shut with a bang. A key grated in the heavy lock that guarded the treasures of the church; and the footsteps of the church's humblest servant died away in the distance, as Dick turned to move on again.

The city rumbled on with its business and its pleasure, its merriment and crime. Guardians of the law protected the citizens by seeing to it that no ill-dressed persons sat too long upon the depot benches, sheltered themselves from the bitter wind in the open hall-way, or looked too hungrily in at the bakery windows.

On the avenue the homes grew hushed and still, with now and then a gleam of light from some library or sitting-room window, accompanied by the tones of a piano or guitar,—or sound of laughing voices. And the house of God stood silent, dark and cold, with the figure of the Christ upon the window and the spire, like a giant hand, pointing upward.

CHAPTER III

"I declare to goodness, if that ain't the third tramp I've chased away from this house to-day! I'll have father get a dog if this keeps up. They do pester a body pretty nigh to death." Mrs. Wilson slammed the kitchen door and returned to her dish-washing. "The ide' of givin' good victuals to them that's able to work—not much I won't—Let 'em do like I do." And the good lady plied her dish-cloth with such energy that her daughter hastily removed the clean plates and saucers from the table to avoid the necessity of drying them again.

"But this man wanted work, didn't he mother?" asked Clara, "And I heard you tell father at dinner that you wanted someone to fix the cowshed and clean up the back yard."

"There you go again," angrily snapped the older woman, resting her wet hands upon her hips and pausing in her labor, the better to emphasize her words; "Allus a criticisin' and a findin' fault—Since you took up with that plagy church there aint been nothin' right."

"Forgive me mother, I didn't think," said the daughter, looking into the wrathful black eyes of her parent.

"Didn't think," whined the woman, "You never think of nothin' but your blamed Young Folks' Society or Sunday School. Your mother an' father and home aint good enough fer your saintship now-a-days. I wish to goodness you'd never heard tell of that preacher; the whole set's a batch of stingy hypocrites." She turned to her dish-washing again with a splash. "An' there's George Udell, he aint going to keep hanging around forever, I can tell you; there's too many that'ud jump at his offer, fer him to allus be a dancin' after you; an' when you git through with your foolishness, you'll find him married and settled down with some other girl, an' what me and your father'll do when we git too old to work, the Lord only knows. If you had half sense you'd take him too quick."

Clara made no reply, but finishing her work in silence, hung up her apron and left the kitchen.

Later, when Mrs. Wilson went into the pleasant little sitting-room, where the flowers in the window *would* bloom, and the pet canary *would* sing in spite of the habitual crossness of the mistress of the house, she found her daughter attired for the street.

"Where are you going now?" she asked; "Some more foolishness, I'll be bound; you just take them things off and stay to home; this here weather aint fit fer you to be trapsin round in. You'll catch your death of cold; then I'll have to take care of you. I do believe, Clara Wilson, you are the most ungratefulest girl I ever see."

"But mother, I just must go to the printing office this afternoon. Our society meets to-morrow night and I must look after the printing of the constitution and by-laws."

"What office you goin' to?" asked the mother sharply.

"Why, George's, of course," said Clara; "You know I wouldn't go anywhere else."

"Oh well, get along then; I guess the weather won't hurt you; its clearin' off a little anyway. I'll fix up a bit and you can bring George home to supper." And the old lady grew quite cheerful as she watched the sturdy figure of her daughter making her way down the board walk and through the front gate.

George Udell was a thriving job printer in Boyd City, and stood high in favor of the public generally, and of the Wilson family in particular, as might be gathered from the conversation of Clara's mother. "I tell you," she said, in her high-pitched tones, "George Udell is good enough fer any gal. He don't put on as much style as some, an' aint much of a church man; but when it comes to makin' money he's all there, an' that's the main thing now-a-days."

As for Clara, she was not insensible to the good points in Mr. Udell's character, of which money-making was by no means the most important, for she had known him ever since the time, when as a long, lank, awkward boy, he had brought her picture cards and bits of bright-colored printing. She was a wee bit of a girl then, but somehow, her heart told her that her friend was more honest than most boys, and, as she grew older, in spite of her religious convictions, she had never been forced to change her mind.

But George Udell was not a Christian. Some said he was an infidel; at least he was not a member of any church; and when approached on the subject, always insisted that he did not know what he believed; and that he doubted very much if many church members knew more of their beliefs.

Furthermore; he had been heard upon several occasions to make slighting remarks about the church, contrasting its present standing and work with the law of love and helpfulness as laid down by the Master they professed to follow.

True, no one had ever heard him say that he did not believe in Christ or God. But what of that? Had he not said that he did not believe in the church? And was not that enough to mark him as an infidel?

Clara, in spite of her home training, was, as has been shown, a strong church member, a zealous Christian, and an earnest worker for the cause of Christ. Being a practical girl, she admitted that there were many faults in the church of today; and that Christians did not always live up to their professions. But, bless you, you could not expect people to be perfect; and the faults that existed in the church were there because all churches were not the same, which really means, you of course understand-"all churches are not of *my* denomination." And so, in spite of her regard for the printer, she could not bring herself to link her destiny with one whose eternal future was so insecure, and whose life did not chord with that which was to her, the one great keynote of the universe, the church. And then, too, does not the good book say: "Be ye not unequally yoked with unbelievers." What could that mean if not, "Do not marry an infidel?"

While Clara was thinking of all these things and making her way through the mud of Boyd City streets, Udell, at the printing office, was having a particularly trying time. To begin with, his one printer had gone off on a spree the Saturday before and failed to return. Then several rush jobs had come in; he had tried in vain to get help; the boy had come late to the office, and, altogether it seemed as though everything had happened that could happen to make things uncomfortable.

Clara arrived on the scene just when the confusion was at its height; the room was littered with scraps of paper and inky cloths; the famous printer's towel was lying on the desk; the stove, with its hearth piled full of ashes, emitted smoke and coal gas freely; and the printer was emptying the vials of his wrath upon the public in general, because all wanted their printing done at the same instant; while the boy, with a comical look of fear upon his ink-stained face, was dodging here and there, striving as best he could to avoid the threatening disaster.

The young girl's coming was like a burst of sunlight. In an instant the storm was past. The boy's face resumed at once its usual expression of lofty indifference; the fire burned freely in the stove; the towel was whisked into its proper corner; and she was greeted with the first smile that had shown on the printer's face that day. "You're just in time," he cried gaily, as he seated her in the cleanest corner of the office.

"I should think so," she answered, smiling, and glancing curiously about the room; "looks as though you wanted a woman here."

"I do," declared George. "I've always wanted *a* woman; haven't I told you that often enough?"

"For shame, George Udell. I came here on business," Clara answered with glowing cheeks.

"Well, that's mighty important business for me," Udell answered. "You see—" but Clara interrupted him.

"What's the matter here anyway?" she asked.

"Oh—nothing; only my man is off on a drunken spree, and everybody wants their stuff at the same time. I worked until two o'clock last night; that's why I wasn't at your house; and I must work tonight too. I'm— Yes, there's another;" as the telephone rang. "Hello!—Yes, this is Udell's job office—We have the matter set up and will send you proof as soon as possible—I'm sorry, but we are doing the best we can—Yes—all right—I'll get at it right away—three o'clock—can't possibly get it out before"—bang! He hung up the receiver.

"I tell you this is making me thin. If you had half the influence at headquarters that you profess to have, I wish you'd pray them to send me a printer."

"Why don't you get help?"

"Get help?—Get nothing! I tell you I've prayed, and threatened, and bribed, and promised, as well as the best prayer-meeting church member you've got, and I can't get the sign of an answer. Reckon the wire must be down," he added, a queer shadow of a smile twitching up the corners of his mouth; "Y-e-s," as the phone rang again. "I wish that wire was down."

The girl noted the worn look on his rugged face, and when he had hung up the receiver again, said: "I wish I could help you, George."

"You can, Clara,—you know you can," he answered quickly. "You can give me more help than the ghost of Franklin himself. I don't mind the hard work, and the worry wouldn't amount to anything if only—if only—" he stopped, as Clara shook her head.

"George, you know I have told you again and again—"

"But Clara," he broke in,—"I wouldn't in any way interfere with your church work. I'd even go with you every Sunday, and you could pay the preacher as much as you liked. Don't you see, dear, it couldn't possibly make any difference?"

"You don't understand, George," she answered, "and I can't make you see it; there's no use talking, I *can't*, until you change your ideas about—"

The door opened and a weary, hungry, unshaven face looked in.—The door opened wider and a figure came shuffling timidly toward the man and girl.

"What do you want?" said Udell, gruffly, a little put out at such an interruption.

"Are you the foreman of this office?" said the newcomer.

"Yes, I'm the boss."

"Do you need any help? I'm a printer."

"You a printer?" exclaimed Udell. "What's the matter?—No,"—he interrupted himself.-"Never mind what the matter is. I don't care if you're wanted for horse stealing. Can you go to work now?" The man nodded. Udell showed him to a case and placed copy before him. "There you are, and the faster you work the better I'll pay you."

Again the other nodded, and without a word caught up a stick and reached for the type.

George turned back to Clara who had risen. "Don't go yet," he said.

"Oh, yes, I must; I have been here too long now; you have so much to do; I only wanted to get that society printing." George handed her the package. "Who is he?" she whispered, with a look toward the newcomer.

"Don't know; some bum I suppose; looks like he had been on a big spree. I only hope I can keep him sober long enough to help me over this rush."

"You're wrong there," said the girl, moving toward the door, "He asked for work at our house early this morning; that man is no drunkard, neither is he a common tramp."

"How do you know?"

"Same as I know you, by the looks," laughed Clara. "Go talk to him and find out. You see your prayer was answered, even if you did pray like a church member. Who knows, perhaps the wire is not down after all," and she was gone.

The printer turned to his work again with a lighter heart for this bit of brightness. Somehow he felt that things would come out all right some day, and he would do the best he could to be patient; and, for Clara's sake, while he could not be all she wished, he would make of himself all that he could.

For a while, he was very busy with some work in the rear of the office; then remembering Clara's strange words about the tramp, he went over to the case where the new man sat perched upon his high stool. The stranger was working rapidly and doing good work. George noticed though, that the hand which held the stick trembled; and that sometimes a letter dropped from the nervous fingers. "What's the matter?" he asked, eyeing him keenly.

The man, without lifting his head, muttered, "Nothing."

"Are you sick?"

A shake of the head was the only answer.

"Been drinking?"

"*No*." This time the head was lifted and two keen gray eyes, filled with mingled suffering and anger, looked full in the boss's face. "I've been without work for some time and am hungry, that's all." The head bent again over the case and the trembling fingers reached for the type.

"Hungry!—Good God, man!" exclaimed Udell. "Why didn't you say so?"—and turning quickly to the boy he said, "Here, skip down to that restaurant and bring a big hot lunch. Tell 'em to get a hustle on too."

The boy fled and George continued talking to himself; "Hungry—and I thought he had been on a spree. I ought to have known better than that. I've been hungry myself—Clara's right; he is no bum printer. Great shade of the immortal Benjamin F! but he's plucky though—and proud—you could see that by the look in his eye when I asked him if he'd been drunk—poor fellow—knows his business too—just the man I've been looking for, I'll bet—Huh—wonder if the wire is down." And then as the boy returned with the basket of hot eatables, he called cheerily, "Here you are; come and fill up; no hungry man in this establishment, rush or no rush." He was answered by a clatter as half a stick full of type dropped from the trembling hand of the stranger. "Thank you," the poor fellow tried to say, as he staggered toward the kind-hearted infidel, and then, as he fell, Dick's outstretched fingers just touched Udell's feet.

CHAPTER IV

It was a strange coincidence that the Rev. James Cameron should have preached his sermon on "The Church of the Future," the Sunday following the incidents which have been related in the preceding chapters. If he had only known, Rev. Cameron might have found a splendid illustration, very much to the point, in the story of Dick Falkner's coming to Boyd City and his search for employment. But the minister knew nothing of Dick or his trouble. He had no particular incident in mind; but simply desired to see a more practical working of Christianity. In other words, he wished to see Christians doing the things that Christ did, and using, in matters of the church, the same business sense which they brought to bear upon their own affairs. He thought of the poverty, squalor and wretchedness of some for whom Christ died, and of the costly luxuries of the church into whose hands the Master had given the care of these. He thought of the doors to places of sin, swinging wide before the young, while the doors of the church were often closed against them. He thought of the secret societies and orders, doing the work that the church was meant to do, and of the honest, moral men, who refused to identify themselves with the church, though professing belief in Jesus Christ; and, thinking of these things and more like them, he was forced to say that the church must change her methods; that she must talk less and do more; that she must rest her claims to the love of mankind where Christ rested his; upon the works that He did.

He saw that the church was proving false to the Christ; that her service was a service of the lips only; that her worship was form and ceremony—not of the heart—a hollow mockery. He saw that she was not touching the great problems of life; and that, while men were dying for want of spiritual bread, she was offering them only the stones of ecclesiastical pride and denominational egotism. He saw all this, and yet,—because he was a strong man—remained full of love for Christ and taught that those things were not Christianity but the lack of it; and placed the blame where it justly belonged, upon the teaching and doctrines of men, and not upon the principles of Christ; but upon the shepherds, who fattened themselves, while the starving sheep grew thin and lean; and not upon Him who came to seek and save that which was lost.

Adam Goodrich walked out of the church with his aristocratic nose elevated even beyond its usual angle. He was so offended by the plebeian tastes of his pastor that he almost failed to notice Banker Lindsley who passed him in the vestibule.

"Fine discourse—fine discourse, Mr. Goodrich."

"Uh—" grunted Adam, tossing his head.

"Just the kind of sermon we need;" went on Mr. Lindsley, who was not a church member. "Practical and fearless; I'm glad to have heard him. I shall come again;" and he hurried out of the house.

It was not often that a sermon was honored by being discussed at the Goodrich table; nor indeed, that any topic of religion was mentioned; but Adam could not contain himself after the unheard of things which his pastor had preached that morning. "It's a pity that Cameron hasn't better judgment," he declared, in a voice that showed very plainly the state of his mind. "He could easily make his church the first church in the city if he would only let well enough alone and not be all the time stirring things up. He is a good speaker, carries himself like an aristocrat, and comes from a good family; but he is forever saying things that jar the best people. He might be drawing half as much again salary if only he would work to get those people who are worth something into the church, instead of spending all his time with the common herd."

"Perhaps he thinks the common herd worth saving too," suggested Miss Amy, a beautiful girl of nineteen, with dark hair and eyes.

"What do you know about it?" replied the father. "You're getting your head full of those silly Young People's Society notions, and your friends will drop you if you don't pay more attention to your social duties. The common classes are all right of course, but they can't expect to associate with us. Cameron has his mission schools; why isn't that enough? And he makes three times as many calls on South Broadway and over by the Shops, as he does on our street."

"Perhaps he thinks, 'they that are whole have no need of a physician,'" again suggested the young lady.

"Amy," said Mrs. Goodrich, "how often have I told you that it's not the thing to be always repeating the Bible. No one does it now. Why will you make yourself so common?"

"You agree with Cameron perfectly, mother," put in Frank, the only son; "he said this morning that no one used their Bibles now-a-days."

"It's not necessary to be always throwing your religion at people's heads," answered the father, "and as for Cameron's new-fangled notion about the church being more helpful to those who need help, he'll find out that it won't work. We are the ones who pay his salary, and if he can't preach the things we want to hear, he'll find himself going hungry, or forced to dig along with those he is so worried about. I don't find anything in the Bible that tells me to associate with every low-down person in the city, and I guess I'm as good a Christian as anyone in the church."

"Brother Cameron said that helping people and associating with them were two different things," said Amy.

"Well, it means the same, anyway, in the eyes of the world," retorted the father.

"Fancy," said Frank, "my going down the street with that tramp who called at the office last week. According to Cameron, you ought to have invited him home and asked him to stay with us until he found a job, I suppose. Amy would have liked to meet him, and to make his visit with us pleasant. He was not bad-looking, barring his clothes and a few whiskers."

"Who was that, Mr. Goodrich?" inquired the wife.

"Oh, an impudent fellow that Frank let into the office the other day; he claimed that he was a printer and wanted work; said that he was thrown out of employment by the Kansas City strike; anyone could see that he was a fraud through and through, just Cameron's kind. If I had my way I would give him work that he wouldn't want. Such people are getting altogether too numerous, and there will be no room for a respectable man if this thing keeps up. I don't know what we'll come to if we have many such sermons as that this morning; they want the earth now."

"They'd get Heaven too if Cameron had his way," put in Frank again.

"Won't it be fine when the church becomes a home for every wandering Willie who happens along?"

"Did not Christ intend His church to be a home for the homeless?" asked the sister.

"Amy," interrupted Mrs. Goodrich, "you are getting too many of those fanciful notions; you will learn in time that the church is meant to go to on Sundays, and that people who know what is demanded of them by the best society, leave socials, aids, missions, and such things to the lower classes."

"Yes," answered Frank, as he arose to leave the table—"and don't go looking up that bum printer to teach him the way of the Lord."

The reader must not think that the Goodrichs were unworthy members of the church; their names were all on the roll of membership, and Frank and Amy were also active members of the Young People's Societies. Beside this, Adam contributed liberally (in his own eyes at least) to the support of the gospel; and gave, now and then, goodly sums set opposite his name on subscription lists, for various charitable purposes; although he was very careful, withal, that his gifts to God never crippled his business interests, and managed, in religious matters, to make a little go a long way.

The pastor of the Jerusalem Church, having been called to attend a funeral, was not present at the meeting of the Boyd City Ministerial Association, following his sermon, and the field was left open for his brethren, who assembled in the lecture room of the Zion Church on Monday morning. After the Association had been called to order by the president, the reports of the work given by the various pastors had been heard, and some unfinished business transacted, good old Father Beason arose, and, in his calm, impassioned manner, addressed the Chair.

"Brethren," he said, "I don't know how you all feel about it, but I would like to know what the Association thinks about Brother Cameron's sermon yesterday. Now, I don't want to be misunderstood, Brethren; I haven't a particle of fault to find with Brother Cameron. I love him as a man; I admire him as a preacher; and I believe that whatever he has said he meant for the best. But, Brother Cameron is a young man yet, and I have heard a good deal of talk about the things he said Sabbath morning; and I would just like to know what you Brethren think about it. Have any of you heard anything?" Six reverend heads nodded that they had, and the speaker continued:

"Well, I thought probably you would hear something, and with no harm meant toward our Brother, I would like to have you express yourselves. I have been in the ministry nearly forty years now, and I have never heard such things as people say he said. And, Brethren, I'm awfully afraid that there is a good deal of truth in it all—a good deal of truth in it all;" and slowly shaking his head the old man took his seat.

The Rev. Jeremiah Wilks was on his feet instantly, and, speaking in a somewhat loud and nervous manner, said: "Mr. Chairman, I was coming down town early this morning, after some thread and ribbons and things for my wife, and Sister Thurston, who runs that little store on Third Street—you know she's a member of my church, you know—and always gives me things lots cheaper than I can get them anywhere else, because she's a member of my church, you know—she says to me that Brother Cameron said that the average church of to-day was the biggest fraud on earth. Now she was there and heard him. I don't know of course, whether he really said that or not; that is, I mean, you know,—I don't know whether he meant it that way or not. But I've heard him say myself, that he didn't think the church was doing all she might along some lines. I don't know whether he means all the churches or only his own. *My* people gave fifteen dollars for foreign missions last year, and the Ladies' Aid paid fifty dollars on my salary. Besides that, they bought me a new overcoat last winter, and it will last me through next winter too. They paid eighteen dollars for that, I'm told; and of course they got it cheap because it was for me, you know. And we gave a pound social to Sister Grady, whose husband died some time ago, you know. It took almost all her money to pay funeral expenses—She's a member of my church you know; so was he, poor man; he's gone now. I'm sure I don't know about Brother Cameron's church; we're doing all *we* can; and I don't think it's right for him to talk against the work of the Lord." The reverend gentleman resumed his seat with the satisfied air of a school boy who has just succeeded in hitting a hornet's nest, and devoutly wishes that someone would come along to share the fun.

Little Hugh Cockrell arose, and, crossing his hands, meekly spoke: "Now, Brethren, I don't think we ought to be hasty in regard to this matter. I would advise caution. We must give the subject due and careful consideration. We all respect and love Brother Cameron. Let us not be hasty in condemning him. You know the Scriptures say, Judge not, and I believe we ought to be careful. We don't know what Cameron meant exactly. Brethren, let us try to find out. I know I have heard a great many things, and some of my members say that he spoke rather slightingly of the ministry as a whole, and seemed to think that the church was not practical enough, and my wife is a good deal hurt about some things that he said about the clergy. But, let's be careful. I don't want to believe that our Brother would cast a slur in any way upon us or the church. Let's be cautious and work in a Christianlike manner; find out by talking with people on the street and in their homes, what he said, and above all, don't let Cameron know how we feel. We ought not to be hasty, Brethren, about judging our Brother."

There were nods of approval as the minister took his seat, for he was much admired in the Association because of his piety, and much respected for his judgment. All knew that nothing could possibly harm them if they followed Rev. Cockrell's advice.

Then the Rev. Dr. Frederick Hartzell reared his stoop-shouldered, narrow-chested, but commanding figure, and, in a most impressive and scholarly manner addressed the Association.

"Of course I don't know anything about this matter, Brethren; it's all news to me. I am so confined by my studies that I go on the street very little, and, when I do go out, my mind is so full of the deep things of the Scriptures, that I find it hard to retain anything that has to do with the commonplace in life; and in-as-much as the reverend gentleman failed to consult me as to his sermon, which I understand he calls The Church of the Future, I am unable to say at present whether his position is orthodox or not. But Brethren, of one thing I am sure, and I don't care what Cameron or any other man thinks; the orthodox church of to-day is the power of God unto salvation. God intended that we ministers should be His representatives on earth, and as such, we ought to have a keen appreciation of the grandeur and nobility of our calling. After years of study on the part of myself, and after much consultation with other eminent men, I give it as my opinion that the church of the future will be the same as the church of the past. All denominations—that is, all evangelical denominations, are built upon a rock. Upon this rock I will build my church, Matthew 16-18. Brethren, we are secure; even the gates of Hades cannot prevail against us; and it is proven by the scholarship of the world, that we shall be the same in the future as we have been in the past. Rev. Cameron, whatever may be his opinions, cannot harm so glorious an institution. Why, Brethren, we represent the brains and culture of the world. Look at our schools and seminaries; we must be right. No change can possibly come; no change is needed. As to the gentleman's remarks about the ministry; if he made any, I don't think his opinion matters much anyhow, I understand that he is not a graduate of any regular theological institution; and I'm sure that he cannot harm *my* reputation in the least."

Secure in the impregnable position of his own learning and in the scholarship of his church; amid a hush of profound awe and admiration, the learned gentleman took his seat.

Rev. Hartzell's speech practically finished the discussion of the sermon by the Association. Indeed, the Rev. Frederick nearly always finished whatever discussion he took part in. One or two of the remaining preachers tried to speak, but subsided as soon as they caught the eye of the scholar fixed upon them, and the Association was adjourned, with a prayer by the president that they might always be able to conduct the Master's business in a manner well pleasing in his sight; and that they might have strength to always grapple boldly with questions concerning the church, ever proving true to the principles of the Christ, and following in His footsteps.

While the members of the Ministerial Association were engaged in discussing Rev. Cameron's much-abused sermon, the printer, George Udell, dropped in at the office of Mr. Wicks, to make the final payment on a piece of property which he had purchased some months before. Mr. Wicks, or as he was more often called, Uncle Bobbie, was an old resident of the county, an elder in the Jerusalem Church, and Rev. Cameron's right-hand man.

"Well," he said, as he handed George the proper papers, "that place is your'n, young man, what are ye goin' to do with it?"

"Oh I don't know," replied Udell, "it's handy to have round; good building spot, isn't it?"

"You bet it is," returned the other. "There aint no better in Boyd City, an' I reckon I know. Ye must be goin' to get a wife, talking about buildin'?"

Udell shook his head. "Well, ye ought to. Let's see—this is the third piece of property I've sold ye, aint it?—all of 'em good investments too—You're gettin' a mighty good start fer a young man. Don't it make ye think of the Being what's back of all these blessin's? Strikes me ye'r too blame good a man to be livin' without any religion. George, why don't you go to church anyway? Don't ye know you ought to?"

"Why don't I go to church," said Udell thoughtfully; "Well, Mr. Wicks, I'll tell you why I don't go to church. Just because I've got too much to do. I make my own way in the world and it takes all the business sense I have to do it. The dreamy, visionary, speculative sort of things I hear at meeting may be all right for a fellow's soul, but they don't help him much in taking care of his body, and I can't afford to fill my mind with such stuff. I am living this side of the grave. Of course I like to hear a good talker, and I enjoy the music, but their everlasting pretending to be what they are not, is what gets me. You take this town right here now," he continued, pushing his hat back from his forehead; "we've got ten or twelve churches and as many preachers; they all say that they are following Christ, and profess to exist for the good of men and the glory of God. And what are they actually doing to make this place better? There's not a spot in this city, outside a saloon, where a man can spend an hour when he's not at work; and not a sign of a place where a fellow down on his luck can stay all night. Only last week, a clean honest young printer, who was out of money through no fault of his own, struck me for a job, and before night fainted from hunger; and yet, the preachers say that Christ told us to feed the hungry, and that if we didn't it counted against us as though we had let him starve. According to their own teaching, what show have these churches in Boyd City when they spend every cent they can rake and scrape to keep their old machines running and can't feed even one hungry man? Your church members are all right on the believe, trust, hope, pray and preach, but they're not so much on the do. And I've noticed it's the *do* that counts in this life. Why, their very idea of Heaven is that it's a loafing place, where you get more than you ask for or have any right to expect."

"Gettin' a little excited, ain't ye?" smiled Uncle Bobbie, though there was a tear twinkling in his sharp old eyes.

"Yes I am," retorted the other. "It's enough to excite anyone who has a heart to feel and eyes to see the misery in this old world, and then to be asked eternally, 'Why don't you go to church?' Why look at 'em; they even let their own preachers starve when they get too old to work. Societies and lodges don't do that. I don't mean to step on your toes though," he added hastily. "You know that, Uncle Bobbie. You've proven yourself a Christian to me in ways I'll never forget. My old mother was a member of the church and they let her go hungry, when I was too little to take care of her; and if it hadn't been for you she would have died then. But you fed her, and if there's a Heaven, she's there, and you'll be there too. But what makes me mad is, that these fellows who *never* do anything, are just as sure of it as you who do so much."

"Ah, George," said Wicks; "that help I give your maw warn't nothin'. Do you think I'd see her suffer? Why, I knowed her when she was a girl."

"I know, Uncle Bobbie, but that isn't the question. Why, don't the church *do* some of the things they are always talking about?"

"Do infidels do any more?" asked Mr. Wicks.

"No, they don't," answered George, "but they don't thank God that Jesus Christ was crucified, so that they might get to Heaven, either."

"Thar's one fellow that I didn't feed," said the old man, after a long pause. "That same printer called here and I didn't give him nothin' to do. I've thought of it many a time since though, and asked the Lord to forgive me for sech carelessness. And so he's got a job with you, has he? Well, I'm mighty glad. But say, George, were you at our church yesterday?"

"No," answered Udell, "Why?"

"Oh, nothin'; only I thought from the way you've been preachin' Cameron's sermon, that you'd heard him give it, that's all."

CHAPTER V

"There's only one girl in this world for me," whistled Dick, as he made a form ready for the press. Only in his own mind he rendered it, "There's not one girl in this world for me;" and from Dick's point of view his version was the better one. Thus far in his life there had come no woman's influence; no loving touch of a girlish hand to help in moulding his character; no sweet voice bidding him do right; no soft eyes to look praise or blame. He had only the memory of his mother.

It was less than a week ago that the poor outcast had fainted from lack of food, but he had already become a fixture in the office. George Udell confided to Miss Wilson that he did not know how he could get along without him, and that he was, by long odds, the best hand he had ever had. He was quick and sure in his work, and as George put it, "You don't have to furnish him a map when you tell him to do anything." With three good meals a day and a comfortable cot in the office for the night, with the privilege of spending his evenings by the fire, and the assurance that there was work for him for many weeks ahead, it was no wonder that Dick whistled as he bent over the stone. Locking up the form, he carried it to the press and was fixing the guide pins, when the door opened and a young lady came in.

Dick's whistle stopped instantly and his face flushed like a school girl as he gave her a chair and went to call Udell, who was in the other room trying to convince the boy that the stove needed a bucket of coal.

"Faith," said Dick to himself, as he went back to the press, "If there is one girl in this world for me I hope she looks like that one. What a lovely voice," he added, as he carefully examined the first impression; "and a heavenly smile;" as he finished his work and went back to the composing case; "and what eyes," —he turned sideways to empty his stick—"And what hair;" trying to read his copy—"a perfect form;" reaching for the type again. "I wonder who—"

"Dick!" shouted Udell. Crash went the overturned stool, and, "Yes Sir," answered the young man, with a very red face, struggling to his feet.

A merry light danced in the brown eyes, though the girlish countenance was serious enough.

Udell looked at his assistant in mingled wonder and amusement. "What's the matter, Dick?" he asked, as the latter came toward him.

"Nothing, Sir—I only—I was—" he looked around in confusion at the overturned stool, and the type on the floor.

"Yes, I see you were," said his employer with a chuckle. "Miss Goodrich, this is Mr. Falkner; perhaps he can help us out of our difficulty. Mr. Falkner is just from Kansas City," he added, "and is up in all the latest things in printing."

"Oh yes," and Amy's eyes showed their interest. "You see, Mr. Falkner, we are trying to select a cover design for this little book. Mr. Udell has suggested several, but we cannot come to any decision as to just the proper one. Which would you choose?"

Dick's embarrassment left him at once when a matter of work was to be considered. "This would be my choice," he said, selecting a design.

"I like that too," said the young lady; "but you see it is not *just* what I want;" and she looked not a little worried, for above all things, Miss Goodrich liked things *just* as she liked them; and besides, this was *such* an important matter.

"I'll tell you what," said Dick. "If you'll let me, and Mr. Udell does not object, I'll set up a cover for you to-night after supper."

"O, indeed, you must not think of it," said Amy.

"But I would enjoy it," he answered.

"You need to rest after your day's work," she replied; "and besides, it would be so much trouble for you to come way down here in the night. No, you need not mind; this will do very well."

"But we often work after hours, and I—I—do not live far from here," said Dick.

"What do you think, Mr. Udell?"

"I am sure, Miss Goodrich, that Mr. Falkner would enjoy the work, for we printers have a good bit of pride in that kind of thing you know, and, as he says, we often work after supper. I think you might let him do it, without too great a feeling of obligation."

After some further talk, the matter was finally settled as he had suggested, and Dick went back to his work; as he picked up his overturned stool, he heard the door close and then Udell stood beside him, with a broad grin on his face.

"Well, I'll be shot," ejaculated the printer, "I've seen fellows take a tumble before, but hang me if I ever saw a man so completely kerflummuxed. Great shade of the immortal Benjamin F—! But you were a sight—must be you're not used to the ladies. Seemed all right though when you got your legs under you and your mouth agoing. What in time ailed you anyway?"

"Who is she?" asked Dick, ignoring the other's laughter, and dodging his question.

"Who is she? Why I introduced you to her, man; her name is Amy Goodrich. Her daddy is that old duffer who keeps the hardware store, and is so eminently respectable that you can't get near him unless you have a pedigree and a bank account. Amy is the only daughter, but she has a brother though who takes after the old man. The girl takes after herself I reckon." Dick made no reply and Udell continued: "The whole family are members of the swellest church in the city, but the girl is the only one who works at it much. She teaches in the Mission Sunday School; leads in the Young People's Society and all that. I don't imagine the old folks like it though; too common you know." And he went off to look after the boy again, who was slowly but painfully running off the bill-heads that Dick had fixed on the press.

"What's the matter with him, George?" asked that individual, leaning wearily against the machine; "Did he faint agin, or was he havin' a fit?"

"You shut up and get that job off sometime this week," answered Udell, as he jerked the lever of the electric motor four notches to the right.

Just before the whistles blew for dinner, he again went back to Dick and stood looking over his shoulder at a bad bit of copy the latter was trying to decipher. "Well, what do you think about it?" he asked.

"She's divine," answered Dick absently, as he carefully
placed a capital A upside down.

George threw back his head and roared; "Well, you've got it sure," he said, when he could speak.

"Got what?" asked Dick in wonder.

"Oh, nothing," replied the other, going off with another shout. "But look here;" he said, after a moment; very serious this time; "Let me give you a piece of good advice, my friend; don't you go to thinking about *that* girl too much."

"What girl? Whose thinking about her? You need have no fears on that score," said Dick, a little sharply.

"Oh, you needn't get mad about it, a fellow can't help but think a chap is hit when he falls down, can he?" And with another laugh, George removed his apron and left for dinner.

"Yes, it did look bad;" said Dick to himself, as he dried his hands on the office towel; "but I never saw such eyes; and she's as good as she looks too; but Adam Goodrich's daughter, Whew—" And he whistled softly to himself as he thought of his first meeting with the wealthy hardware merchant.

That evening while Miss Goodrich was entertaining a few of her friends at her beautiful home on the avenue, and while Udell, with Clara Wilson, was calling on old Mother Gray, whose husband had been injured in the mines, Dick worked alone in the printing office. The little book, as Amy called it, was a pamphlet issued by the literary club of which she was the secretary, and never since the time when he set his first line of type, had Dick been so bothered over a bit of printing. The sweet brown eyes and smiling lips of the young woman were constantly coming between him and his work, and he paused often to carry on an imaginary conversation with her. Sometimes he told her funny incidents from his adventurous past and heard her laugh in keen appreciation. Then they talked of more earnest things and her face grew grave and thoughtful. Again he told her all his plans and ambitions, and saw her eyes light with sympathy as she gladly promised her helpful friendship. Then, inspired by her interest, he grew bolder, and forgetting the task before him altogether, fought life's battles in the light of her smiles, conquering every difficulty, and winning for himself a place and name among men. And then, as he laid his trophies at her feet, her father, the wealthy merchant, appeared, and Dick walked the floor in a blind rage.

But he managed to finish his work at last, and about three o'clock, tumbled on to his cot in the stock room, where he spent the rest of the night trying to rescue Amy from her father, who assumed the shape of a hardware dragon, with gold eyes, and had imprisoned the young lady in a log cabin near the river, beneath a hill upon which grew a pine tree tipped with fire, while a lean hound sat at the water's edge and howled.

CHAPTER VI

Uncle Bobbie Wicks pulled down the top of his desk and heard the lock click with a long sigh of satisfaction, for a glance at his large, old-fashioned hunting-case watch told him that it was nearly eleven o'clock. It was a dismal, dreary, rainy night; just the sort of a night to make a man thank God that he had a home; and those who had homes to go to were already there, except a few business men, who like Mr. Wicks, were obliged to be out on work of especial importance.

Locking the rear door of the office and getting hastily into his rain coat, the old gentleman took his hat and umbrella from the rack and stepped out into the storm. As he was trudging along through the wet, his mind still on business, a gleam of light from the window of Udell's printing office caught his eye. "Hello!" he said to himself; "George is working late tonight; guess I'll run in and see if he's got that last batch of bill-heads fixed yet; we'll need 'em tomorrow morning. Howdy, George," he said, a few seconds later; and then stopped, for it was not Udell, but Dick, who was bending over the stone; and in place of working with the type, he was playing a game of solitaire, while he pulled away at an old corn-cob pipe.

"Good evening," said the young man, pausing in his amusement, "What can I do for you?"

"I see ye got a job," said Uncle Bobbie.

"Yes," Dick replied, as he shuffled the cards; "and a very good one too."

"Huh! looks like ye weren't overworked just now."

"Oh, this is out of hours; we quit at six, you know."

"Strikes me ye might find somethin' better to do than foolin' with them dirty pasteboards, if 'tis out of hours;" said Mr. Wicks, pointedly.

"They are rather soiled," remarked Dick, critically examining the queen of hearts; and then he continued, in a matter-of-fact tone, "you see I found them back of the coal box; some fellow had thrown them away, I guess. Lucky for me that he did."

"Lucky for you? Is that the best you can do with your time?"

"Perhaps you would suggest some more elevating amusement," smiled Dick. "Well, why don't you read somethin'?"

The young man waved his pipe toward a lot of month-old papers and printers journals—"My dear sir, I have gone through that pile three times and have exhausted every almanac in this establishment."

"Visit some of your friends."

"Not one in the city except Udell," answered the other, "and if I had—" he glanced down at his worn clothing.

Mr. Wicks tried again; "Well, go somewhere."

"Where?" asked Dick. "There is only one place open to *me*—the saloon—I haven't money enough for that, and if I had, I wouldn't spend it there now. I might go to some respectable gambling den, I suppose, but there's the money question again, and my foolish pride, so I play solitaire. I know I am in good company at least, if the sport isn't quite so exciting."

Uncle Bobbie was silent. The rain swished against the windows and roared on the tin roof of the building; the last car of the evening, with one lone passenger, scurried along Broadway, its lights brightly reflected on the wet pavement; a cab rumbled toward the hotel, the sound of the horses' feet dull and muffled in the mist; and a solitary policeman, wrapped in his rubber coat, made his way along the almost deserted street. As Uncle Bobbie stood listening to the lonely sounds and looking at the young man, with his corn-cob pipe and pack of dirty cards, he thought of his own cheery fireside and of his waiting wife. "To-be-sure," he said at last, carefully placing his umbrella in a corner near the door, and as carefully removing his coat and hat; "To-be-sure, I quit smokin' sometime ago—'bout a month, I reckon—used to smoke pretty nigh all the time, but wife she wanted me to quit—I don't know as there is any use in it." A long pause followed, as he drew a chair to the stove and seated himself. "To-be-sure, I don't know as there's any great harm in it either." There was another pause, while Dick also placed his chair near the stove—"and I git so plaguey fat every time I quit."

Dick tilted back and lazily blew a soft cloud into the air. Uncle Bobbie arose and placed the coal bucket between them. "Told mother last night I was gettin' too fat again—but it made me sick last time I tried it—I wonder if it would make me sick now."—A longer pause than usual followed—then: "It's really dangerous for me to get so fat, and smokin' 's the only thing that keeps it down. D'ye reckon it would make me sick again?" He drew a cigar from his pocket, almost as big as a cannon fire-cracker and fully as dangerous. "I got this t'day. Looks like a pretty good one. It didn't use to make me sick 'fore I quit the last time." Dick handed him a match and two minutes later the big cigar was burning as freely as its nature would permit.

"What an awful wasteful habit it is to-be-sure, ain't it?" went on the old gentleman between vigorous puffs. "Just think, there's school books, and Bibles and baby clothes and medicine for the sick, and food for the hungry, and houses and stores, and farms, and cattle, all a' goin' up in that smoke;" he pointed with his cigar to the blue cloud that hung between them. "If I had half the money church members burn, I could take care of every old worn-out preacher in the world, and have a good bit left over for the poor children. I wisht I was as young as you be; I'd quit it fer good; but it sure does take a hold on an old feller like me."

Dick's face grew thoughtful. "I never looked at it in that way before," he said, as he took his pipe from his mouth; "It's a big comfort to a chap who is all alone, though I suppose it does get a strong hold on a man who has used it most of his life; and a fellow could do a lot of good with the money it costs him." He arose to his feet and went to the window, where he stood for a moment looking out into the rain. Presently he came back to his chair again; "Look out," cried Uncle Bobbie, as Dick took his seat, "You've dropped your pipe into the coal bucket."

"Oh, that's all right; its worn-out anyway, and I have another." But he smoked no more that evening.

"Where are you from?" asked Wicks abruptly.

"Everywhere," answered Dick, shortly, for he did not relish the thought of being questioned about his past.

"Where you goin'?" came next from his companion.

"Nowhere," just as short.

"Folks livin'?"

"No."

"How long been dead?"

"Since I was a little fellow."

"Ain't you got no relations?"

"Don't want any if they're like an aunt of mine."

Uncle Bobbie nodded in sympathy.

"How'd you happen to strike this place?"

Dick told him in three words, "Lookin' for work."

"Udell's a mighty fine fellow."

"You're right he is."

"Not much of a Christian though." And the old man watched Dick keenly through the cloud of smoke.

"No, good thing for me he isn't," the young man answered bitterly, his face and voice betraying his feelings.

"I know; yes, I know," nodded Uncle Bobbie. "To-be-sure, I used to look at things just like you, and then I got more sense and learned a heap better, and I tell you right now that you'll do the same way. I know there is church members that are meaner'n a mule with shoulder galls. They won't pull nothin' and would kick a man's head off quicker'n greased lightnin'. But they ain't goin' to Heaven, be they? Not much they ain't; no more'n my dog's goin' to the Legislature. And there's them outside the church that's a whole lot worse. Taint Christianity that makes folks mean, but they're mean in spite of it, though you can't get such fellers as you to see it that way, no more'n you can foller a mosquito through a mile o' fog. To-be-sure, I aint blamin' you much though."

Dick's face changed. This was not just what he expected. "I'll tell you," he said, when he saw that the old gentleman expected him to reply. "Ever since I can remember, I've been kicked and cuffed and cursed by saint and sinner alike, until I can't see much difference between the church members and those whom they say are in the world."

"Except that the members of the church do the kickin' and cuffin' and let the sinners do the cussin'," broke in Uncle Bobbie. "To-be-sure, ye can't tell me nothin' about that either."

"I'm not saying anything about the teaching of Christ," continued Dick; "that's all right so far as it goes, but it don't seem to go very far. I have not made much of a success of life, but I've worked mighty hard to earn a living and learn my trade, and I don't know but that I am willing to take my chances with some of the church members I have seen."

"To-be-sure," said Uncle Bobbie; "and I reckon your chance is just as good as their'n. But it strikes me that I want to stand a little better show than them fellers. How about the folks that be Christians? You know there is them that do follow the Master's teachin'; what about their chances, heh?"

"You see it's just this way," continued Uncle Bobbie, settling himself more comfortably in his chair; "I had a whole lot of brothers and sisters at home, back in Ohio; an' they was all members of the church but me. To-be-sure, I went to Sunday School and meetin' with the rest—I jing! I had to!—Huh!—My old dad would just naturally a took th' hide off me if I hadn't. Yes sir-ee, you bet I went to church. But all the same I didn't want to. An' they sorter foundered me on religi'n, I reckon, Jim and Bill and Tom and Dave. They'd all take their girls and go home with them after meetin', an' I'd have to put out the team and feed the stock all alone; an' Sunday evenin' every one of 'em would be off to singin' and I'd have to milk and feed again. An' then after meetin' of course the boys had to take their girls home, and other fellows would come home with our girls, and I'd have to put up the team and take care of the boys' horses that come sparkin'. An' somehow I didn't take to Christianity. To-be-sure, 'twas a good thing fer the stock I didn't."

He carefully knocked the ashes from his cigar and continued: "To-be-sure, I know now that wasn't no excuse, but it looked that way then. After a while the boys married off and I staid to home and took care of the old folks; and purty soon the girls they got married too; and then pa and ma got too old to go out, and I couldn't leave 'em much, and so I didn't get to meetin' very often. Things went on that way a spell 'til Bill got to thinkin' he'd better come and live on the home farm and look after things, as I didn't have no woman; to-be-sure, it did need a good bit of tendin'. Six hundred acres all in fine shape and well stocked—so I told pa that I'd come west an let 'em run things at home. I got a job punchin' steers out here in James County, and they're all back there yet. The old folks died a little bit after I came west, and Bill—well—Bill, he keeps the home place 'cause he took care of 'em ye know—well, I homesteaded a hundred and sixty, and after a spell, the Santa Fe road come through and I got to buyin' grain and hogs, and tradin' in castor-oil beans and managed to get hold of some land here when the town was small. To-be-sure, I aint rich yet, though I've got enough to keep me I reckon. I handle a little real estate, get some rent from my buildin's, and loan a little money now and then. But you bet I've worked for every cent I've got, and I didn't fool none of it away either, 'cept what went up in smoke."

The old gentleman's voice sank lower and lower as he recalled the years that had flown. And as Dick looked at the kindly face, seamed and furrowed by the cares of life, and the hair just whitened by the frost of time, now half hidden in a halo of smoke, he felt his heart warm with sympathy, which he knew was returned full measure by the boy who had left his Ohio home to battle with life alone in that strange western country.

"But what I wanted to tell ye," said Uncle Bobbie, coming suddenly back to the present and speaking in his usual abrupt manner, "you'll find out, same as I have, that it don't much matter how the other feller dabbles in the dirt, you've got to keep your hands clean anyhow. An' taint the question whether the other feller's mean or not, but am I livin' square? I know that Christ is the Saviour of men, but he can't save 'em 'less they want him to, no more'n I can catch a jack-rabbit a-foot. Christianity's all right, but it aint a goin' to do no good 'less people live it, and there's a heap more living it too than we think. What such fellers as you want to do is to listen to what Christ says and not look at what some little two by four church member does. They aint worth that;" and he tossed his cigar stub to keep company with Dick's pipe.

Dick said nothing, because he could find no words to express himself, and the older man, seeing how it was, rose to his feet.

"Well, I must be goin'. Wife'll think I've clean gone back on her. Come up to the house and see me sometime. I reckon you know you're welcome after what I've been sayin'." And then as the young man gave him a lift with his coat; "keep a stiff upper lip; you'll strike pay dirt after a while; just keep a hangin' on, like a puppy to a root. Good-night," and Dick was alone again.

"Wife," said Mr. Wicks next morning, just before getting up to build the fire; "wife, I made a discovery last night."

"You were out late enough to discover something," returned Mrs. Wicks, with a laugh; "what is it?"

And Uncle Bobbie replied slowly as he arose and began dressing, "There's some fellers go to the devil just because they aint got nowheres else to go."

Later, the old gentleman sat at his desk in his office, tilted back in his revolving chair, his feet among the papers where his hands should have been. No one came in to disturb his revery for it was still early in the morning, and the only sound was the clicking of a typewriter in the next room. Suddenly the feet came down to their proper place with a bang, and leaning forward, he wrote rapidly for a few moments, then called, "Charlie." The noise of the typewriter stopped and a young man entered the room. "Charlie, I've been gettin' out a little advertisin' stuff here, and I wish you'd take it over to George Udell's an' wait until they fix it up, so you can bring me back the proof. You can let them letters rest a spell."

The young man took his hat and umbrella, for it was still raining, and started on his errand, but his employer stopped him. "Wait a bit, Charlie. Do you remember that young feller what called here for a job week before last, the time I sold that Johnson property, you know?"

"Said he was a printer from Kansas City?" asked Charlie.

The other nodded.

"Yes, sir, I remember him."

"Well, he's got a job with Udell. I was there last night and had a talk with him. He aint got no friends and stays in the office nights alone. I just thought I'd tell you. He's shy of Christians though, and proud as an old turkey gobbler in the spring. But he needs somebody to talk to more'n anything else, that's all." And the old man turned back to his papers.

This was the beginning. The end is easily foreseen; for, given a young man of Dick's temperament, longing for companionship, and another young man of Charlie's make-up, with a legitimate business to bring the two together, and only a friendship of the David and Jonathan order could result.

Dick was distant at first, but Charlie was too wise to force himself upon him, and as Mr. Wicks found many excuses for sending his young assistant to the printing office, the two slowly grew better acquainted. Then came a time when Charlie dared to ask Dick what he did evenings, and Dick answered in his proud way, "Smoke and play solitaire. Couldn't Charlie come up and chat with him sometimes? He couldn't play cards and didn't care to smoke, but he did like to talk. Yes, Charlie could if he chose, but he would find it a dull place to spend an evening."

Dick was pulling away at his corn-cob pipe the first time Charlie came, but moved to hide it from sight as the latter entered the room. Then thinking better of it, with a proud lifting of his chin, he stuck the pipe in his mouth again. However, Charlie noticed that the smoke soon ceased to come from his companion's lips, and guessed that the tobacco was not burning well. This was the last time that he ever saw Dick smoking. Indeed, it was the last time that Dick ever used tobacco in any form. "For," said he to himself, "I can't afford to do anything that robs babies and mothers, and makes me disagreeable to my friends."

The ice once broken, Charlie's calls grew more and more frequent, until the two met and talked like old friends, and often left the office to walk about the city, arm in arm, after dark.

"Mr. Udell," said Dick, one Saturday night, as the latter handed him his wages for the week, "Where's the best place to go for clothing?"

And George, with a pleased look on his face, which Dick could not help but notice, directed him to a clothing store on the corner of Fourth and Broadway.

CHAPTER VII

The quiet of a Sunday morning in early May was over the city. Stores and business houses were closed, save here and there a meat market, which opened for careless citizens who had neglected to lay in their supply the night before. A group of negro loafers sat on the stone steps of the National Bank, and lounged about the entrance of the Opera House. A little farther up the street a company of idle whites sat in front of a restaurant; and farther on, in the doorway of a saloon, a drunkard was sleeping in the sun. Old Dr. Watkins, in his buggy, came clattering down the street and stopped in front of the Boyd City Drug Store, and a man with his arm in a sling followed him into the building. Then the church bells rang out their cheery invitation, and the children, neat and clean in their Sunday clothes, trooped along the street to the Sunday Schools. An hour later the voices of the bells again floated over the silent city, and men and women were seen making their way to the various places of worship.

In the throng which passed through the door of the Jerusalem Church was a gentleman dressed in gray. It was not difficult to guess from his manner, as he stood in the vestibule as though waiting for someone, that he was a stranger in the place. His figure was tall, nearly if not quite six feet, well formed, but lithe rather than heavy, giving one the impression not only of strength, but of grace as well; the well-set head and clear-cut features; the dark hair and brows, overshadowing, deep-set, keen gray eyes; the mouth and chin, clean-shaven and finely turned; all combined to carry still farther the impression of power. Even the most careless observer would know that he would be both swift and sure in action, while a closer student would say, "Here is one who rules himself, as he leads others; who is strong in spirit as well as body; who is as kind as he is powerful; as loving as he is ambitious; this is indeed a man whom one would love as a friend and be forced to respect as an enemy."

Charlie Bowen, one of the ushers, came hurrying up and caught the stranger by the hand. "Good," he whispered, looking him over admiringly; "Glad to see you, old man. Whew, but you do look swell. Folks will think you're a Congressman sure, in that outfit."

"Do I take my hat off when I go in?" whispered Dick, who already had his hat in his hand, "Or do I wait till after prayers?"

"You come along and do as the Romans do, of course," replied Charlie.

"Didn't know I was getting into a Catholic church," retorted the other. "Say, don't rush me way up in front, will you?"

"Never you mind that. Come on." And before Dick could say more the usher was half way up the aisle.

"Who is that stranger Charlie Bowen is seating?" said old Mrs. Gadsby in a low voice, to her neighbor. The neighbor shook her head. "Isn't he handsome?" whispered a young school teacher to her chum. "Some distinguished strangers here to-day," thought the pastor as he glanced over his congregation. And Adam Goodrich turned his head just in time to look into the face of the tramp printer, who was being seated in the pew behind him. Miss Goodrich was with her father and Dick heard nothing of the opening part of the service, only coming to himself when Cameron was well started in his discourse. The preacher's theme was, "The Sermon on the Mount," and the first words that caught the young man's ear were, "Blessed are the poor in spirit, for theirs is the kingdom of Heaven." He glanced around at the congregation. Mrs. Gadsby was inspecting the diamonds in the ears of the lady by her side, who was resting her powdered and painted face on the back of the pew in front, as though in devotion.

"Blessed are they that mourn, for they shall be comforted," read the minister. Dick thought of the widows and orphans in the city, and of the luxurious homes of the people he saw about him. "Blessed are the meek, for they shall inherit the earth." Dick looked straight at Adam Goodrich, the very back of whose head showed haughty arrogance and pride. "Blessed are they that do hunger and thirst after righteousness, for they shall be filled." Dick lifted up his eyes and looked at four members of the choir who were whispering and giggling behind their books, and noted the beautiful frescoed ceiling, the costly stained-glass windows, the soft carpets and carved furniture on the rostrum, and the comfortable, well-cushioned pews. "Is all this righteousness?" he asked himself. And he thought of the boys and girls on the street, of the hungry, shivering, starving, sin-stained creatures he had seen and known, who would not dare present themselves at the outer door of this temple, consecrated to the service of Him who said, "Come unto me and I will give you rest." And then, lest men might be mistaken, added, "Whosoever will may come."

"Blessed are the pure in heart, for they shall see God." Dick's eyes rested on the girl in the next seat. Yes, Amy was pure in heart. There was no shadow of evil on that beautiful brow. Innocence, purity and truth were written in every line of the girlish features, and Dick's heart ached as he thought of his own life and the awful barrier between them; not the barrier of social position or wealth; *that*, he knew, could be overcome; but the barrier he had builded himself, in the reckless, wasted years. And then and there the strong young man fought a battle in the secret chamber of his own soul; fought a battle and won; putting from himself forever, as he believed, the dreams he had dared to dream in the lonely evening hours in the printing office.

His struggle with himself seemed to make Dick feel more keenly the awful mockery of the worshippers; and to him, who all his life had been used to looking at things as they really were, without the glasses of conventionalism or early training, the very atmosphere of the place was stifling.

When the services were over, he rushed from the building without even returning Charlie's salutation, only drawing a long breath when he was safe on the street again; and rejoiced in his heart when at dinner, the restaurant keeper cursed his wife in the kitchen, and a drunken boarder fell from his chair. "This, at least, is real," he said to himself; "but what a world this would be if only the Sermon on the Mount were lived, not simply talked about."

The Monday night following Dick's visit to the church, Charlie Bowen had gone back to the office after supper, as he often did when business was brisk, forgetting that it was the first Monday in the month, and that the official board of the Jerusalem Church would hold their regular business meeting there.

The matter was only brought to his mind when Elder Wicks, with Rev. Cameron, entered, followed soon after by two or three others. Charlie's first impulse was to leave the office, but it was necessary that his work be done. His employer knew that he was there and could easily give him a hint if it would be better for him to retire. Shrewd old Uncle Bobbie, however, had his own plans in regard to this particular meeting, and it was not a part of them to have his young assistant leave the office. So nothing was said, and the meeting opened in the regulation way, with a prayer by Elder Gardner, the Chairman of the Board. The pastor and the different standing committees, with the treasurer, made their reports; some general matters were passed upon, and then the much-talked-of, long-deferred subject of building an addition to their place of worship was introduced.

"You know, Brethren," said the pastor, "our house does not begin to hold the people at the regular services, and we must have more Sunday School room. It seems to me that there will be no better time than the present. The church is in a prosperous condition; we are out of debt; and if we ever expect to enlarge our work we must begin."

"I know, Brother Cameron," said Deacon Godfrey, stating the standard objection, as it had been stated for the past two years, "but where's the money to come from? The members are paying all they can now to keep out of debt, and I don't believe they will do any more."

"We do need more room," said Elder Chambers; "that's a fact. The Sunday School is too crowded, and lots of people can't get to hear the preaching. But I'm like Brother Godfrey, I don't see how it's to be done. I'm giving every cent I can now, and I know lots of the Brethren who are doing the same."

"The Lord will provide," said Deacon Wickham, with a pious uplifting of his eyes, and a sanctimonious whine in his voice. "The Lord will provide. Brethren, I'm ashamed for you to talk in this doubting manner. What would the congregation think if they should hear you? Can't you trust the Lord? Don't, oh, don't doubt His precious promises. He will provide. If we need an addition to the church let us ask Him. He will provide."

"Yes, the Lord will provide, but we've got to do the hustlin'," said Uncle Bobbie. "He'll provide common sense and expect us to use it."

"Couldn't the women folks do something?" timidly suggested another.

"Of course they could," said Deacon Sharpe. "They could get up a social, or fair, or an entertainment of some kind. They used to do a lot that way before Brother Cameron came."

"Yes, and spent twenty-seven cents to make seventeen, while their boys run the streets and their husbands darn their own britches," broke in Uncle Bobbie again. "I tell you, I don't believe that so much of this Ladies' Aid business is business. Christ wouldn't run a peanut stand to support the church, ner pave a sinner's way to Heaven with pop-corn balls and molasses candy—" A half smothered cough came from the next room and everybody started. "Oh, it's only Charlie. He's got some work to do to-night," said the old man, reassuringly.

"Everybody does it though," said Deacon Sharpe, encouraged by the nods of Chambers and Godfrey. "All the churches depend upon the women, with their fairs and such, to pay their way. I don't see what's the harm. It gives the women something to do, and keeps us from paying out so much cash."

"Yes, an' that's what ails the churches," retorted Elder Wicks again. "There's too many of 'em run on the lemonade and ice cream basis; and as fer givin' the women somethin' to do, my wife's got her hands full takin' care o' me and her home. That's what I got her for, ain't it? She didn't marry the church—to-be-sure, though, it does look like it sometimes."

"We must all work in the Master's vineyard. None shall lose his reward," said Deacon Wickham again. "We all have our talents and God will hold us responsible for the use we make of them. We all have our work to do." To which sentiment Uncle Bobbie's reply was, "Yes; that means all the women have our work to do, and that we'll get our reward by makin' 'em do it. I ain't got no use fer a man who lets a woman do his work, even in church. There's enough for 'em to do that we can't, without their spoilin' their eyes and breakin' their backs makin' sofa pillows, carpet rags, and mince meat, to pay the runnin' expenses of the church, and the debt besides."

"I know of only one way," said the pastor, anxious to prevent these too frequent clashes between the pious deacon and the sharp old elder.

"What's that?" asked Chairman Gardner.

"The Young People's Society."

There was a slight rustle and the sound as of a book falling to the floor in the other room.

"Umph," said Godfrey; "what can *they* do?"

"Have you ever attended their meetings?" asked Cameron. "They have done more practical, Christian work this past year than all the rest of the church put together. And if the truth must be told, are more to be depended upon at regular services, and prayer meeting, than some members of the official board."

"Better turn the church into a Young Folks' Society then," said Wickham, angrily; "and throw away the Bible altogether. Christ didn't say, 'Upon this rock I'll build my Young People's Society.' For my part, I won't have nothing to do with it. There is not a single passage of Scripture that says we shall have such things; and until you can show me, book, chapter and verse, I'll fight it."

"I'll give ye book, chapter and verse," said Uncle Bobbie; "Phillippians, iv: 8."

There was a painful silence and then one of the deacons asked, "But would the young folks help?"

"I think so," said the pastor.

"We might ask Charlie Bowen 'bout that," suggested Mr. Wicks. "Charlie," he called, "are you most through with them books?"

"Yes, sir," answered the young man.

"Well, lock 'em up and come in here."

When they had laid the matter before him Charlie said, "Yes, I am sure the Society would take the matter up but for one thing; ever since Brother Cameron's sermon, on the Church of the Future, we have been planning to furnish a reading room somewhere, and it may be that they wouldn't want to give up the idea. If it was arranged so that we could have a room in the church when the addition was built, I am sure the Society would be glad to take hold."

Uncle Bobbie's eyes twinkled as he watched his young helper. He had not misjudged his man. This was just what he had expected. But Deacon Wickham was on his feet almost before Charlie finished speaking.

"Brethren, this is entirely out of order. We have no right to listen to the counsel of this boy. He has not a single qualification, for either a deacon or an elder. I believe we ought to go according to the Scriptures or not at all; and as for this new-fangled idea of a reading room in the church, it's all wrong. The Bible don't say a thing about reading rooms and there is no authority for it whatever. If the inspired apostles had wanted reading rooms in the church they would have said so. Paul didn't have them. Let us stand for the religion of our fathers and let the young people read at home if they want to. Brethren, I am opposed to the whole thing. This boy has no right to speak here."

Wicks whispered to Charlie, "Never you mind him. He's got just so much sputtering to do anyway. I'll fix him in a minute, and then he'll wash his hands of the whole matter." "I think it's a fine plan," he said aloud.

"So do I," agreed Deacon Sharpe. "Why not let the young folks have the room? We could charge ten cents admission and make a good thing for the church. I believe we ought to watch these corners and make a little now and then. Paul worked to support himself."

"Make not my Father's house an house of merchandise," said Cameron, but faintly concealing his disgust. "I tell you, Brethren, this thing must be free. I am sure that is the plan of the young folks. The Young People's Society is not in the business to make money. Am I right, Charlie?"

"Yes, sir," answered the young Christian eagerly. "We wanted to fix some place where the young men of the town could spend their evenings, without going to the bad. There are lots of them who don't have homes, but live in boarding houses and have no place to go."

"And a pretty crowd you'll have too," said Wickham.

"Yes, and if you had to pay the preacher you'd want to rent the room," said Sharpe.

Cameron's face flushed at the hard words.

"Come, come, Brethren, what shall we do about this?" said the Chairman.

"I move," said Elder Wicks, "that we ask the Young People's Society to assist us in building the addition to the church, and that we give them one of the rooms."

"I second the motion," said Cameron; and it was carried. Then the meeting adjourned with the usual prayer.

"Well," said Wickham, "I wash my hands of the whole matter."

Uncle Bobbie nudged Charlie in the side as he started for his hat; and later, as he walked down the street, arm in arm with his pastor and his bookkeeper, he said: "Poor old Wickham; his heart's all right, but he's got so much Scripture in his head that his think machine won't work."

"Friends," said Cameron, as they paused in front of the parsonage; "this is the day I have looked forward to for a long time. This step will revolutionize our methods. It's hard to get out of old ruts, but the world needs applied Christianity. Thank God for the young people." And Uncle Bobbie said, "Amen."

CHAPTER VIII

Charlie Bowen ran into the printing office one day on his way home to dinner. "Dick," he said, "it's time you got out of this. I want you to put on your best bib and tucker to-night and go with me to meet some young people."

Dick carefully spread a pile of letterheads on the drying rack; then shutting off the power, stood watching the machine as its movements grew slower and slower. "Young people," he thought; "the Young People's Society of the Jerusalem Church. I saw the announcement in to-day's Independent. Church members—*she'll* be there, and I'll have the joy of seeing how near I can come to the candle without getting my wings singed. Well, I suppose a fellow can't stay in the dark all the time," he said aloud, as he turned from the now motionless press.

"Of course not," cried Charlie. "You've hidden yourself long enough. It will do you a world of good to get out; and, beside, I always do feel like a sneak when I'm having a good time and you're moping up here in this dirty old place."

Dick looked around. "I've moped in worse places," he said. "But I'll go with you to-night and be as giddy as you please. I'll whisper pretty nothings to the female lambkins and exchange commonplace lies with the young gentlemen, and then—why then—we'll come away again and straightway forget what manner of things we said and did, and they won't count when we meet on the street before folks."

"That's all right," returned the other. "You just come anyway and see how badly you're mistaken. I'll call for you at seven-thirty sharp." And he left him cleaning up for his mid-day lunch.

When Charlie returned to the office that evening he found Dick dressed ready to go, and a strange contrast the latter presented to the poorly-clad, half-starved tramp who had walked into Boyd City only a few weeks before. Some thought of this flashed through Dick's mind as he read the admiration in his friend's face, and his own eyes glowed with pleasure. Then a shadow swiftly came, but only for a moment. He was determined to forget, for one evening at least. "Come on," he cried gaily, squaring his shoulders as though looking forward to a battle, "my soul seemeth anxious for the fray."

Charlie laughed as he answered, "I only hope that you'll come off whole. There will be some mighty nice girls there to-night. Look out you don't get your everlasting."

When the two young men reached the home of Helen Mayfield, where the social was to be held, they were met at the door by Miss Clara Wilson, who was Chairman of the reception committee.

"Glory," whispered that young lady to herself. "Here comes Charlie Bowen with that tramp printer of George's. Wish George could see him now." But not a hint of her thought found expression in her face, and the cordial, whole-hearted way in which she offered her hand in greeting, carried the conviction that no matter what might be his reception from others, this, at least, was genuine.

The guests gathered quickly, and soon there was a house full of laughing, chattering, joking young people; and Dick, true to his promise, laughed and chattered with the rest.

"Who is that tall, handsome man with the dark hair, talking to those girls with Nellie Graham and Will Clifton?" whispered Amy Goodrich to Miss Wilson, who had been asking her why Frank was not at the gathering.

"Haven't you met him yet?" answered Clara, secretly amused, for George had told her of the incident at the office. "That's Mr. Falkner, from Kansas City. Come, you must meet him. Mr. Falkner," she said, skillfully breaking up the group, "I wish to present you to a very dear friend. Miss Goodrich, Mr. Falkner." Poor Dick felt the room spin round and everybody looking at him, as he mumbled over some nonsense about the great honor and happiness of having met Miss Goodrich before.

Amy looked at him in astonishment. "I think you are mistaken, Mr. Falkner," she said. "I do not remember having met you. Where was it; here in town?"

With a mighty effort, Dick caught hold of himself, as it were, and gazed around with an air of defiance. To his amazement, no one was paying the least attention to him. Only his fair partner was looking up into his face with mingled amusement, wonder and admiration written on her features.

"In California; I think it was year before last," he said glibly.

Amy laughed—"But I never was in California in my life, so you must be mistaken." Then, as Dick swept the room with another anxious glance: "What is the matter, Mr. Falkner; are you looking for someone?"

"I was wondering where Charlie Bowen went to," he answered desperately. "I didn't know but what he would want me to turn the ice-cream freezer or something."

Miss Goodrich laughed again. "You're the funniest man," she said, and something in her voice or manner brought Dick to his senses with a jar.

"Well," he said, with a smile, "if I am mistaken I am very sorry, I assure you."

"About the ice cream?"

"No, about having met you before."

"Oh, sorry that you thought you had met me?"

Dick protested to some length with much unnecessary earnestness, and at last suggested that they find seats. Miss Goodrich agreed, and leading the way to an adjoining room, discovered a cushioned corner near the window. "Do you know," she said, when they were seated, "I, too, feel as you do?"

"About the ice-cream?" retorted Dick.

"No," she laughed, "about having met you before."

"Indeed, I am glad."

"Glad?"

"Yes, that you feel as I do."

"Truly," she said, ignoring his reply, "you *do* remind me of someone I have seen somewhere. Oh, I know; it's that tramp printer of Mr. Udell's, I—Why, what is the matter, Mr. Falkner? Are you sick? Let me call someone."

"No, no," gasped Dick. "I'll be all right in a moment. It's my heart. Please don't worry." He caught up a basket of pictures. "Here, let's look at these. I find nothing that has a more quieting effect than the things one finds on the center tables of our American homes."

Amy looked uneasy but began turning over the pictures in the basket. There were some commonplace photos of commonplace people, a number of homemade kodaks, one or two stray views of Yellowstone Park, the big trees of California, Niagara Falls, and several groups that were supposed to be amusing. "Oh, here's a picture of that printer," she cried, picking up one which showed the interior of an old-fashioned printing office, with a Washington hand-press and a shock-headed printer's devil sitting on a high stool, his face and shirt-front bespattered with ink. "That looks just like him. Why,—why, Mr. Falkner, you've torn that picture! What *will* Helen Mayfield say?"

"Awfully sorry," said Dick, "I'll find her another. It was very awkward of me, I am sure." Then in desperation, "But tell me more about this printer of whom I remind you; what was his name?"

"Oh, I don't know that," replied Amy, "but he was very kind to me and sat up at night to design a cover for a little booklet I was having printed. I never saw him to thank him though, for he was out when I called the next day. I heard that Mr. Udell had a tramp working for him and I suppose it was he, for he acted very strangely—he may have been drinking. It is too bad for he must have been a splendid workman. There ought to be one of those books here," and she began turning over the things on the table. "Yes, here it is." And she handed Dick the pamphlet that had caused him so much trouble that night in the office.

It is hard to say where the matter would have ended had not Miss Jameson, another member of the social committee, appeared just then, and ordered them to the parlor, where Amy was wanted to play.

After the company had listened to several instrumental pieces and one or two solos by different girls, one of the young men asked, "Don't you sing, Mr. Falkner?"

"Of course he does," and all began calling for a song.

A sudden thought struck Dick, and stepping quickly to the piano, he played his own accompaniment and sang, in a rich baritone voice, a street song:

> "They tell me go work for a living,
> And not round the country to stamp;
> And then when I ask for employment,
> They say there's no work for a tramp."

The song was by no means a classic one, but the manner in which Dick rendered it made it seem so, and as he sang:

> "There's many a true heart beating,
> Beneath the old coat of a tramp."

A strange hush fell over the little audience, and when the song was finished a subdued murmur of applause filled the room, while eager voices called for more. Dick responded with another selection and then declaring that he had done his share, left the instrument and seated himself by Charlie's side.

"Good, old man," said that young gentleman, in a whisper, "but where in the world did you learn all that?"

"Dance hall and variety," whispered Dick. "Never thought I'd air that accomplishment at a church social."

Charlie's reply was lost in a call to the dining room, where light refreshments were served to the hungry young people by waiters from among their number; then turn about, and the waiters were waited upon; and through it all ran the laugh and jest of happy young folks, who thoroughly enjoyed each other's company, and who for one evening met on common ground. After supper, came games and more music, while a few of the more earnest ones, in an out-of-the-way corner, discussed the reading room and planned for its future. Then came a call for everyone to sing, and with Amy at the piano, they sang song after song until it was time to go. Then the bustle of leave-taking—good nights—lovely time—my house next month—and Dick found himself walking downtown, arm in arm with his friend. "Well," said the latter, "how about it?"

"Thank you for a pleasant evening," replied Dick. "But say, those folks don't know me, do they?"

"Some of them do; some don't. What does it matter?"

"Well, tell me, did those who know how I came to town, know that I would be there tonight?"

"*No, sir,*" said Charlie, emphatically. "What do you take me for, Dick?"

"Forgive me," said Dick. "I ought to have known better, only you see my experience with church people, and—well—I'm a bit sore I guess. I couldn't believe there were any like those. I didn't know, that's all," and with a "good-night," he turned down the street toward his humble lodging place, while Charlie went on toward home.

"Yes, that's all," said the latter to himself. "Dick didn't know; and that's what's the matter with hundreds of fellows just like him; they don't know what real Christianity is like; they see so much of the sham; but he'll find out though, or I'm mistaken. My, what a worker he would make, with his experience and talents, if only once he got started right. He just made that old street song burn its way into the heart, and I felt like I wanted to be a brother to every poor, homeless chap in the world."

Meanwhile, Dick had reached the office, and throwing off his coat, laid aside his collar, tie and cuffs. Then seating himself in the rickety old chair, he tilted back as far as possible and fixed his feet as high as he could get them, against the big Prouty press. Five—ten—fifteen-minutes went by, Dick sat without moving a muscle. The clanging bell of the eleven-thirty train on the "Memphis" pulling into the depot, sounded plainly in his ear, but still he sat immovable. A night-hawk cab rattled over the brick pavement, and a drunkard yelled beneath the window; still Dick held his place. So still that a little mouse that lived in one corner of the office, crept stealthily out, and glancing curiously with his bead-like eyes, at the motionless figure, ran, with many a pause, to the very legs of Dick's chair. Crash—as Dick's feet struck the floor. The shaky old piece of furniture almost fell in ruins and the poor frightened mouse fled to cover. Kicking the chair to one side, the young fellow walked to the window and stood with his hands in his pockets, looking into the night. Then, in sullen tones, he addressed the lamp that twinkled in the bakery across the way: "I'm a fool. I know I'm a fool; a great big fool. I ought to have told her who I was. I ought to get out a poster and label myself *dangerous*, so people would know they were talking to a tramp. Oh, but when she finds out, as she must—and her father—." Here Dick's imagination failed him, and he laughed again and again in spite of himself, as he thought of the tramp who had applied to Adam Goodrich for work, chatting with his beautiful daughter as an equal. "Whew—but there'll be a hot time in the camp of the enemy when they learn the truth," and he took himself off to bed.

CHAPTER IX

The opinions on the part of Rev. Cameron's flock regarding the proposed reading room, were numerous and varied. Adam Goodrich, in his usual pompous manner, gave it as his judgment that Cameron would be running a free lodging house next, as though that were the greatest depth of infamy to which a poor preacher could sink, and Mrs. Goodrich declared that it would ruin the social influence of the church forever. Amy was heart and soul with the movement, but prudently refrained from discussing the matter in the presence of her parents; while Frank, though he attended all the meetings of the society and would not openly oppose their efforts for fear of being unpopular, lost no opportunity to secretly throw a stumbling block in their way, and made all manner of sneering allusions to the work when he thought it would not come to the ears of the young people.

When at last the room was finished and ready to be occupied, the committee appointed met to select a manager. The church, with the usual good judgment shown by churches in such matters, had named Elder Wicks and Deacon Wickham, and the young people had selected Charlie Bowen and two young ladies, to represent the Society. They met in the new rooms one evening and Deacon Wickham took the floor at once.

"I hope our young friends won't take offense at what I am about to say, but you know I am one of the kind who always say just what I think, for I believe that if a man has anything on his mind, it had better come out. This business ought to be in the hands of the church board; you young folks have no Scriptural rights to speak on the subject at all." The three young Christians looked at Uncle Bobbie, whose left eye remained closed for just the fraction of a second, and the speaker wondered at the confident smile with which his words were received. "There's not one of you that has the proper qualifications for an elder or a deacon," he continued. "You girls have no right to have the oversight of a congregation, anyway, and Charlie Bowen here is not even the husband of one wife."

"Give him time, Brother Wickham; give the boy time," broke in Uncle Bobbie, with a chuckle, much to the delight of the girls, and the confusion of Charlie. "You just wait; he may surprise you some day in his qualifications."

But the deacon continued with a frown at the interruption, "As far as that goes, the whole thing is unscriptural and I was opposed to it at the first, as Brother Wicks here can tell you." Uncle Bobbie nodded. "But you've gone ahead in spite of what I and the Scriptures teach, and you've got your reading rooms; and now I mean to see to it that you have a good Brother, who is eminently qualified to teach, at the head of the concern; a good man who is thoroughly grounded in the faith, and who has arrived at years of discretion; a workman that needeth not to be ashamed of his handiwork, rightly dividing the word of truth. Such a man could get the young Christians together evenings and lay out their Bible reading for them, spending an hour or two perhaps, each week, in explaining the more difficult passages. If I had time I would be glad to do the work myself, for there's nothing I like better than teaching. I don't know, I might possibly find time if the Brethren thought best for me to take the work. I am always ready to do what the Lord wants me to, and I promise you that I'd teach those young people the Scriptures, and make them interested, too. Why, when I was in Bear City, down in Oklahoma, I had a—"

"But, Brother Wickham," interrupted Uncle Bobbie, who knew from experience that if the good deacon ever got started on his work in Oklahoma they never would get to the business of the evening, "it strikes me you ain't got jist the right ide' of this. Tain't to be a Sunday School, ner a place to teach the Bible, as I understand it, though I reckon it's in line with the teachin' of Christ. It is—"

"Not to teach the Bible?" ejaculated the astonished deacon. "What on earth can you teach in the church except the Bible, and what kind of a reading room can you have in the Lord's house I'd like to know?"

"The ide', Brother Wickham," said the old elder, as gently as he could, "is to furnish some place where young men of the town can go and spend their time when they aint working. This room will be stocked with the latest books, magazines and papers; there will be tables with writin' material and sich stuff, if a feller wants to write to his girl, you know, and the room in there will be fixed with easy chairs and sofas for them that wants to talk er play games, er have a good time generally. Seems to me what we want fer a manager is some young man who's got good boss sense, and who could make things pleasant, even if he don't know so much Scripture."

"And it's to be free to every loafer who wants to come in and use the place?"

"Yes, just as free as Christ's invitation to come and be saved."

"But you'll fill the church with a lot of trash who don't know anything about the Bible, or the plan of salvation. How can you, when the Scriptures say, have no fellowship with such?"

"We'll save a few young men who are startin' fer Hell by way of the saloons and bawdy houses."

"No you won't. The Gospel and the Gospel alone, is the power of God unto salvation. God never ordained that men should be saved by reading rooms and such."

"I believe I know just the man we want," said Uncle Bobbie, turning to the young people, when the deacon had at last subsided into an attitude of sullen protest.

"Who?" asked one of the young ladies, with the hint of a laugh in her eyes, as she looked at their stand-by.

"That printer of Udell's. He's a clean, strong young feller, and I believe would be glad of some sech place to spend his evenin's. Of course he aint a Christian, but—"

"Not a Christian," cried Wickham, starting to his feet again; "not a Christian? And you propose to let an alien take charge of the Lord's work? I wash my hands of the whole matter."

"Are you sure he will be all right?" asked the other girl on the committee.

"Sure," replied Wicks, "if he will take it, and I think we can get Charlie here to see to that."

Charlie nodded. "It will be a splendid thing for him," he said; and then he told them how Dick spent his evenings alone in the office, rather than go to the only places open to him.

"Well," said Uncle Bobbie, "let's fix it that way. Brother Wickham, we have decided to ask Richard Falkner to take charge of the rooms."

"I've got nothing to say about it, sir," answered the good deacon. "I don't know anything about it. I wash my hands of the whole matter."

And so the work at the Jerusalem Church was established. It took no little power of persuasion on the part of Charlie Bowen, to bring his friend to the point of accepting the committee's offer, even when it was endorsed by the entire Young People's Society, and a large part of the congregation. But his arguments finally prevailed and Dick consented to be at the rooms between the hours of seven and eleven every evening, the time when a strong, tactful man in authority would be most needed.

The rooms were furnished by friends of the cause and were cheery, comfortable, homelike apartments, where everyone was made welcome. Many a poor fellow, wandering on the streets, tired of his lonely boarding house, and sorely tempted by the air of cheerfulness and comfort of the saloons, was led there, where he found good books and good company; and at last, for what was more natural, became a regular attendant at the only church in the city which did not close its doors to him during the week.

Dick enjoyed the work, and in a short time had many friends among the young men. He treated everybody in the same kindly, courteous manner, and was always ready to recommend a book, to introduce an acquaintance, or to enter into conversation with a stranger. Indeed he soon grew so popular among the young folks that George Udell told Miss Wilson it seemed as though he had always lived in Boyd City, he knew so many people, and so many knew him. And of course Clara answered, "I told you so." What woman could resist such an opportunity? "Didn't I say that he was no common tramp? You needn't tell me I don't know a man when I see him."

The two were driving in the evening, on the road that leads south from town, down a hill, across a bridge, and along the bank of a good-sized creek, where the trees bend far over to dip the tips of their branches in the water, and the flowers growing rank and wild along the edges, nod lazily at their own faces reflected in the quiet pools and eddies.

"You may know a man when you see him," replied George, letting the horse take his own time beneath the overhanging boughs, "but you take precious good care that you don't see too much of one that I could name."

"Who do you mean; Mr. Falkner?" replied Clara, with a provoking smile, as she tried in vain to catch one of the tall weeds that grew close to the side of the road.

"Hang Mr. Falkner," returned Udell impatiently. "You know what I mean, Clara. What's the use of you and me pretending? Haven't I told you ever since I was ten years old that I loved you, and would have no one else to be my wife? And haven't you always understood it that way, and by your manners toward me given assent?"

The girl looked straight ahead at the horse's ears as she answered slowly, "If my manner has led you to have false hopes it is very easy to change it, and if accepting your company gives assent to all the foolish things you may have said when you were ten years old, you'd better seek less dangerous society."

"Forgive me dear, I spoke hastily," said George, in a much softer tone. "But it's mighty hard to have you always just within reach and yet always just beyond."

The sun had gone down behind the ridge. The timbers of an old mining shaft, and the limbs and twigs of a leafless tree showed black against the tinted sky. A faint breath of air rustled the dry leaves of the big sycamores and paw-paw bushes, and the birds called sleepily to each other as they settled themselves for the coming night. A sparrow-hawk darted past on silent wings, a rabbit hopped across the road, while far away, the evening train on the "Frisco" whistled for a crossing; and nearer, a farm boy called to his cattle. After a long silence, George spoke again, with a note of manly dignity in his voice, which made his fair companion's heart beat quicker. "Clara, look at me; I want to see your eyes," he insisted. She turned her face toward him. "Clara, if you can say, I do not love you as a woman ought to love her husband, I will promise you, on my honor, never to mention the subject to you again. Can you say it?"

She tried to turn her head and to hide the tell-tale color in her cheeks, but he would not permit it. "Answer me," he insisted. "Say you do not love me and I will never bother you again."

At last the eyes were lifted, and in their light George read his answer. "All right," he said, picking up the whip, "I knew you could not lie; you do love me, and I'll never stop asking you to be my wife." He turned the horse's head toward the city.

That same evening, Adam Goodrich, with his family and two or three neighbors, sat on the veranda of the Goodrich home, enjoying the beauties of the hour, and passing the evening in social chat. In the course of the conversation, someone mentioned the rooms at the Jerusalem Church. Adam grunted. "What a splendid thing it is for the young men," said one of the lady callers. "I don't see why more of the churches don't adopt the plan. I wish ours would."

"Yes," chimed in another, "and isn't that Mr. Falkner, who has charge of the rooms in the evening, a splendid fellow? My brother speaks of him so highly, and all the young men seem to think so much of him."

"Where is he from; St. Louis, is it?" asked the first lady.

"Kansas City," said Frank. "At least that's what *he* says. He bummed his way into town last spring and got a job in that infidel Udell's printing office. That's all anybody knows of him."

"Except that he has never shown himself to be anything but a perfect gentleman," added his sister.

"Amy," said Mrs. Goodrich, a note of warning in her voice.

"I don't care, mamma, it's the truth. What if he *was* out of money and hungry and ragged when he came to town? He was willing to work, and Mr. Udell says that he is a splendid workman, and—" But her father interrupted her. "Well, what of it? No one knows anything about his family or how he lived before he came here. He's only a tramp, and you can't make anything else out of him. Some folks are never satisfied unless they are trying to make gentlemen out of gutter snipes. If we let such fellows get a foothold, there won't be any respectable society after a while; it will be all stable boys and boot-blacks."

Later, when the visitors had said good-night and Amy and her mother had entered the house, Frank said, "Father, I'll tell you one thing about that man Falkner, you've got to watch him."

"What do you mean?" asked Adam.

"I mean Amy," replied the other, moving his chair nearer the old gentleman and speaking in a guarded tone. "He takes every chance he can to talk with her, and she is altogether too willing to listen."

"Pshaw," grunted the older man, "she never sees him."

"That's where you are mistaken, father. They met first last spring in the printing office; and afterwards, when he had gotten in with that soft fool, Charlie Bowen, they met again at the Young People's social. He was all dressed up in a new suit of clothes and of course Amy didn't know him. They were together all that evening, and since then, though she has found out who he is, she talks with him at every opportunity. They meet at the Society, at church, at picnics and parties, and sometimes in the printing office. I tell you you'd better watch him. He's doing his level best to get in with her, and just look how he's working everybody else. Half the town is crazy over him."

Low spoken as were Frank's words, Amy heard every one, for she had not retired as her brother supposed, but was lying on a couch just inside the doorway of the darkened parlor. With burning cheeks, she rose cautiously and tiptoed out of the silent room. Making her way upstairs and entering her own chamber, she closed and bolted the door, and then, throwing herself on the floor by the low seat of an open window, rested her head on her arm while she looked up at the stars now shining clear and bright. Once she started impatiently and her eyes filled with angry tears. Then she grew calm again, and soon the girlish face was worthy of a master's brush as she gazed reverently into the beautiful heavens, her lips moving in a whispered prayer; a softly whispered prayer for Dick. And as she prayed, in the shadow of the Catalpa trees, unseen by her, a man walked slowly down the street. Reaching the corner, he turned and slowly passed the house again; crossing the street, he passed once more on the opposite side, paused a moment at the corner, and then started hurriedly away toward the business portion of the city.

CHAPTER X

November, with its whispered promises of winter fun, was past, and the Christmas month, with snow and ice, had been ushered in. Usually in the latitude of Boyd City, the weather remains clear and not very cold until the first of the new year; but this winter was one of those exceptions which are met with in every climate, and the first of December brought zero weather. Indeed, it had been unusually cold for several weeks. Then, to make matters worse, a genuine western blizzard came howling across the prairie, and whistled and screamed about the streets, from which it had driven everything that could find a place of shelter. The stores on Broadway were vacant, save a few shivering clerks. In the offices, men sat with their feet on the stove and called to mind the biggest storms they had ever known; while street cars stood motionless and railway trains, covered with ice and snow, came puffing into the stations three or four hours behind time. In spite of the awful weather, George Udell spent the evening at the Wilson home on the east side. He had not seen Clara for nearly two weeks and the hour was rather late when he arose to prepare for the long, cold walk to his boarding house. "And I must wait, Clara?" he asked again, as they stood in the hallway, and the girl answered rather sharply, "Yes, you must wait. I do wish you would be sensible, George." The printer made no reply, but paused for some time with his hand on the door-knob, as though reluctant to leave her in such a mood. Then with an "Alright, goodnight," he stepped out into the storm, his mind filled with bitter thoughts that had best be left unspoken. The man did not know how heavy was the heart of the girl who stood at the window watching long after his form had vanished into the night.

The wind was terrific and the snow cut the printer's face like tiny needles, while he was forced again and again to turn his back to the blast in order to breathe, and in spite of his heavy clothing was chilled to the bone before he had gone three blocks. On Broadway, he passed saloon after saloon, brilliant with glittering chandeliers and attractive with merry music, inviting all the world to share the good-fellowship and cheer within. He thought of his rooms, how cold and lonely they would be, and had half a mind to stop at the hotel for the night. For an instant he hesitated, then with a shake, "What folly," pushed on again. As he struggled along, fighting every inch of the way, with head down and body braced to the task, warm lights from the windows of many cozy homes fell across his path, and he seemed to feel the cold more keenly for the contrast. Then through the storm, he saw a church, dark, grim and forbidding, half-hidden in the swirling snow, the steps and entrance barricaded with heavy drifts. A smile of bitter sarcasm curled his lip as he muttered to himself: "How appropriate; what a fine monument to the religious activity of the followers of Christ," and he almost laughed aloud when he remembered that the sermon delivered there the Sunday before was from the text, "I was a stranger and ye took me not in." Suddenly he stopped and stood peering through the storm. In the light of an electric arc, which sizzled and sputtered on the corner, he saw a dark form half hidden in the snow piled about the doorway of the building. Stepping closer, he reached out and touched it with his foot, then bending down, he discovered to his horror that it was the body of a man.

George tried to arouse the fallen one and lift him to his feet, but his efforts only met with failure, and the other sank back again on his bed of snow. The printer studied a moment. What should he do? Then his eyes caught a gleam of light from a house near by. "Of course," he thought, "Uncle Bobbie Wicks lives there." Stooping again, he gathered the man in his arms, and with no little effort, slowly and painfully made his way across the street and along the sidewalk to Mr. Wicks's home.

Uncle Bobbie was sitting before the fire, dozing over his Sunday School quarterly, when he was aroused by the sound of heavy feet on the porch and a strange knock, as though someone was kicking at the door. Quickly he threw it open, and Udell, with his heavy burden, staggered into the room.

"Found him on the church steps," gasped the printer, out of breath, as he laid the stranger on a couch. "I'll go for a doctor," and he rushed out into the storm again, returning some thirty minutes later with Dr. James at his heels. They found Uncle Bobbie, who had done all that was possible, sitting beside the still form on the couch. "You're too late, Doc," he said. "The poor chap was dead before George left the house."

The physician made his examination. "You're right, Mr. Wicks," he answered, "we can do nothing here. Frozen to death. Must have died early in the evening."

The doctor returned to his home to get what sleep he could before another call should break his rest, and all that night the Christian and the infidel sat together, keeping watch over the dead body of the unknown man.

The next morning the coroner was summoned; the verdict was soon handed in, "Death by exposure." Or the body was found a church statement that there had been paid to the current expense fund, in the quarter ending August first, the sum of three dollars, but the name written with lead pencil was illegible. Besides this, was a prayer-meeting topic-card, soiled and worn, and a small testament, dog-eared, with much fingering, but no money. A cheap Christian Endeavor pin was fastened to the ragged vest. There was nothing to identify him, or furnish a clew as to where he was from. The face and form was that of a young man, and though thin and careworn, showed no mark of dissipation. The right hand was marked by a long scar across the back and the loss of the little finger. The clothing was very poor.

Among those who viewed the body in the undertaking rooms where it lay for identification, was Dick, and Udell, who was with him, thought that he seemed strangely moved as he bent over the casket. George called his attention to the disfigured hand, but Dick only nodded. Then, as they drew back to make room for others, he asked in a whisper, "Did they search thoroughly for letters or papers? Sometimes people hide important documents in their clothing, you know."

"No, there was nothing," answered George. "We even ripped out the linings."

When they reached the open air Dick drew a long breath. "I must hurry back to the office," he said. "I suppose you'll not be down to-day."

"No, I must arrange for the funeral; you can get along I guess."

"Oh yes, don't worry about that," was the reply, and the young man started off down the street, but at the corner he turned, and walking rapidly, in a few moments reached the church where the body of the stranger was found.

The steps and walks had been carefully cleaned and the snow about the place was packed hard by the feet of the curious crowd who had visited the scene earlier in the morning.

Dick looked up and down the street. There was no one in sight. Stepping swiftly to the pile of snow which the janitor had made with his shovel and broom, he began kicking it about with his feet. Suddenly, with an exclamation, he stopped and again glanced quickly around. Then stooping, he picked up a long, leather pocketbook, and turning, walked hurriedly away to the office.

The body was held as long as possible, but when no word could be had as to the poor fellow's identity, he was laid away in a lot purchased by the printer, who also bore the funeral expenses. When Uncle Bobbie would have helped him in this, George answered: "No, this is my work. I found him. Let me do this for his mother's sake."

The funeral was held in the undertaking rooms. Dick Falkner, Uncle Bobbie and his wife, and Clara Wilson, with George, followed the hearse to the cemetery.

To-day, the visitor to Mt. Olive, will read with wonder, the inscription on a simple stone, bearing no name, but telling the story of the young man's death, and followed by these words, "I was a stranger and ye took me not in."

The church people protested loudly when it was known how the grave was to be marked, but George Udell answered that he wanted something from the Bible because the young man was evidently a Christian, and that the text he had selected was the only appropriate one he could find.

The evening after the funeral, Charlie Bowen and Dick sat alone in the reading room, for the hour was late and the others had all gone to their homes. Charlie was speaking of the burial. "I tell you," he said, "it looks mighty hard to see a man laid away by strangers who do not even know his name, and that too, after dying all alone in the snow like a poor dog. And to think that perhaps a mother is watching for him to come home; and the hardest part is that he is only one of many. In a cold snap like this, the amount of suffering among the poor and outcast is something terrible. If only the bad suffered, one might not feel so."

Dick made no reply, but sat staring moodily into the fire.

"I've studied on the matter a good bit lately," continued Charlie. "Why is it that people are so indifferent to the suffering about them? Is Udell right when he says that church members, by their own teaching, prove themselves to be the biggest frauds in the world?"

"He is, so far as the church goes," replied Dick; "but not as regards Christianity. This awful neglect and indifference comes from a *lack* of Christ's teaching, or rather from a lack of the application of Christ's teaching, and too much teaching of the church. The trouble is that people follow the church and not Christ; they become church members, but not Christians."

"Do you mean to say that the church ought to furnish a lodging place for every stranger who comes to town?" asked Charlie.

"I mean just this," answered Dick, rising to his feet and walking slowly back and forth across the room, "there is plenty of food in this world to give every man, woman and child enough to eat, and it is contrary to God's law that the *helpless* should go hungry. There is enough material to clothe every man, woman and child, and God never intended that the needy should go naked. There is enough wealth to house and warm every creature tonight, for God never meant that men should freeze in such weather as this; and Christ surely teaches, both by words and example, that the hungry should be fed, the naked clothed, and the homeless housed. Is it not the Christian's duty to carry out Christ's teaching? It is an awful comment on the policy of the church when a young man, bearing on his person the evidence of his Christianity and proof that he supported the institution, dies of cold and hunger at the locked door of the house of God. That, too, in a city where there are ten or twelve denominations, paying at least as many thousand dollars for preachers' salaries alone each year."

"But we couldn't do it."

"The lodges do. There is more than enough wealth spent in the churches in this city, for useless, gaudy display, and in trying to get ahead of some other denomination, than would be needed to clothe every naked child in warmth to-night. You claim to be God's stewards, but spend his goods on yourselves, while Christ, in the person of that boy in the cemetery, is crying for food and clothing. And then you wonder why George Udell and myself, who have suffered these things, don't unite with the church. The wonder to me is that such honest men as you and Mr. Wicks can remain connected with such an organization."

"But," said Charlie, with a troubled look on his face, "would not such work encourage crime and idleness?"

"Not if it were done according to God's law," answered Dick. "The present spasmodic, haphazard sentimental way of giving does. It takes away a man's self-respect; it encourages him to be shiftless and idle; or it fails to reach the worthy sufferers. Whichever way you fix it, it kills the man."

"But what is God's law?" asked the other.

"That those who do not work should not eat," replied Dick; "and that applies on the avenue as well as in the mines."

"How would you do all this, though? That has been the great problem of the church for years."

"I beg your pardon, but it has *not* been the problem of the church. If the ministry had spent one-half the time in studying this question and trying to *fulfill* the teaching of Christ, that they have wasted in quarreling over each other's opinions, or in tickling the ears of their wealthy members, this problem would have been solved long ago. Different localities would require different plans, but the purpose must always be the same. To make it possible for those in want to receive aid without compromising their self-respect, or making beggars of them, and to make it just as impossible for any unworthy person to get along without work."

For some minutes the silence in the room was only broken by the steady tramp, tramp, as the speaker marched up and down.

"Dick," said Charlie, "do you believe that anything could be done here?"

Dick started and looked sharply at his companion. "Of course it could, if only the church would go about it in a businesslike way."

Charlie shook his head. "That's hopeless. The church will never move in the matter. Brother Cameron has preached again and again on those subjects and they do nothing."

"But has your pastor presented any definite plan for work?" asked Dick. "It's one thing to preach about it, and another thing to present a plan that will meet the need. That's the great trouble. They're all the time preaching about Christianity and trying to live as they talk, in a sickly, sentimental fashion; when of all things in the world Christianity is the most practical, or it is nothing."

"The young folks would take it up, I am sure," said Charlie.

"Say, will you suggest a plan to the Society?"

"I'm like the rest," said Dick, with a slight smile. "I'm preaching when I have no remedy," and he began locking up for the night. "But," as they stepped out into the street, he added, "I'll not go back on my statement though. I believe it can be done."

Nothing more was said on the subject so much in the hearts of the young men, until the Saturday before the regular monthly business meeting of the Young People's Society. Then Charlie broached the matter to Dick as together they walked down the street at the close of their day's work.

"No," said Dick, "I have not forgotten, and I believe I have a plan that would meet the needs of the case as it is in this city."

"Will you go before the Young People's Society at their meeting next Tuesday night, and explain your scheme?"

Dick hesitated. "I fear they would not listen to me, Charlie," he said at last. And then added, as he rested his hand affectionately on the other's shoulder, "You see, old man, people here don't look at me as you do. They can't, or won't forget the way I came to town, and I fear they would not attach much weight to my opinion, even should they consent to hear me."

"That's where you're wrong, Dick, all wrong. I know there are some who look at things in that light, but they wouldn't do anything if Paul himself were to teach them. But there are many who want only someone to lead the way. Take myself for instance. I realize what's needed, and I honestly want to do something, but I don't know how to go at it; and Dick, if this problem is ever solved, it will be through someone like you, who knows from actual experience; not from occasional slumming expeditions; whose heart is filled with love for men; who is absolutely free from ecclesiastical chains, and who is a follower of no creed but Christ, a believer in no particular denomination."

Dick smiled at his friend's manner. "You too, have been doing a little thinking," he said quietly. "But had this come to you, that the man must also be a Christian?"

"Yes, a Christian so far as he is a believer in the truths that Christ teaches; but not in the generally accepted use of that word; which is, that a man can't be a Christian without hitching himself up in some denominational harness."

"If you believe that, why do you wear the badge?" asked Dick, drily.

"Because I believe that while the man who takes the initiative must owe allegiance to no particular congregation, the work must be carried on by the church; there are many Christians who are thinking on these lines, and I hope that you will some day see that the church with all its shortcomings and mistakes, is of divine origin; and that she needs just such men as yourself to lead her back to the simplicity of Christ's life and teaching. But that's not the question," he continued, as he saw a slight shadow cross the face of his companion. "The question is: Will you go before the Young People's Society next Tuesday night and submit your plan as a suggested way to do Christ's work here in the city? You see, you'll not be going before the church, and I will give you such an introduction that there will be no danger of a mistaken notion as to your presence."

The two walked on in silence until they reached the door of Dick's restaurant. "Won't you come in and eat with me?" he said.

"Not unless you need more urging," answered Charlie, with a laugh, "for I have other fish to fry just now."

"Well," said Dick, "I'll go."

CHAPTER XI

Needless to say that Charlie Bowen, who was the president of the Young People's Society at this time, took particular pains to notify each member that there would be a matter of unusual importance to discuss at the next meeting. And so, when he called the Society to order at eight o'clock Tuesday evening, in the lecture room of the church, almost the entire membership, including Rev. Cameron, was present. Dick remained in the reading room, but it was understood between the two that he was to be called in at the proper time.

After the regular routine business had been disposed of, the president stated that he wished to introduce a matter of great importance, which he felt sure would interest every Christian present. He then called to their minds some of the teaching they had heard from their pastor, along lines of practical Christianity; noticed briefly the condition of things in Boyd City; and asked if they would not be glad to remedy such evils. The nodding heads and earnest faces told Charlie of their interest. After recalling the death of the young man found by George Udell, he told of his conversation with Dick. "I am aware that Mr. Falkner makes no profession of Christianity," he said, "but you know him and need no word from me to tell you of the strength of his character." He then explained how he had asked Dick to speak to them, and after delicately stating the latter's objections, asked if they would receive him and listen to his ideas of Christian work.

At the close of Charlie's talk, the Society gladly voted to invite Dick in, and three of the boys started to find him, when Rev. Cameron rose to his feet, and in a voice full of emotion, said: "My dear young people. Wait just a moment. My heart is moved more than I can say, by the Christian spirit you are showing. And now, before your invitation is carried to Mr. Falkner, let us bow our heads in prayer, that we may be guided by the Holy Spirit in listening to the things he may have to put before us, and in any discussion of this subject that may follow."

A deep hush fell on the little band of young people as they followed their pastor's example, and it seemed as if a wonderful presence filled all the room. The thought flashed through Cameron's mind, "This must be another step in the new era of Christian work in this city." And then, in a few beautiful words, he voiced the prayer in the hearts of the young people, and the committee appointed went to call Dick. They found him nervously pacing up and down the passageway between the reading room and the parlor. Making known the wish of the Society, they escorted him to the meeting in the other part of the building. He was greeted by smiling faces, nods of encouragement, and just a faint ripple of applause, that sprung from a desire on the part of the young people to let him know that they were glad to bid him welcome, and ready to give him their attention.

The president stated simply that he had explained to the Society the purpose of Mr. Falkner's visit, and that he could assure the latter he was most heartily welcome. At Charlie's words, the ripple of applause became a wave, which in its strength, left no doubt on Dick's mind as to their earnestness and interest. Bowing his thanks he began, while both Charlie and Cameron wondered at his ease of manner, and the strange power of his simple, but well-chosen words.

"I have no means of knowing what your president may have said by way of introduction of myself, or as a preface to my remarks, but judging from your faces, the manner in which you receive me, and my knowledge of him, I feel that I am safe in assuming that he has said all that is necessary, and that I may proceed at once with my plan. But let me add simply this: What I have to say to you is in no way new or startling. I claim no originality, for I have simply gathered from the works of better men that which seems to me best fitted for the needs of this particular city. And understand, farther, that I speak in no sense as a Christian, but from the standpoint of one to whom has been given opportunities for study along these lines, I hope may ever be denied you.

"As I understand it, the problem that we have to consider is, briefly, how to apply Christ's teaching in our own town. Let me suggest first: That there are in this city, as in every city, two classes who present their claims for assistance; the deserving and undeserving. Any plan which does not distinguish between these two classes must prove a failure, because it would encourage the idle in their idleness, and so prove a curse instead of a blessing. It would make fraud profitable by placing a premium rather than a penalty on crime; and it would make the sufferings of the truly unfortunate much keener by compelling them to yield their self-respect as the price of their succor. The only test that can possibly succeed in distinguishing between these two classes is the test of work.

"The first thing necessary would be a suitable building. This building should have sleeping rooms, dining room, sitting room, kitchen, store-room and a bath room. There should also be a large yard with an open shed in the rear. I would have the sleeping rooms small, and a single cot in each, for you know it is sometimes good for a man to be alone. It ought not to be hard to find twenty-five people in the church who would furnish a room each, at a cost of say three dollars. The reading room supplies could be donated by friends who would be glad to give their papers and magazines when they were through with them, just as your present room is supplied. Now if you stop to think, in this mining city everyone burns coal, and kindling wood ought to find a ready sale. I believe the merchants would be glad to give away their old packing cases, boxes and barrels. These could be collected, hauled to the yard, there worked up into kindling and delivered to the customer. The whole establishment to be under the supervision of some man who, with his family, could occupy rooms in the building. All the work of the house, kitchen, dining room, care of the sleeping rooms, and all, must be done by the inmates. When a man applied for help he would be received on these conditions: that his time belonged wholly to the institution, and that he receive for his work only food and bed, with the privilege of bath and reading room of course. If he refused to comply with these conditions, or to conform to the rules of the institution, no food would be issued, nor would he be admitted.

"This briefly is my plan. I would be glad to have you ask questions and make objections or suggestions, for I believe that would be the best way to thoroughly understand the matter." Dick paused and one of the young people asked: "What would be the cost of the building and its furnishings?"

"That I cannot say," replied Dick. "It would depend of course upon how large an establishment you wished to conduct. I should think a house might be found in some convenient locality, which could be converted into the right thing, for I would not think of a large institution at the start. It would grow as fast as the people came to believe in it."

"You spoke of a store-room—what for?"

"Let the people contribute clothing, which could be kept and issued by the superintendent in charge. I said store-room, that the material might always be on hand when needed."

"Would you receive women?"

"No; they would require a separate institution with a different kind of employment."

"Would we not need women to do the housework?"

"No, everything could be done by the men under the direction of the superintendent's wife."

"Would the merchants contribute boxes enough?"

"That," with a bow and a smile, "is a matter for the Society to look after. The workers at the institution would gather them up and haul them to the yard. Old side-walks, fences, tumbled-down buildings, could also be used, so the supply need not run short, and the city would be much improved if these things were gathered up and utilized."

"Would the people buy the kindling-wood?"

"That again, is the business of the Society. Every member should be a salesman. The kindling would be put up in bundles of uniform size, warranted to be dry and to give satisfaction and delivered at the door by the workers of course. It ought not to be difficult for you to secure a sufficient number of regular customers to insure the success of the business. You see, it is not a church-begging scheme, for it benefits every person connected with it, and every person pays for what he gets. The citizens would have the pleasure of feeling that they were assisting only the worthy sufferers, and the satisfaction of knowing that they were receiving their money's worth."

"Would the income be sufficient to pay all bills?" asked Cameron.

"The food, of course, could be of the plainest, and could be bought in quantities. Twenty cents will feed a man a day. It is possible, of course, to live on less," Dick added, with a whimsical smile, which was met with answering smiles from the company of interested young people. "Now suppose you had for the start, one hundred regular customers, who would pay, each, ten cents per week for their kindling! that would bring you ten dollars per week, which would feed seven people. Not a large thing I grant you, but a start in the right direction, and much more than the church is doing now. The other expenses would not be large, and I am confident that the institution would be self-supporting. But bear in mind that the Society must own the grounds and building, so that there would be no rent. *That* must be the gift of the people to the poor."

"How would the superintendent and his wife be paid?"

"They would receive their house rent, provisions, and a small weekly salary, paid either by the Society, the church, or the institution. There are many men and women who would be glad to do such work."

"Would kindling-wood be the only industry?"

"I believe other things would suggest themselves. I am only planning a start you know. I said kindling-wood because that seems to be the most practical thing for this particular city."

"Would not men impose on the institution by working just enough to get their food and remain idle the rest of the time?"

"That," said Dick, "is the greatest danger, but I believe it would be met in this way: You remember I said that the time of the inmates must be given wholly to the institution. The men could be kept busy at the housework, scrubbing and cleaning when not in the yard. Then too, they could be hired out to do odd jobs of rough work for the citizens; the wages all to go to the institution. Thus, if every man was kept busy eight hours each day, and received only his food and a place to sleep, there would be no temptation to remain longer than necessary. The institution would also act as an employment agency, and when a man was offered work of any kind he would no longer be permitted to remain in the home. Much of this would necessarily be left to the discretion of the managers and directors."

This question seemed to bring the matter to a close as far as Dick was concerned, and after asking if there was anything more, and again calling attention to the fact that the greatest obstacle in the way was a suitable building, he thanked them for their attention and took his seat.

Then followed a warm discussion. Several spoke enthusiastically in favor of the scheme. One or two thought it very good, but feared it would be impossible because of the building needed. A few offered amendments to the plan. Finally a committee was appointed to see if a suitable building could be secured, and the meeting was adjourned.

At once the young people crowded about Dick, shaking his hand, thanking him, asking questions, making suggestions, with now and then a happy laugh or jest. Much to Charlie's delight, Dick, for the time being, forgot himself and talked and laughed and prophesied with the rest about *our* institution and the things we would do. But in the midst of it all, his manner suddenly changed, and making his way quickly to Charlie's side he whispered, "Good-night, old man, I must go."

"So soon?" asked his friend in a tone of surprise.

"Yes," replied Dick hurriedly, "I must." And Charlie was left wondering at the pain in his face, which a moment before had been so bright, for he did not know that Dick had heard Frank Goodrich saying to his sister, "Come, we must go home. We can't afford to associate with that tramp," and that he had seen Amy leaving the room on her brother's arm, without even acknowledging his presence by so much as a glance.

The next morning bright and early, Deacon Wickham might have been seen knocking at the door of the parsonage. "Why, good morning, Brother," cried Cameron, throwing wide the door and extending his hand. "What good fortune brought you out so early? Come in. Come in."

"No good fortune, sir," replied the deacon, and seating himself very stiffly on the edge of the straightest-backed chair in the room, he glared with stern eyes at the pastor, who threw himself carelessly into an easy rocker. "No good fortune, sir; I came to inquire if it is true that you are encouraging that unscriptural organization in their foolish and world-wise plans."

Cameron put on a puzzled look. "What organization, and what plans?" he asked.

"There," said the good deacon, with a sigh of great relief. "I told Sister Jones that there must be some mistake, for though you and I don't always agree, and lock horns sometimes on certain passages of the Scriptures, I did not believe that you were so far from the teaching of the Word as that."

"As what?" asked Cameron again, but this time with a faint glimmer of understanding in his voice. "Please explain, Brother Wickham."

"Why, Sister Jones came over to my house early this morning and told me that at the meeting of the Young People's Society last night, that young upstart Falkner, laid down plans for doing church work, and that you were there and approved of them. That rattle-headed boy of hers is all carried away."

The preacher nodded, "Well?"

"I could not believe it of course, but she said, as near as I could gather, that you were going to have the church buy a house and keep all the tramps who came to Boyd City. A more unscriptural thing I never heard of. Were you at the meeting last night?"

"Yes, I was there," said Cameron slowly.

The official frowned again as he said sharply: "You'll do more good for the cause, Brother Cameron, if you spend your time calling on the members. There is Deacon Godfrey's wife hasn't been out to services for three months because you haven't been to see her; and you're ruining the church now by your teaching. You've got to build on a Scriptural foundation if you want your work to last. All these people you've been getting in the last two years don't know a thing about first principles."

The minister tried to explain: "The plan suggested last night by Mr. Falkner, who was there at the invitation of the Society, was simply for an institution that would permit a man who was homeless, cold and hungry, to pay for food and lodging until he could do better. In short, to prevent deaths like that of the young man found frozen a few weeks ago."

"You don't know anything about that fellow," said the deacon. "If he had followed the teaching of the Scriptures he wouldn't have been in that fix. The Word says plainly: 'He that provideth not for his own is worse than an infidel.' You don't know whether he was a Christian or not. He may have never been baptized. Indeed, I am ready to prove that he never was, for the Scripture says that the righteous are never forsaken, nor their seed begging for bread. I've lived nearly fifty years now and I never went hungry and never slept out-doors either."

Cameron sat silently biting his lip; then looking his parishioner straight in the eye, said: "Brother Wickham, I cannot harmonize your teaching with Christ's life and character."

"My teaching is the Scripture, sir; I'll give you book, chapter and verse," snapped the deacon.

"Christ taught and lived a doctrine of love and helpfulness toward all men, even enemies," continued Cameron. "When I remember how he pointed out the hungry and naked and homeless, and then said: 'Inasmuch as ye did it not unto one of the least of these, ye did it not unto me,' I cannot help but feel sure in my heart that we are right, and I must tell you that Mr. Falkner's plan for doing just that work is the most practical and common-sense one I have ever heard. The only thing I find to wonder at is the stupidity of the church and myself, that we did not adopt it long ago."

"Then I am to understand that you support and encourage this unscriptural way of doing things?"

"I most certainly have given my support to the young people in this effort; and as far as possible, will encourage and help them in their labor of love."

"Labor of love, fiddlesticks," said the deacon; "Labor of foolishness. You'll find, sir, that it will be better to take my advice and the advice of the sacred writers, instead of going off after the strange teaching of an outcast and begging infidel."

"Stop!" said Cameron, springing to his feet, and speaking in a tone that few people ever heard him use. "I beg of you be careful that you do not go too far. Whatever his religious convictions may be, Mr. Falkner is neither an outcast nor a beggar; and although I am only your pastor, it might be well for you to remember that I am also a gentleman, and will allow no man to speak of my friends in any such language."

"Well, well," whined Wickham hastily, holding out his hand, "The Scriptures say that there must be love between brethren, and I want you to know that I bear you no ill will whatever, no ill will whatever; but I warn you, I wash my hands of the whole matter. I don't want to know anything about it."

Cameron took the proffered hand and replied, "That's the best thing you can do, Brother Wickham. You have discharged your duty faithfully as an officer in the church and are released from all responsibility whatever."

"Yes, yes," said the other, as he stood on the porch; "And don't let them call on me for any money. Remember I wash my hands of the whole thing. How much did you say it would cost?"

"I don't know yet, exactly."

"Well, you know I can't give anyway. I'm already doing more than my share in a scriptural way, and I must wash my hands of this."

"Yes," said Cameron to himself, as he shut the door; "A certain Roman governor washed his hands once upon a time." And then the pastor took himself to task for his uncharitable spirit.

Later in the day, Rev. Cameron had another visitor. Old father Beason, whose hair had grown white in the Master's service. He had been with his congregation over twenty years and they would not give him up; for while his sermons may have lost some of their youthful fire, they were riper for the preacher's long experience, and sweeter for his nearness to the source of love.

The old man met Cameron's outstretched hand of welcome with a smile that, in itself, was a benediction. Though identified with a different denomination, he was a close friend to the pastor of the Jerusalem Church, and always stood ready to draw from his wealth of experience for the benefit of his younger brother. When they were seated in Cameron's cozy den with a basket of fruit between them, Rev. Beason began:

"Brother Jim, what's this about the proposed work of your young people? Suppose you tell me about it, if you don't mind. I've heard a good many things to-day, and I just thought I'd run over and get the straight of it."

Cameron laughed as he carefully selected a rosy-cheeked apple. "You're the second caller I've had to-day who needed straightening out. I've been wishing you would run in, and if you had not, I would have been over to see you this evening. This work is right along lines that you and I have talked over many times." And then he told the whole story.

When Cameron had finished, the older man asked a few questions, and then slowly nodding his head, repeated softly: "Thy kingdom come, thy will be done, on earth as it is in Heaven."

"Brother Cameron, you know that I belong to a church that is noted for its conservative spirit, but I have been preaching more years than you have lived, and have been at it too long to be bound altogether by the particular belief of any particular people, and I want to say to you that if I were a younger man, I would take just your course exactly. There is no use, Brother Jim, of our flinching or dodging the question. The church is not meeting the problems of the day, and it's my candid opinion that ninety-nine out of every hundred preachers know it. But I'm too old to make the fight. I haven't the strength to do it. But my boy, do you go in to win, and may God's richest blessing rest upon you. And you'll stir this city as it never was stirred before. I only wish I were twenty years younger; I'd stand by you. But this needs young blood and I am an old, worn-out man. It is almost time that I was going home, and I dare not take up any work like this that will need years of patient labor to complete." He arose to his feet, and grasping Cameron's hand, said, "Good night, Brother Jim; we older men must turn our work, all unfinished, over to younger, stronger hands to complete. My boy, see that you keep that which is committed unto you, and don't, Oh don't, be sidetracked by the opinions of men. The victory will be yours, through Jesus Christ, our Lord. Good-night Jim, I thank God for this day."

CHAPTER XII

The sun sank into the prairie and tinted the sky all red and green and gold where it shone through the rents in the ragged clouds of purple black. The glowing colors touching dull, weather-beaten steeples and factory stacks, changed them to objects of interest and beauty. The poisonous smoke from smelter and engine, that hung always over the town like a heavy veil, shot through with the brilliant rays, became a sea of color that drifted here and there, tumbled and tossed by the wind, while above, the ball of the newly painted flag-staff on the courthouse tower gleamed like a signal lamp from another world. And through it all, the light reflected from a hundred windows flashed and blazed in wondrous glory, until the city seemed a dream of unearthly splendor and fairy loveliness, in which the people moved in wonder and in awe. Only for a moment it lasted. A heavy cloud curtain was drawn hurriedly across the west as though the scene in its marvelous beauty was too sacred for the gaze of men whose souls were dwarfed by baser visions. For an instant a single star gleamed above the curtain in the soft green of the upper sky; then it too vanished, blotted out by the flying forerunners of the coming storm.

About nine o'clock, when the first wild fury of the gale had passed, a man, muffled in a heavy coat and with a soft hat pulled low over his face, made his way along the deserted streets. In front of the Goodrich hardware and implement store, he stopped and looked carefully about as though in fear of some observer. Then taking a key from his pocket, he unlocked the door and entered. Walking quickly through the room to the office, as though familiar with the place, he knelt before the big safe, his hand upon the knob that worked the combination. A moment later the heavy door yielded to his hand. Taking a bunch of keys from his pocket, he selected one without hesitation, and upon applying it, the cash box opened, revealing a large sum of money. Catching up a package of bills, he placed it in his side coat pocket, and locking the cash box again, was closing the safe, when he paused as though struck with a sudden thought. The storm without seemed to be renewing its strength. The dashing of sleet and snow against the windows, the howling of the wind, the weird singing of the wires, and the sharp banging of swinging signs and shutters, carried terror to the heart of the man kneeling in the dimly lighted office. Sinking on the floor, he buried his face in his hands and moaned aloud, "My God—What am I doing? What if I should fail?"

Again there came a lull in the storm; everything grew hushed and still, almost as if the very spirit of the night waited breathlessly the result of the battle fought in the breast of the tempted man. Rising slowly to his knees, he swung back the heavy doors and once more unlocking the cash box reached out to replace the package of bills; but with the money before his eyes he paused again. Then with a sudden exclamation, "I won't fail this time; I can't lose always," he quickly closed the safe, and with the money in his pocket, sprang to his feet and hurried out of the building, where the storm met him in all its fury, as though striving to wrest from him that which he had taken from another. But with set face and clenched fists, he pushed into the gale, and a few minutes later knocked at the door of a room on the top floor of a big hotel. He was admitted and greeted cordially by two men who were drinking and smoking.

"Hello Frank," they exclaimed; "We thought you had crawfished this time sure. What makes you so late; it is nearly ten?"

"Oh, the old man had some work for me, of course. What a beastly night. Where's Whitley?" He tried to speak carelessly, but his eyes wavered and his hands trembled as he unbuttoned his heavy coat.

"You're right; this storm's a ripper. Jim will be back in a minute; he just stepped down to the corner drug-store to see a man. Here he is now;" as another low knock sounded on the door, and the fourth man entered, shaking the snow from his fur-trimmed coat.

"Pile out of your duds, boys, and have a drink. Good liquor hits the spot a night like this."

Whitley grasped the proffered glass eagerly and emptied it without a word, but Frank refused.

"You know I don't drink," he said, shortly; "take it yourself if you need it, and let's get to work." He drew a chair to the table in the center of the room.

The others laughed as they took their places, and one said, as he shuffled a deck of cards: "We forgot you were a church member." And the other added, with a sneer, "Maybe you'd like to open the services with a song and prayer."

"You drop that and mind your own business," retorted young Goodrich, angrily. "I'll show you tonight that you can't always have your own way. Did you bring my papers with you?" The others nodded and one said, "Whitley here told us you wanted a chance to win them back before we were obliged to collect. It's to be cash tonight though," added the other; "good cold cash, against the notes we hold."

"For God's sake, shut up and play," growled Frank in reply. "I guess there's cash enough," and he laid the package of bills on the table. Four eyes gleamed in triumph. Whitley looked at the young man keenly and paused with the cards in his hands. Then he dealt and the game began.

Meanwhile Adam Goodrich and his wife were entertaining the whist club, of which they were enthusiastic members, for it was the regular weekly meeting; and though the weather was so rough not a few of the devoted lovers of the game were present.

In the conversation that preceded the play, the Young People's Society, with Dick Falkner's plan of work, was mentioned. Nearly all of the guests being members of different churches, expressed themselves quite freely, with a variety of opinions, until the host, with annoyance plainly expressed on his proud face and in his hard cold voice, said: "You must not think, ladies and gentlemen, that because I and my family are members of the Jerusalem Church, that we agree with Rev. Cameron in his outlandish ideas. We have never been accustomed to associating with such low characters as he delights in forcing us to meet in the congregation; and if he don't change his line of work some, he will drive all the best people to other churches."

The guests all nodded emphatic approval and each silently resolved to send his pastor to interview the Goodrich's without delay.

Adam continued: "As for that tramp printer and his fool plan, I say that it's just such stuff that causes all the discontent among the lower classes and makes them unfit to serve their betters, and that *my* children shall have nothing to do with it. I have not brought them up to follow the lead of a vagabond and a nobody."

Amy's face flushed painfully and she lifted her head as though to speak, when Mrs. Goodrich silenced her with a look, and skilfully changed the subject by saying: "It's too bad Frank won't be here to-night. He enjoys these evenings so much and plays so well. But he and Mr. Whitley are spending the evening with a sick friend. The dear boy is so thoughtful of others and is always ready to give up his own pleasures. And Mr. Whitley too; he will miss the game so much, and Amy loses a strong partner." The company took the hint and talked of other things until the all-absorbing game began.

And so, while the son played with his friend Whitley, and the two professional gamblers at the hotel, played with fear in his face and a curse in his heart, to save himself from sure disgrace, his fond parents and beautiful sister at home, forgot his absence in their eager efforts to win with the cards the petty prize of the evening, a silver-mounted loving cup.

One, two, three hours passed. The storm had spent its strength; Mr. Goodrich had won the coveted prize, and the guests of the evening had returned to their homes. The last of the pile of ills before Frank was placed in the center of the table. The silence was unbroken save for the sound of the shuffling cards and the click of a whiskey glass as one of the men helped himself to a drink.

Suddenly young Goodrich leaped to his feet with a wild exclamation: "Tom Wharton, you're a liar and a cheat!" As he spoke, a heavy chair whirled above his head and fell with a crashing blow upon the man who sat at his right. Instantly all was confusion; the table was overturned; the cards, money and glasses scattered over the room. Whitley and the other man stood in blank astonishment at the sudden outburst. Frank leaped at his prostrate victim, with a chair again raised to strike, and had the second blow fallen, he would have been a murderer, for the intent to kill shone from his glittering eyes. But Whitley, just in time, caught his arm, while the other drew a knife and stepped between the crazed man and his victim.

"Stop, you fool!" said Whitley. "And you, Jack, put up that knife and look after Tom. This is a nice mess for us to be caught in." The gambler did as he was bid, but Frank struggled in his friend's grasp. "Let me go, Jim. Let me at him. I'm ruined anyway and I'll finish the man that did it before I go myself." But Whitley was the stronger and forced him backward, while the other man was busy with his fallen partner.

"Ruined nothing," said Jim in Frank's ear. "I'll stand by you. You get out of this quick and go to my room. I'll come when I've settled with them." He unlocked the door and pushed Frank into the hall, just as the man on the floor struggled to his feet.

The two gamblers turned on Whitley in a rage when they saw Frank had escaped. Standing with his back to the door, he let them curse a few minutes and then said calmly: "Now if you feel better let's take a drink and talk it over."

When he had them quiet again he continued, in a matter-of-fact tone: "Suppose you fellows raise a row about this, what will you gain?"

"We'll teach that young fool a lesson he won't forget soon," snarled the one who had fallen.

"Yes, and you'll pay big for the lesson," replied Whitley quietly.

"What do yon mean?"

"I mean that if this gets out young Goodrich is ruined and you won't get a cent on the paper you hold."

Wharton's friend nodded, "That's straight, Tom," he said.

"Well," growled the other; "What of it, the old man won't pay it anywray."

"Yes he would," returned Jim quickly, "if you didn't make it public; but I don't happen to want him to know about this little deal."

"What's it to you?"

"Never mind what it is to me. I know what I'm doing, and I don't want this to get out."

"How'll you help it?"

"This way." He took a check-book from his pocket. "Make the notes over to me and I'll add two hundred to the amount. Go after Frank and you get nothing. Go to the old man and you get what the paper calls for. Keep your mouth shut and sell me the notes and you get an extra hundred apiece. What do you say?"

"I say yes," exclaimed Jack, with an oath; "I'm no fool." And the other grumbled a surly "All right. But I'd like to get one crack at that kid's head."

"You'll have to pass that little pleasure this time." said the other with a laugh. "Write your check, Whitley and let's get out of this. I'm sleepy."

When Whitley reached his room after settling with the two gamblers, he found Frank pacing the floor, his face white and haggard.

"Sit down. Sit down, old man; and take things easy. You're all right. Look here." And he drew the notes from his pocket.

Frank sank into a chair. "What have you done?" he gasped. "How did you get those?"

Whitley laughed. "Just invested a little of my spare cash, that's all," he said.

"But I tell you I'm ruined. I can't pay a third of that in six years."

"Well, perhaps you won't have to." Frank stared. "What do you mean?"

"I mean Amy," the other replied coolly. "You poor idiot, can't you see. I can't afford to have you disgraced before the world under the circumstances. If I wasn't in it, I'd let you go to thunder and serve you right. But a fine chance I'd have to marry your sister if she knew about this business tonight. If it wasn't for her I'd let you hang your fool self too quick, before I'd spend a dollar on your worthless carcass; but I've said that I would marry that girl and I will, if it costs every cent I've got, and you'll help me too."

Frank was silent for a time, completely cowed by the contempt in the other's voice, too frightened to protest. But at last he managed to say: "There's more than those notes."

"I know that too," quickly returned Whitley, with an oath. "How much did you steal from the old man's safe tonight?"

"What—How—How do you know?" stammered the other.

"Saw you," returned Whitley, shortly; and then added, as Frank rose to his feet and began walking the floor again. "Oh, for Heaven's sake quit your tragedy and sit down. You make me tired. You're not cut out for either a gambler or a robber. You haven't the nerve."

Frank was silent, while the other went to a small cupboard and leisurely helped himself to a glass of whiskey; then lit a fresh cigar.

"What can I do?" ventured Frank at last, in a voice but little above a whisper.

Jim crossed the room, and unlocking a drawer in his desk, returned with a handful of bills. "You can put that money back in the safe before morning and keep your mouth shut." And then when Frank attempted to grasp his hand, while stammering words of gratitude, he said, "No thanks," and put his own hands behind his back in a gesture that there was no mistaking. "Be a good boy, Frankie. Listen with more care to your pastor's sermons; keep your Young People's Society pledge; read your Bible and pray every day, and take part in all the meetings, and when I marry your sister I'll make you a present of these papers. But Oh Lord," he added, with a groan, "you'll make a healthy brother-in-law, you will."

"How much did you say?"

Frank muttered the amount he had stolen.

Jim quickly counted it out and threw the bills on the table. "There you are. And now you better go quickly before you slop over again and I kick you." And turning his back he poured himself another glass of liquor while Frank, with the money in his hand, sneaked from the room like a well-whipped cur. And over his head, as he crept stealthily down the street toward his father's store, the stars shone clear and cold in their pure, calm beauty, while the last of the storm-cloud on the far horizon covered the face of the bright new moon.

CHAPTER XIII

The committee appointed by the Society called on Mr. Wicks at his office, and found him deep in a letter to an old lady, whose small business affairs he was trying to straighten out. He dropped the matter at once when they entered, and, after shaking hands, as though he had not seen them for years, said: "Now tell me all about it. To-be-sure, Charlie here has had some talk with me, but I want to get your ide's."

"Our brightest idea, I think," said the leader, with a smile, "is to get your help."

Uncle Bobbie laughed heartily. "I reckoned you'd be around," he said. "I'm generally kept posted by the young folks when there's anything to do. To-be-sure, I aint got much education, 'cept in money matters an' real estate, but I don't know—I reckon education is only the trimmings anyhow. It's the hoss sense what counts. I've seen some college fellers that was just like the pies a stingy old landlady of mine used t' make; they was all outside—To-be-sure, they looked mighty nice though. Now tell me what ye want."

When the young people had detailed to him Dick's plan, and he had questioned them on some points, the old gentleman leaned back in his chair and thoughtfully stroked his face. Then—"Now I tell ye what ye do. Mebbe I can handle the property end of this a little the best. To-be-sure, folks would talk with me when they might not listen to you; 'cause they'd be watchin' fer a chance to get me into a deal, you see; fer business is a sort of ketch-as-ketch-can anyhow you fix it. So jes' let me work that end an' ye get Charlie here and some more to help, and drum up the store-keepers to find out if they'll let ye have their barrels and boxes. An' then go fer the citizens and see how many will buy kindlin'-wood. Tell 'em about what it will cost—say ten cents a week fer one stove. To-be-sure, some will use more'n others, but give 'em an ide'. Then we'll all come together again and swap reports, an' see what we've got."

For the next few days, the young people went from store to store, and house to house, telling their plan, and asking the citizens to support it by their patronage. Some turned them away with rudeness; some listened and smiled at their childish folly; some said they couldn't afford it; and some gave them encouragement by entering heartily into the scheme. With but few exceptions, the merchants promised the greater part of their boxes and barrels, and one man even gave them the ruins of an old cow shed, which he said he would be glad to have cleared away.

Meanwhile, Uncle Bobbie interviewed the business men, members of the church, and those who were not Christians. He argued, threatened and plead, studied plans, consulted architects and contractors, figured and schemed, and, when besieged by the young people for results, only shook his head. "Jes' hold your hosses and wait till the meetin'. It don't pay to fire a gun before ye load it." And none but Charlie Bowen noticed that the old gentleman's face grew grim whenever the subject was introduced, and the young man guessed that the outlook was not so promising as Uncle Bobbie would like. Then one Wednesday night, the Society met again in the church. The weather was cold and stormy, but, as at the previous meeting, nearly every member was present. When the committee had made their report and it was known that the merchants and citizens would support the movement by their patronage and contributions, a wave of enthusiasm swept over the room while the call for Mr. Wicks was enforced by loud applause.

Uncle Bobbie, who had been sitting by Rev. Cameron's side, arose and came slowly forward. Turning, he faced the little company and his honest old eyes were wet as he said in a trembling voice: "I didn't want to come here tonight, young folks; I jes' tell ye I was ashamed to come; but I knew I ought to; and now I am ashamed that I didn't want to. I might have known better. Fer I can see right now as I look into your faces, that Brother Cameron is right, and that what I have to tell won't make no difference." An ominous hush fell upon the company. "To-be-sure, we may have to wait a bit, but God will show a way, and we'll conquer this old devil of indifference yet." He paused and drew a long breath. "Well, I found a big house that is for sale; jes' the thing we need; and it could be bought and fixed up in first-class shape fer about nine hundred dollars. I sold the property myself to Mr. Udell, fer fifteen hundred, 'bout a year ago; an' I want to tell you young folks, right now, that whether he's a Christian er not, George Udell is the whitest man in this city, and the fellow what says anythin' again him's got me to whip." The old gentleman paused and glared about him, without a thought of how his words sounded; but the young people, who knew him well, only answered with a clapping of hands, which was a tribute to Uncle Bobbie's heart and character, rather than to his unconscious recklessness of speech or love for the man whom he championed. But when he went on to say that of all the men he had interviewed, church members and all, only Udell had met him half way, and had agreed to give the lot if they would raise the money to pay for the house, they applauded with a vim, the generosity of the printer.

"Just think," said Uncle Bobbie, "that among all the church members in this city, I couldn't raise two hundred dollars fer such a cause. One of 'em said no, because he'd jes' bought a new span of carriage hosses. Huh! I told him he might ride to Hell behind fine bosses but he'd not feel any better when he got there. 'Nother said he'd jes' put five hundred dollars into the new lodge temple, and that he couldn't spend any more. I asked him if Jesus was a member of his lodge, and he said he reckoned not. I said, Well, we want to build a home for Christ, and you say you can't. Seems to me if I was you I wouldn't call Christ my redeemer in prayer meeting so much. 'Nother had just fixed his home. 'Nother had just put in a new stock of goods; and so with 'em all. They all had some excuse handy, and I don't know what to do. I'm up a stump this time fer sure. We've got the material to work up; we've got the people to buy the goods; we've got the lot; and there we're stuck, fer we can't get the house. *I* can't anyway. We're jes' like the feller that went fishin'; had a big basket to carry home his fish; a nice new jointed pole with a reel and fixin's, a good strong linen line, an' a nice bait box full of big fat worms, an' when he got to the river he didn't have no hook, and the fish just swum 'round under his nose an' laughed at him 'cause he couldn't touch 'em—and still I believe that God will show us the way yet, 'though mebbe not. Perhaps taint fer the best fer us to do this; to-be-sure though I thought it was, and so did Brother Cameron; and so did you. But I don't know—" And the old man took his seat.

After a long silence, one or two offered suggestions but could not help matters. Rev. Cameron was called for and tried to speak encouragingly, but it was hard work, and it seemed that the plans were coming to an inglorious end, when Clara Wilson sprang to her feet.

"I'm not a bit surprised at this," she said, while the young people, forgetting the praise they had just bestowed upon George Udell, thought that her rosy cheeks and sparkling eyes were caused by her excitement. "I don't wonder that the business men won't go into such a scheme. They haven't any faith in it. It isn't so much that they've not got the money or don't want to help, but it's because they don't trust the church. They have seen so many things started, and have supported so many, and still no real good comes of it, that they're all afraid. They put money into their lodges because they see the results there. I believe there has been more wealth put into the churches than has ever been put into lodges; but all we've got to show for it is fine organs, fine windows, and fine talk, while the lodges do practical work. We can't expect folks to take hold of our plan until we show what we are going to do. We are starting at the wrong end. We haven't done anything ourselves yet. I wish I was a man, I'd show you," with a snap of her black eyes.

"Yo're a pretty good feller if you ain't a man," chuckled Uncle Bobbie. This raised a laugh and made them all feel better.

"That's all right; you can laugh if you want to," said Clara, "but I tell you we can do it if we have a mind to. Why, there is enough jewelry here tonight to raise more than half the amount. Let's not give up now that we've gone so far. Let's have a big meeting of the Society, and have speeches, and tell what has been done, and see what we can raise. Just make the people believe we are going to have this thing anyway. Mr. President, I move you that we have an open meeting of the Society one week from next Sunday, and that a special committee be appointed to work up a good program."

Cameron jumped to his feet. "With all my heart, I second that motion." And before the president could speak, a storm of Ayes was followed by prolonged applause. Clara was promptly named chairman of the committee, and in a few minutes they were trooping from the building, out into the storm, but with warm hearts and merry voices.

George Udell had not been to call on Miss Wilson since the night he found the man frozen in the streets. Indeed, he had not even spoken to her since the funeral. He had seen her though, once when she had met him on the street with several friends, and several times when he had glanced up from his work by the window as she had passed the office. All this was strange to Clara. What could be the matter? George had never acted so before. She wanted to talk to him about the incident of that stormy night when they had parted so abruptly. She wanted him to know how proud she was that he had proven so kind in the matter of the funeral. "What a warm heart he has beneath all his harsh speeches," she thought; and could not help but contrast him, much to his credit, with many professed Christians she knew. And then, Mr. Wicks had spoken, in the business meeting, of his generosity, and had talked so strongly of his goodness; no wonder her cheeks burned with pride, while her heart whispered strange things.

When the young woman had said Good-night to her companions, after the meeting, and had shut herself in her room, she asked again and again, was she right in always saying No? Was she not unnecessarily cruel to the friend who had shown, and was showing himself, so worthy of her love? Oh why was he not a Christian? And when Mrs. Wilson crept into her daughter's room that night, to get an extra comfort from the closet, to put over the little boy's crib, she was much surprised to see a big tear, that glistened in the light of the lamp, roll from beneath the dark lashes, as her eldest child lay sobbing in her sleep.

The next morning the girl was strangely silent and went about her work without the usual cheery whistle—for Clara would whistle; it was her only musical accomplishment. But toward noon, after arousing from a prolonged spell of silent staring into the fire, during which her mother tried in vain to draw her into conversation, she suddenly became her own bright self again, and went about getting dinner in her usual manner. Then when the dishes were washed, she appeared in her street dress and hat.

"Land sakes alive, child, you aint going out to-day, be you?" said Mrs. Wilson, her hands on her hips, in her usual attitude of amazement or wrath.

"Yes mother, I've got a little business down-town that I can't put off. I won't be gone long. Is there anything that I can do for you?"

"But look how it's snowing; you'll be wet through and catch your death sure. I wish to goodness you'd have more sense and try to take some care of yourself."

"Not the first time I've been wet. The walk will do me good." And soon the determined young lady was pushing her way through the snow and wind toward the business part of the city.

The boy in the printing office had gone out on an errand and George and Dick were both at the composing case, setting up a local politician's speech, which was to be issued in the form of a circular, when Clara walked in, stamping her feet and shaking the snow from her umbrella and skirt. Udell started forward.

"Great shade of the immortal Benjamin F!" he shouted. "What in the name of all that's decent are you doing here?" And he placed a chair near the stove with one hand as he captured the umbrella with the other.

"I'm going to get warm just now," Clara replied, with an odd little laugh, and Dick noticed that the wind, or cold, or something, had made her face very red. "Come here and sit down," she commanded. "I want to talk business to you. Don't stand there as though you had never seen me before."

"Well, it has been ages since I saw you," he declared, seating himself on the edge of the waste-box.

"Yes, all of twenty-four hours. I passed you yesterday and you looked me right in the face, and never even said 'Howdy.' If you were anyone else, George Udell, I'd make you wait awhile before you got another chance to do me that way."

George drummed on the edge of the box and whistled softly. Then looking anxiously toward Dick, said: "How are you getting along with that stuff, old man?"

"Almost through," answered Dick, with a never-to-be-forgotten wink. "But I believe I'll run off those dodgers on the big press, and let you finish the politics."

"All right, I reckon that'll be better," answered Udell; and soon the whir of the motor, and the stamp of the press filled the room.

"We are awfully busy now," said Udell, turning to Clara again. "I ought to be at work this minute."

"Why haven't you been to see me, George?" persisted the girl, a strange light coming into her eyes. "There are so many things I want to talk to you about."

"Thought I'd let you come and see me awhile; turn about is fair play. Besides, I don't think it would be safe in this cold weather. It's chilly enough business even in the summer time."

Clara held out manfully—or—womanly—"George Udell; you knew very well that I would come here if you staid away from my home; and it's real mean of you, when you knew how bad I wanted to see you, to make me come out in all this snow."

George looked troubled. "I'll take my death of cold, and then how'll you feel?—" George looked still more worried—"I've not felt very well lately anyway—" George looked frightened; "and I—came all the way—down here—just to see what was the matter." The printer looked happy. "And now you don't want me to stay, and I'll go home again." She moved toward her umbrella, Udell got it first. Whir—Whir—went the motor, and clank—clank—clank—sounded the press. Dick was feeding the machine and must necessarily keep his eyes on his work, while the noise prevented any stray bits of the conversation from reaching his ears. Besides this, Dick was just now full of sympathy. Clara let go her end of the umbrella, and George, with an exaggerated expression of rapture on his face, kissed the place where her hand had held it. The young lady tried to frown and look disgusted. Then for several moments neither spoke. At last Clara said, "I wanted to tell you how proud and glad I am of the things you have been doing. You are a good man, George, to take care of that poor dead boy the way you did."

"Why, you see I had a sort of fellow-feeling for him," muttered the printer. "I had just been frosted myself."

"And that Young People's Society business, it is just grand," went on Clara. "Only think, you have given more than all the church members even."

Udell grunted, "No danger of me losing on that offer. They'll never raise the rest."

"Oh yes we will. I'm chairman of the committee." And then she told him of the meeting, and how Uncle Bobbie had praised him.

Udell felt his heart thaw rapidly, and the two chatted away as though no chilly blast had ever come between them.

"And yet, Clara, with all your professed love for me, you won't allow me a single privilege of a lover, and I can have no hope of the future. It had better stop now."

"Very well, George; it can stop now if you like; but I never could have lived without talking it out with you and telling you how glad I am for your gift to the Society."

"Look here, don't you go and make any mistakes on that line. I'm giving nothing to the Society or the church. That bit of land goes to the poor, cold, hungry fellows, who are down on their luck, like Dick here was. I tell you what though, Clara, if you'll say yes, I'll add the house and enough to furnish it besides."

The girl hesitated for just a moment. Here was temptation added to temptation. Then she pulled on her rubbers and rose to go. "No, George, No, I cannot. You know you would not need to buy me if I felt it right to say yes."

"But I'm going to keep on asking you just the same," said George. "You won't get angry if I keep it up, will you?"

"I—guess—not. I feel rather badly when you don't. I don't like to say no; but I would feel awful if you didn't give me a chance to say it. Good-bye George."

"Good-bye dearest. You can't forbid me loving you anyway, and some day you'll take me for what I am."

Clara shook her head. "You know," she said.

As the door closed, Dick wheeled around from the press, holding out his ink-stained hand to George.

"What's the matter?" said the other wonderingly, but grasping the outstretched hand of his helper.

"I want to shake hands with a man, that's all," said Dick. "Why don't you join the church and win her?"

"Because if I did that I wouldn't be worthy of her," said George.

"You have strange ideas for this day and age."

"Yes, I know; but I can't help it; wish I could."

"You're a better man than half the church members."

George shook his head. "It won't do, Dickie, and you know it as well as I. That's too big a thing to go into for anything but itself. What is it mother used to say? No other Gods before me, or something like that."

And Dick said to himself as he turned back to the press, "I have indeed, shaken hands with a man."

CHAPTER XIV

The night was at hand when the young people were to hold their special meeting in the interest of the new movement. Clara Wilson had worked incessantly, and when at last the evening arrived, was calm and well satisfied. Whether the effort proved a success or not, she would be content, for she had done her best.

The incident of the man found frozen to death on the steps of the church, still so fresh in the minds of the citizens, the flying rumors about Dick's visit to the Society, and the plans of the young people, all served to arouse public curiosity to such a pitch that the place of meeting was crowded, many even standing in the rear of the room. After the opening services, which were very impressive but short, and the purpose of the Society and the proposed plan of work had been fully explained, Uncle Bobbie told, in his simple way, of the work that had been done; how the young people had called on him; how they had gone from house to house, through the cold and snow; and how he had interviewed the business men, many of whom he saw in the audience. "To-be-sure," he said, "I don't suppose you understood the matter fully or you would have been glad to help; but we'll give ye another chance in a minute." Then he told of the last business meeting; how they were encouraged when the reports came in that the citizens had responded so liberally; and how he had been forced to tell them that he had met with nothing but failure in his attempt to secure a house. "I just tell you, it made my old heart ache to see them young folks tryin' to do some practical work for Christ, come up agin a stump like that. I wish you church members could have seen 'em and heard 'em pray. I tell you it was like Heaven; that's what it was; with the angels weepin' over us poor sinners 'cause we won't do our duty."

The old gentleman finished, amid a silence that was almost painful, while many were leaning eagerly forward in their seats. The great audience was impressed by the scheme and work so practical and Christ-like. This was no theory, no doctrine of men, no dogma of a denomination.

The pastor of the Jerusalem Church stepped to the front of the rostrum and raised his hand. Without a word the people reverently bowed their heads. After a moment of silent prayer, the minister voiced the unuttered words of all, in a few short sentences: "God help us to help others," and then in clear, earnest tones began to speak. He recalled to their minds the Saviour of men, as he walked and talked in Galilee. He pictured the Christ feeding the hungry and healing the sick. He made them hear again the voice that spake as never man spake before, giving forth that wonderful sermon on the mount, and pronouncing his blessing on the poor and merciful. Again the audience stood with the Master when he wept at the grave of Lazarus, and with him sat at the last supper, when he introduced the simple memorial of his death and love. Then walking with him across the brook Kedron, they entered the shadows of the Olive trees and heard the Saviour pray while his disciples slept. "If it be possible, let this cup pass from me. Nevertheless, not my will, but thine be done." And then they stood with the Jewish mob, clamoring for his blood; and later with the Roman soldiery, grouped at the foot of the cross, where hung the brother of men, and heard that wonderful testimony of his undying love. "Father forgive them, they know not what they do." Then under the spell of Cameron's speech, they looked into the empty tomb and felt their hearts throb in ecstasy, as the full meaning of that silent vault burst upon them. Looking up they saw their risen Lord seated at the right hand of the Father, glorified with the glory that was his in the beginning; and then, then, they looked where the Master pointed, to the starving, shivering, naked ones of earth, and heard with new understanding, those oft repeated words, "Inasmuch as ye did it unto one of the least of these, ye did it unto me." "Men and brethren," cried the pastor, stretching out his arms in the earnestness of his appeal, "what shall we do? Shall there be no place in all this city where the least of these may find help in the name of our common Master? Must our brothers perish with cold and hunger because we close the doors of the Saviour's church against them? These young people, led by a deep desire to do God's will, have gone as far as they can alone. Their plan has been carefully studied by good business men and pronounced practical in every way. They have the promised support of the merchants in supplying material. They have the promised patronage of the citizens; and a man, not a professed Christian, but with a heart that feels for suffering humanity has given the land. In the name of Jesus, to help the least of these, won't you buy the house?"

   The deacons, with the baskets and paper and pencils, started through the congregation. In a moment Mr. Godfrey went back to Cameron and placed something in his hand. The pastor, after listening a moment to the whispered words of his officer, turned to the audience and said: "At our last meeting, one of the young people made the remark that there were jewels enough on the persons of those present to pay half the amount needed. Brother Godfrey has just handed me this diamond ring, worth I should say, between forty and fifty dollars. It was dropped into the basket by a member of the Young People's Society. Friends, do you need any more proof that these young folks are in earnest?"

At last the offering was taken, and the deacons reported one thousand dollars in cash, and pledges, payable at once. "And perhaps," said the leader, "I ought to say, in jewelry also." And he held up to the gaze of the audience a handful of finger rings, scarf-pins, ear-rings and ornaments, and a gold watch, in the case of which was set a tiny diamond.

Again for a moment a deep hush fell over the vast congregation as they sat awed by this evidence of earnestness. Then the minister raised his voice in prayer that God would bless the offering and use it in his service, and the audience was dismissed.

Dick did not sleep well that night. Something Cameron had said in his talk, together with the remarkable gifts of the young people, had impressed him. He had gone to the church more from curiosity than anything, and had come away with a feeling of respect for Christians, that was new to him. As he thought of the jewelry, given without the display of name or show of hands, he said to himself, "Surely these people are in earnest." Then, too, under the spell of Cameron's talk, he saw always before him the figure of the Christ as he lived his life of sacrifice and love, and heard him command, "Follow thou me." In the meantime at the church he had seen people doing just that, following Him; doing as He did; and the whole thing impressed him as nothing had ever done before. So, when he went to the office next morning and found Udell strangely silent and apparently in a brown study, he was not at all surprised, and asked, "What's the matter, George? Didn't you sleep well last night either? Or did the thoughts of having been so generous with your property keep you awake?"

"The property hasn't anything to do with it," answered Udell. "It's what that preacher said; and not so much that either, I guess, as what those young folks did. I've been thinking about that handful of jewelry; if I hadn't seen it I wouldn't have believed it. Say, do you know that a few sermons like those gold trinkets would do more to convert the world than all the theological seminaries that ever bewildered the brains of poor preachers?"

"Right you are, George, but is it true?"

"Is what true?" asked the other.

"Why, what Cameron said about Christ being the Saviour of men, and all that."

The printer paused in his work. "What do *you* say?" he asked as last, without answering Dick's question.

"Well," answered Dick slowly, "I've tried hard for several years, to make an infidel of myself, because I couldn't stand the professions of the church, and their way of doing things. But that meeting last night was different, and I was forced to the conclusion, in spite of myself, that Cameron spoke the truth, and that Christ is what he claimed to be, the Saviour of mankind, in the truest, fullest sense of the word. I'm sure of this. I have always wished that it were true, and have always believed that the Christian life, as Christ taught it, would be the happiest life on earth. But there's the rub. Where can a fellow go to live the life, and why are you and I not living it as well as the people who have their names on the church books? Must I join a company of canting hypocrites in order to get to Heaven?"

"Seems to me that word is a little strong for those who put up their rings and stuff last night," said Udell; "and anyway, I know one in the crowd who was in earnest."

"You are right, George," returned Dick. "I spoke harshly. I know there are earnest ones in the church, but I don't see how they stand it. But you're dodging my question. Do you believe in Christ as the Saviour of men?"

"Folks say that I'm an infidel," answered George.

"I don't care what folks say, I want to know what you think about it."

"I don't know," said George. "Sometimes, when I listen to the preachers, I get so befuddled and mixed up that there's nothing but a big pile of chaff, with now and then a few stray grains of truth, and the parson keeps the air so full of the dust and dirt that you'd rather he wouldn't hunt for the grain of truth at all. Then I'm an infidel. And again I see something like that last night, and I believe it must be true. And then I think of Clara, and am afraid to believe because I fear it's the girl and not the truth I'm after. You see, I want to believe so bad that I'm afraid I'll make myself believe what I don't believe. There, now you can untangle that while you run off that batch of cards. It's half-past eight now and we have not done a blessed thing this morning." He turned resolutely to his task of setting up another speech for the local politician.

"George, what in the world does this mean?" asked Dick, about two hours later, holding up a proof sheet that he had just taken from the form George had placed on the stone, and reading: "When Patrick Henry said, Give me liberty or give me Clara, he voiced a sentiment of every American church member."

George flushed. "Guess you'd better set up the rest of this matter," he said gruffly. "I'll run the press awhile." He laid down his stick and put the composing case between himself and Dick as soon as possible.

"That bloomin' politician must be crazy," said the boy, as he scrubbed wearily at an inky roller, with a dirty rag. "Old Pat. Henry never said no such stuff as that, did he George?"

"You dry up," was all the answer he received.

All that week and the week following, Dick's mind fastened itself upon the proposition: Jesus Christ is the Son of God, and the Saviour of men. At intervals during working hours at the office, he argued the question with Udell, who after his strange rendering of the great statesman's famous speech, had relapsed into infidelity, and with all the strength of his mind, opposed Dick in his growing belief. The evenings were spent with Charlie Bowen, in discussing the same question. And here it was Charlie who assumed the affirmative and Dick as stoutly championed Udell's position. At last, one day when Dick had driven his employer into a corner, the latter ended the debate forever, by saying rather sharply, "Well, if I believed as you do, I'd stand before men and say so. No matter what other folks believed, did or said, if a man was so good as to give me all the things that you say Christ has given to the world, I would stand by him, dead or alive. And I don't see why you can't be as honest with Him as you are with men." And Charlie clinched the matter that evening by saying, "Dick, if I thought you really believed your own arguments, I wouldn't talk with you five minutes, for the doctrine you are teaching is the most hopeless thing on earth. But I can't help feeling that if you would be as honest with yourself as you are with others, you wouldn't take that side of the question. Suppose you preach awhile from your favorite, Shakespeare, taking for your text, 'This above all, To thine own self be true, and it must follow as the night the day. Thou canst not then be false to any man.'"

There were no more arguments after that, but Dick went over in his mind the experience of the past; how he had seen, again and again, professed Christians proving untrue to their Christ. He looked at the church, proud, haughty, cold, standing in the very midst of sin and suffering, and saying only, "I am holier than thou." He remembered his first evening in Boyd City, and his reception after prayer-meeting, at the church on the avenue, and his whole nature revolted at the thought of becoming one of them. Then he remembered that meeting of the Young People and the unmistakable evidence of their love, and the words of Uncle Bobbie Wicks in the printing office that rainy night: "You'll find out, same as I have, that it don't matter how much the other fellow dabbles in the dirt, you've got to keep your hands clean anyway. And it aint the question whether the other fellow is mean or not, but am I living square?"

And so it was, that when he went to church Sunday evening, his heart was torn with conflicting emotions, and he slipped into a seat in the rear of the building, when the ushers were all busy, so that even Charlie did not know he was there. Cameron's sermon was from the text, "What is that to thee? Follow thou me." And as he went on with his sermon, pointing out the evils of the church, saying the very things that Dick had said to himself again and again, but always calling the mind of his hearers back to the words of Jesus, "What is that to thee? Follow thou me," Dick felt his objections vanish, one by one, and the great truth alone remain. The minister brought his talk to a close, with an earnest appeal for those who recognized the evils that existed in the church, because it was not following Christ as closely as it ought, to come and help right the wrongs, Dick arose, went forward, and in a firm voice, answered the question put by the minister, thus declaring before men his belief in Christ as the Son of God, and accepting Him as his personal Saviour.

As he stood there, the audience was forgotten. The past, with all its mistakes and suffering, its doubt and sin, came before him for an instant, then vanished, and his heart leaped for joy, because he knew that it was gone forever. And the future, made beautiful by the presence of Christ and the conviction that he was right with God, stretched away as a path leading ever upward, until it was lost in the glories of the life to come, while he heard, as in a dream, the words of his confessed Master, "Follow: thou me."

CHAPTER XV

George was busy in the stock room getting out some paper for a lot of circulars that Dick had just finished setting up, when the door opened and Amy Goodrich entered. "Good Morning, Mr. Falkner," as Dick left his work and went forward to greet her. "I must have some new calling cards. Can you get them ready for me by two o'clock this afternoon? Mamma and I had planned to make some calls and I only discovered last night that I was out of cards. You have the plate here in the office, I believe."

"Yes," said Dick, "the plate is here. I guess we can have them ready for you by that time."

"And Mr. Falkner," said the girl, "I want to tell you how glad I was when you took the stand you did Sunday night."

Dick's face flushed and he looked at her keenly. "I have thought for a long time, that you would become a Christian, and have often wondered why you waited. The church needs young men and you can do so much good."

"You are very kind." said Dick, politely. "I am sure that your interest will be a great inspiration to me, and I shall need all the help I can get. In fact, we all do, I guess."

A shadow crossed the lovely face, and a mist dimmed the brightness of the brown eyes for a moment before she replied. "Yes, we do need help; all of us; and I am sure you will aid many. Will you enter the ministry?"

"Enter the ministry," replied Dick, forgetting his studied coolness of manner. "What in the world suggested that? Do I look like a preacher?"

They both laughed heartily.

"Well no, I can't say that you do. At least I wouldn't advise you to go into the pulpit with that apron and that cap on; and the spot of ink on the end of your nose is not very dignified."

Dick hastily applied his handkerchief to the spot, while Amy, like a true woman, stood laughing at his confusion. "But seriously," she added, after a moment, "I was not joking. I do think you could do grand work if you were to enter the field. Somehow, I have always felt that you exerted a powerful influence over all with whom you came in touch. Let me make a prophecy; you will yet be a preacher of the Gospel."

"I'm sure," said Dick, "that if I truly came to believe it to be my work, I would not refuse. But that is a question which time alone can answer. Do you remember the first time we met?"

"Indeed I do," the girl replied, laughing again. "It was right here, and you met with an accident at the same time."

Dick's face grew red again. "I should say I did," he muttered. "I acted like a frightened fool."

"Oh, but you redeemed yourself beautifully though. I have one of those little books yet. I shall always keep it; and when you get to be a famous preacher, I'll exhibit my treasure, and tell how the Rev. Mr. Richard Falkner sat up late one night to design the cover for me, when he was only a poor printer."

"Yes," retorted Dick, "and I'll tell the world how I went to my first church social, and what a charming young lady I met, who told me how much I reminded her of someone she knew."

It was Amy's time to blush now, and she did so very prettily as she hurriedly said, "Let's change the subject. I ought not to be keeping you from your work. Mr. Udell will be asking me to stay away from the office."

"Oh, we're not rushed today," said Dick, hastily, "and I'll make up all lost time."

"So you consider this lost time, do you?" with a quick little bow. "Thank you, then it's surely time for me to go;" and she turned to leave the room, but Dick checked her.

"Oh, Miss Goodrich, you know I did not mean that." Something in his voice made her eyes drop as he added, "You don't know how much I enjoy talking with you; not that I have had many such pleasures though, but just a word helps me more than I can say." He stopped, because he dare not go farther, and wondered at himself that he had said even so much.

"Do you really mean, Mr. Falkner, that you care at all for my friendship?"

"More than the friendship of any one in the world," he replied, earnestly.

"Why?"

Dick was startled and turned away his head lest his eyes reveal too much. "Because," he said slowly, "your friendship is good for me and makes me want to do great things."

"And yet, if I were not a member of the church you would not think that way."

"I would think that way, no matter what you were," said Dick.

"You would still value my friendship if I should do some awful wicked thing?" she asked. "Suppose I should leave the church, or run away, or steal, or kill somebody, or do something real terrible?"

Dick smiled and shook his head. "Nothing you could ever do would make me change. But tell me," he added; "you're not thinking of giving up your church work, are you?"

"Why do you ask?" said she quickly.

"You'll pardon me won't you, if I tell you. I can't help noticing that you are not so much at the meetings of the Society as you were; and that—well—you don't seem—somehow—to take the interest you did. And you have given up your class at the South Broadway Mission."

"How do you know that?"

"I asked Brother Cameron if there was any place for me out there, and he said, yes, that your class was without a teacher now."

"So you are to have my boys at the Mission. Oh, I am so glad." And her eyes filled. "Don't let them forget me altogether, Mr. Falkner."

"But won't you come back and teach them yourself?"

"No, no; you do not understand; I must give it up. But you'll do better than I anyway, because you can get closer to them. You understand that life so well."

"Yes," he said, very soberly. "I do understand that life very well indeed."

"Oh, forgive me, I didn't mean to pain you." She laid her hand timidly on his arm. "I admire you so much for what you have overcome, and that's what makes me say that you can do a great deal, now that you are through with it. You must forget those things that are behind, you know."

"Yes," murmured Dick, "those things *are* behind, and I can do all things through Him; but may I also have the help of thinking of you as my friend?"

Amy blushed again. "Please notice," said Dick, quietly, "I said of *thinking* of you as my friend."

The girl put out her hand. "Mr. Falkner, just as long as you wish, you may think of me as your friend. But I want you to pray for me, that I may be worthy your friendship, for I too, have my battles to fight." And she smiled. "Good-bye. You were so funny when you fell off the stool that day, but I like you better as you are now." Then suddenly the room grew dark and close, and as Dick turned again to his work, he heard a voice within whispering, "Only in your thoughts can she be your friend."

Adam Goodrich was just coming out of the express office, which was in the same block as the printing establishment, when he saw his daughter leave the building and cross the street. All that day the incident persisted in forcing itself upon his mind, and that night, after the younger members of the family had retired, and he and Mrs Goodrich were alone, he laid aside his evening paper and asked, "What was Amy doing at Udell's place today?"

"She went to have some calling cards printed. Why, what made you ask?"

"Oh nothing. I saw her coming from the building, and I wondered what she was doing there, that's all." He picked up his paper again, but in a moment laid it down once more. "That fellow Falkner joined the church last Sunday night."

"So Frank told me," answered Mrs. Goodrich. "I do wish Rev. Cameron would be more careful. He gets so many such characters into the church. Why can't he keep them out at the Mission where they belong, and not force us to associate with them?"

Mr. Goodrich spoke again. "I suppose he will be active in the Young People's Society now. Does Amy still take as much interest there as she did?"

"Oh no, not nearly as much as she used to. I have tried to show her that it was not her place to mix in that kind of work, and she's beginning to understand her position, and to see that she can't afford to lower herself and us, by running after such people. I don't understand where she gets such low tastes."

"She don't get them from the Goodrich's, I'm sure," answered Adam. "You know *our* family was never guilty of anything that could compromise their standing in society."

"Well, she will outgrow it all in time, I am sure. I have been as careful in her training as I could, Mr. Goodrich. It is a hard task to raise girls, and make them understand their position when they're Amy's age; but she's taking up her social duties again now. We are to make some calls tomorrow, and Thursday night, she has accepted an invitation to the card party at Mrs. Lansdown's; and Mr. Whitley has called frequently of late. I have great hopes, for she seems to be quite interested in him."

"Yes," agreed Adam. "Whitley is worth while; he is of a good family, and without doubt, the richest man in Boyd City. It would be a great thing for us. It's time he was thinking about a wife too. He must be well on toward forty."

"Oh dear no; he can't be more than thirty-five; he was quite young when he went abroad, and you remember that was only five years ago."

"Well, well, it's no matter; he's young enough. But does she see much of that printer of Udell's?"

"Why, of course not; what a question. She would have nothing to do with him."

"But she has met him at the socials and in the Society. He would naturally pose as a sort of hero, for he was the one who suggested that fool plan that Cameron is working on; and now that he has joined the church, she must see more or less of him. I tell you, he's a sharp fellow. Look how he has been quietly worming himself into decent society since he got hold of that reading room. There is no knowing what such a man will do, and Amy naturally would be a good mark for him."

"I'm sure I am doing the best I can," faltered Mrs. Goodrich; "but you'd better talk to her yourself; with Mr. Whitley so interested, we must be careful. I do wish she would be more like Frank. He has never given us a moment's trouble."

"Yes," said the father, with no little pride manifest in his voice and manner. "Frank is a Goodrich through and through. Amy seems to take more after your people."

Mrs. Goodrich sighed. "I'm sorry, but I don't see how I can help it."

The next day, after dinner, Mr. Goodrich found his daughter alone in the library, where she had gone with a bit of fancy work, which girls manage to have always about them. "Frank tells me that Mr. Falkner has united with the church," he remarked, carelessly.

"Yes," said Amy, "I am so glad. The church needs such young men, I think."

"He is quite a shrewd fellow, isn't he?" continued her father.

"He's very intelligent, I'm sure. You know it was he who proposed the plan for our new institution, and Mr. Wicks and Brother Cameron think it is very fine."

"Does he use good language in his conversation?"

"Oh yes sir, indeed. He is a very interesting talker. He has traveled so much, and read almost everything. I tell him I think he ought to preach."

"Hum. And will he, do you think?"

"He said he would if he were convinced it was his work."

"Where did he live before he came here?"

"Oh, he has lived in nearly all the big cities. He was in Kansas City last."

"And what did his father do?"

"His mother died when he was a little boy, and his father drank himself to death, or something. He won't talk about his family much. He did say though, that his father was a mechanic. I believe that he tells Mr. Udell more about his past than anyone."

"And did Udell tell you all this?"

"No," answered Amy, who suddenly saw what was coming.

"How do you know so much about him then?"

"He told me."

"Indeed. You seem to be on very good terms with this hero. How long were you at the printing office yesterday? I saw you leaving the building."

Amy was silent, but her burning cheeks convinced her father that he had cause to be alarmed.

"Did you talk with him when you were there?"

"Yes sir; he waited on me."

"And do you think it is a credit to your family to be so intimate with a tramp who was kicked out of my place of business?"

"Oh father, that is not true—I mean, sir, that you do not understand—Mr. Falkner is not a tramp. He was out of work and applied to you for a place. Surely that is not dishonest. And that he wanted to work for you ought not to be used against him. He has never in any way shown himself anything but a gentleman, and is much more modest and intelligent than many of the young men in Boyd City who have fine homes. I am sure we ought not to blame him because he has to fight his own way in the world, instead of always having things brought to him. If you knew him better, you wouldn't talk so." She spoke rapidly in her excitement.

"You seem to know him very well when you champion him so strongly that you call your own father a liar," replied Adam, harshly.

"Oh papa," said Amy, now in tears. "I did not mean to say that. I only meant that you were mistaken because you did not know. I cannot help talking to Mr. Falkner when I meet him in the Young People's Society. I have not been anywhere in his company, and only just speak a few words when we do meet. You wouldn't have me refuse to recognize him in the church, would you? Surely, father, Christ wants us to be helpful, doesn't he?"

"Christ has nothing to do with this case," said Adam. "I simply will not have my daughter associating with such characters; and another thing, you must give up that Mission business. I believe that's where you get these strange ideas."

"I have already given up my work there," said Amy, sadly.

"Mr. Falkner has taken my class."

"Which is just the place for him. But don't you go there again. And if you have any printing that must be done at Udell's, send it by Frank, or someone. You understand, I forbid you to have any conversation whatever with that man. I'll see if such fellows are going to work themselves into my family."

Amy's face grew crimson again. "You must learn," went on the angry parent, "that the church is a place for you to listen to a sermon, and that it's the preacher's business to look after all these other details; that's what we hire him for. Let him get people from the lower classes to do his dirty work; he shan't have my daughter. Christianity is all right, and I trust I'm as good a Christian as anyone; but a man need not make a fool of himself to get to Heaven, and I'm only looking out for my own family's interest. If you wish to please me you will drop this Young People's foolishness altogether, and go more into society. I wish you would follow Frank's example. He is a good church member but he don't let it interfere with his best interests. He has plenty of friends and chooses his associates among the first families in the city. *He* don't think it necessary to take up with every vagabond Cameron chooses to drag into the church. Remember, it must stop." And the careful father took his hat and left for the place on Broadway, where on the shelves and behind the counters of his hardware store he kept the God he really worshipped.

CHAPTER XVI

The year following Dick's stand for Christianity, an open air theater was established in the park on West Fourth Street, near the outskirts of the city, which was advertised by its enterprising manager as a very respectable place, well looked after by the police. It is true that the shows were but cheap variety and vulgar burlesque, and of course liquor, as well as more harmless drinks, was sold freely; and equally of course, the lowest of the criminal classes were regular attendants. But, with all that, there was something terribly fascinating in the freedom of the place. And all too often, on a Sunday evening, while the pure, fragrant air of summer was polluted by the fumes of tobacco and beer, while low plays were enacted on the stage, and the sound of drunken laugh or shout went out, young men and women mingled, half frightened, in the careless throng.

Among a certain set of Boyd City's gay young society people, to spend an evening at the park was just the thing to do; and often they might be seen grouped about the tables, sipping their refreshments, while laughing at the actors on the stage, or chatting and joking among themselves.

On an evening in August, when our chapter opens, one such party was even gayer than usual, and attracted no little attention from the frequenters of the place, as well as the employes. Waiters winked at each other and made remarks, as they hurried to and fro attending to the wants of their guests, while people with less wealth looked on in envy at the glittering show. The gentlemen were in evening dress, the ladies gowned in the latest fashion, jewels and trinkets flashed, eyes sparkled, cheeks glowed, as story and jest went round, while the ladies sipped their refreshing sodas and the men drank their wine.

One of the younger girls seemed a little frightened for a moment as she caught the eye of a waiter fastened upon her in anything but a respectful glance, and gave the fellow such a look in return that he dropped a napkin in his confusion. "I tell you, Bill," he said to his companion at the bar, where he had gone to get more drinks for the company, "that's a fast lot all right, but there's one in the bunch that can't go the pace."

But the waiter was evidently mistaken, for that same girl, after a glance around which revealed to her that she and her companions were the center of all eyes, tossed her head as though getting rid of some unpleasant thoughts, and turning to her escort, with a reckless laugh, asked him why he kept the best for himself. "I don't think it fair, girls," she declared in a loud voice. "We have as good a right to that nice wine as the boys have. I move that we make them treat us as well as they treat themselves."

"Done," cried one of the men before the others could object, even had they so desired; and in a moment another bottle, with more glasses, was set before them. The girl who had proposed the thing only drank a little. Something seemed to choke her when she lifted the glass to her lips, and she set it down again almost untasted. "Ugh," she said, "I don't like it," and a laugh went around at her expense.

"Take it. Take it. You must. You started it you know."

"I can't," she protested. "Here Jim," to her companion, who had already taken more than was good for him. "You must help me out." And she handed him the glass.

"Glad to help a lady always," he declared. "Notisch please, gen'lemen, I set y' good example. Alwaysh come to the rescue of fair ones in trouble—" He drained the glass. "Anybody else in trouble?" he said, looking around the table with a half tipsy grin. But the other girls had no scruples and drank their wine without a protest.

At last the party discovered that it was time to go home, and indeed the garden was almost deserted. One of the girls proposed that they walk, it was such a beautiful night; and accordingly they set out, two and two; the men reckless with wine; the ladies flushed and excited; all singing and laughing. Not far from the park entrance, the girl who had proposed the wine, and her companion, who was by this time more than half intoxicated, dropped a little behind the others and soon turned down a side street.

"This is not the way, Jim," she said, in a tone of laughing protest.

"Oh yesh 'tis. I know where'm goin'. Come 'long." And he caught her by the arm. "Nicesh place down here where we can stop and resht," and he staggered against her.

"But I want to go home, Jim," her tone of laughing protest changed to one of earnestness. "Father will be looking for me."

"Hang father," said the other. "Old man don't know. Come on I tell you." And he tried to put his arm about her waist.

The girl was frightened now in earnest. "Stop sir," she said.

"Why? Whash ze matter m' dear?" stammered the other. "Whash ze harm—zash all—I'll take care you all right—Ol' man never know." And again he clutched her arm.

This was too much, and giving the drunken wretch a push, which sent him tumbling into the gutter, where cursing fiercely he struggled to regain his feet, the frightened girl, without pausing to see his condition, or listening to his calls and threats, fled down the street. When her companion had at last managed to stagger to the sidewalk and could look around by clinging to the fence, she was out of sight. He called two or three times, and then swearing vilely, started in pursuit, reeling from side to side. The frightened girl ran on and on, paying no heed to her course, as she turned corner after corner her only thought being to escape from her drunken and enraged companion.

Meanwhile, Dick Falkner was making his way home after a delightful evening at the parsonage, where he had talked with Cameron on the veranda until a late hour. As he was walking leisurely along through the quiet streets, past the dark houses, enjoying the coolness of the evening and thinking of the things that he and Cameron had been discussing, his ear caught a strange sound, that seemed to come from within a half finished house on North Catalpa Street, near the railroad. He paused a moment and listened. Surely he was not mistaken. There it was again. The sound of someone sobbing. Stepping closer and peering into the shadow, he saw a figure crouching behind a pile of lumber. It was a woman.

"I beg your pardon, madam, but can I be of any help to you?"

She started to her feet with a little cry. "Don't be frightened," said Dick, in a calm voice. "I am a gentleman. Come, let me help you." And stepping into the shadow, he gently led her to the light, where she stood trembling before him. "Tell me what—My God! Amy—I beg your pardon—Miss Goodrich."

"Oh Mr. Falkner," sobbed the poor girl, almost beside herself with fear. "Don't let that man come near me. I want to go home. Oh, please take me home?"

"There, there," said Dick, controlling himself and speaking in a steady, matter-of-fact tone. "Of course I'll see you home. Take my arm, please. You need have no fear. You know I'll protect you."

Calmed by his voice and manner, the girl ceased her sobbing and walked quietly down the street by his side.

Dick's mind was in a whirl. "Was he dreaming? How came she here at such an hour. Who was she afraid of? By her dress, she had been to a social party of some kind; what did it all mean? But he spoke no word as they walked on together.

"Oh look," exclaimed Amy, a few moments later, as they turned east on Sixth Street; "there he is again. Oh Mr. Falkner, what shall I do? Let me go." And she turned to run once more.

Dick laid his hand on her arm. "Miss Goodrich, don't you know that you are safe with me? Be calm and tell me what you fear." Something in his touch brought Amy to herself again and she whispered: "Don't you see that man standing there by the light?" She pointed to a figure leaning against a telephone pole.

"Well, what of it?" said Dick. "He won't hurt you."

"Oh, but you don't understand. I ran away from him. He is drunk and threatened me."

Dick's form straightened and his face grew hard and cold. "Ran away from him. Do you mean that that fellow insulted you, Miss Goodrich?"

"I—I—was with him—and—he frightened me—" gasped Amy. "Let's go the other way."

But they were too late. Amy's former escort had seen them, and with uncertain steps approached. "Oh, here you are," he said. "Thought I'd find you, my beauty."

Dick whispered to Amy in a tone she dared not disobey. "Stand right where you are. Don't move. And you might watch that star over there. Isn't it a beautiful one?" He deftly turned her so that she faced away from the drunkard. Then with three long steps, he placed himself in the way of the half-crazed man.

"Who are you?" asked the fellow, with an oath.

"None of your business," replied Dick, curtly. "I'm that girl's friend. Go to the other side of the street."

"Ho, I know you now," cried the other. "You're that bum printer of Udell's. Get out of my way. That girl's a lady and I'm a gentleman. She don't go with tramps. I'll see her home myself."

Dick spoke again. "You may be a gentleman, but you are in no condition to see anybody home. I'll tell you just once more; cross to the other side of the street."

The fellow's only answer was another string of vile oaths, which however was never finished.

In spite of herself, Amy turned just in time to see a revolver glisten in the light of the electric lamp; then the owner of the revolver rolled senseless in the gutter.

"Miss Goodrich, I told you to watch that star. Don't you find it beautiful?" Dick's voice was calm, with just a suggestion of mild reproach.

"Oh Mr. Falkner, have you killed him?"

"Killed nothing. Come." And he led her quickly past the place where the self-styled gentleman lay. "Just a moment," he said; and turning back, he examined the fallen man. "Only stunned," he reported cheerfully. "He'll have a sore head for a few days; that's all. I'll send a cab to pick him up when we get down town."

"Mr. Falkner," said Amy, when they had walked some distance in silence. "I don't know what you think of finding me here at this hour, but I don't want you to think me worse than I am." And then she told him the whole story; how she had gone to the park with her friends to spend the evening; and how they had a few refreshments. Dick ground his teeth; he knew what those refreshments were. Then she told how her companion had frightened her and she had run until she was exhausted and had stopped to hide in the unfinished house. "Oh, what must you think of me?" she said, at the point of breaking down again.

"I think just as I always have," said Dick simply. "Please calm yourself, you're safe now." Then to occupy her mind, he told her of the work the Young People's Society was doing, and how they missed her there and at the Mission.

"But don't you find such things rather tiresome, you know?" she asked. "There's not much life in those meetings seems to me; I wonder now how I ever stood them."

"You are very busy then?" asked Dick, hiding the pain her words caused him.

"Oh yes; with our whist club, box parties, dances and dinners, I'm so tired out when Sunday comes I just want to sleep all day. But one must look after one's social duties, you know, or be a nobody; and our set is such a jolly crowd that there's always something going."

"And you have forgotten your class at the Mission altogether?" Dick asked.

"Oh no, I saw one of the little beggars on the street this summer. It was down near the Mission building, and don't you know, we were out driving, a whole party of us, and the little rascal shouted: 'Howdy, Miss Goodrich.' I thought I would faint. Just fancy. And the folks did guy me good. The gentlemen wanted to know if he was one of my flames, and the girls all begged to be introduced; and don't you know, I got out of it by telling them that it was the child of a woman who scrubs for us."

Dick said nothing. "Could it be possible?" he asked himself, "that this was the girl who had been such a worker in the church." And then he thought of the change in his own life in the same period of time; a change fully as great, though in another direction. "It don't take long to go either way if one only has help enough," he said, half aloud.

"What are you saying, Mr. Falkner?" asked Amy.

"It's not far home now," answered Dick, and they fell into silence again.

As they neared the Goodrich mansion, Amy clasped Dick's arm with both her little hands: "Mr. Falkner, promise me that you will never speak to a living soul about this evening."

Dick looked her straight in the eyes. "I am a gentleman, Miss Goodrich," was all he said.

Then as they reached the steps of the house, she held out her hand. "I thank you for your kindness—and please don't think of me too harshly. I know I am not just the girl I was a year ago, but I—do you remember our talk at the printing office?"

"Every word," said Dick.

"Well, has my prophecy come true?"

"About my preaching? No; not yet."

"Oh, I don't mean that," with a shrug of her shoulders. "I mean about the other. Do you still value my friendship?"

Dick hesitated. "The truth, please," she said. "I want to know."

"Miss Goodrich, I cannot make you understand; you know my whole life has changed the last year."

"Yes."

"But my feelings toward you can never change. I do value your friendship, for I know that your present life does not satisfy you, and that you are untrue to your best self in living it."

The girl drew herself up haughtily. "Indeed, you are fast becoming a very proficient preacher," she said, coldly.

"Wait a moment, please," interrupted Dick. "You urged me to tell the truth. I desire your friendship, because I know the beautiful life you could live, and because you—you—could help me to live it," his voice broke.

Amy held out her hand again. "Forgive me please," she said. "You are a true friend, and I shall never, never, forget you. Oh, Mr. Falkner, if you are a Christian pray for me before it is too late. Good-night." And she was gone; just as her brother Frank came up the walk.

Young Goodrich stopped short when he saw Dick, and then sprang up the steps and into the house, just in time to see his sister going up the stairway to her room.

CHAPTER XVII

The day following Amy's adventure with her drunken escort, and her rescue by Dick Falkner, Frank Goodrich had a long interview with his father, which resulted in Adam's calling his daughter into his library that evening. Without any preface whatever, he began, in an angry tone: "I understand, Miss, that you have disobeyed my express commands in regard to that tramp printer, and that you have been with him again; and that too, late at night. Now I have simply to tell you that you must choose between him and your home. I will *not* have a child of mine keeping such company. You must either give him up or go."

"But father, you do not know the circumstances or you would not talk so."

"No circumstances can excuse your conduct; I know you were with him and that is enough."

"Indeed I have not disobeyed you; father, you do not understand; I was in Mr. Falkner's company only by accident, and—"

"Stop. Don't add a falsehood to your conduct. I understand quite enough. Your own brother saw you bidding him an affectionate good-night at one o'clock, on my doorstep. Such things do not happen by accident. I wonder that you dare look me in the face after roaming the streets at that time of night with such a disreputable character."

"Father, I tell you you are mistaken. Won't you please let me explain?" said Amy, almost in tears.

But the angry man only replied, "No explanation can be made. Frank saw you himself and that's enough; no excuse can justify such conduct. I have only to repeat that I will not own you as my daughter if you persist in keeping such company."

Amy tried again to speak, but he interrupted her. "Silence, I don't want to hear a word from you. Go to your room."

Then the woman asserted herself and there were no tears this time, as she said respectfully, but firmly, "Father, you *shall* hear me. I am not guilty of that of which you accuse me. I was in other company, company of your own choosing, and to save myself from insult I was forced to appeal to Mr. Falkner, who brought me safely home. He is far more a gentleman than the men I was with, even though they are welcome at this home; and he is not. I—"

Adam turned fairly green with rage. "You ungrateful, disobedient girl. How dare you say that this miserable vagabond is a fit associate for you, and more worthy than the guests of my house? You must not think you can deceive me and clear yourself by any trumped-up lie of his teaching. You may have your tramp, but don't call me father. You are no daughter of mine." And he left the room.

It is astonishing how little the proud man knew of the real nature of his child; a nature which rightfully understood and influenced, was capable of any sacrifice, any hardship, for the one she loved; but misunderstood or falsely condemned, was just as capable of reckless folly or despair. A nature that would never prove false to a trust, but if unjustly suspected, would turn to the very thing of which it stood accused.

The next morning Amy did not appear at breakfast and the mother went to her room; while Mr. Goodrich, impatient at the delay, stood with angry eyes awaiting their appearance.

Frank came in. "Good morning, father," he said, glancing about with an assumed expression of surprise. "Where is Amy and mother? I thought I heard the bell."

Adam grunted some reply and the son picked up a week-old daily and pretended to be deeply interested. Suddenly a piercing scream reached their ears, and a sound as of someone falling. With an exclamation of alarm, Mr. Goodrich, followed by his son, hurried from the dining-room and ran upstairs. The door of Amy's apartment was open, and just inside prone upon the floor, lay Mrs. Goodrich, holding in her hand a piece of paper. Adam, with the help of his son, lifted his wife and laid her upon the bed, which they noticed had not been occupied. For an instant the two stood looking into each other's face without a word, and then the older man said, "We must take care of mother first. Call Dr. Gleason."

Under the advice of the physician, who soon came in answer to Frank's telephone call, Mrs. Goodrich was removed to her own room, and in a short time regained consciousness, but fell to moaning and sobbing, "Oh, Amy—Amy—my poor child—my baby girl—what have you done? I never thought that you would do a thing like this. Oh, my beautiful girl—come back—come back—" And then when she became calmer, told them what they already knew; that she had found her daughter's room undisturbed, with a note addressed to herself on the toilet table, containing only a simple farewell message.

"There, there, wife, she's gone," said Adam, clumsily trying to soothe the mother's anguish, but finding that a tongue long accustomed to expressions of haughty pride and bigotry, could but poorly lend itself to softer words of comfort. "There, there, don't cry, let her go. That scoundrel printer is at the bottom of it all. Somehow the girl does not seem to take after the Goodrich's. Madam, please try to control your feelings. You must not make yourself ill over this matter."

Mrs. Goodrich, accustomed to obey, with a great effort, ceased the open expression of her grief.

> "There can be no doubt but that she has gone with that tramp," continued Adam. "I shall do what I can to find her and give her one more chance. If she acknowledges her fault and promises to do better she may come home. If not, she shall never darken these doors again."

"Oh, Mr. Goodrich, don't say that," cried the mother. "Think of that poor child on the streets all alone. Perhaps you are mistaken."

"*What*? Am I to understand that you take her part against me?"

"No, no," murmured the frightened woman.

"I tell you, there can be no mistake. You saw them did you not, Frank?"

"Yes, sir."

"You hear that, Mrs. Goodrich? You will oblige me by not mentioning this matter again." And hurriedly leaving the room, Adam went to his own private apartment, where, after he had turned the key in the door, he paced to and fro, the tears streaming down his cheeks. But in a few moments, while he made his preparations for going down the street, thoughts of the curious faces he must meet aroused the old pride and hardened his heart again. So that when he left the building, not a trace of his worthier feelings showed on his cold, proper countenance, except that to the keen observer, he looked a little older perhaps, and a trifle less self-satisfied.

His first visit was to the store, where he spent an hour or two going over his correspondence, interviewing the head clerk and issuing his orders for the day. Then taking his hat and cane, he left for the printing office.

The boy was away on an errand, and George had stepped out for a few moments, so that Dick was alone when Mr. Goodrich entered. Thinking that it was the printer who had returned, he did not look up from his work until he was startled by the angry voice of his visitor.

"Well, sir, I suppose you are satisfied at last. Where is my daughter?"

"Your daughter," said Dick, who had not heard the news, "I'm sure, sir, that I do not know."

"Don't lie to me, you scoundrel," shouted Adam, losing all control of himself. "You were with her last. You have been trying ever since you came here to worm yourself into the society of your betters. Tell me what you have done with her."

"Mr. Goodrich," said Dick, forcing himself to be calm, "you must explain. It is true that I was with your daughter night before last, but—" he hesitated; should he explain how he had found Amy?—"I left her safely at your door and have not seen her since." He finished. "Is she not home?"

Adam only glared at him. "She did not sleep at home last night," he growled.

Dick's voice failed him for a moment. "Then she must be stopping with some friend; surely there is no need for alarm."

"I tell you she's gone," said the other furiously. "She left a letter. You are to blame for this. You I say; and you shall suffer for it." He shook his clenched fist at the young man. "If you have hidden her anywhere I'll have your life; you miserable, low-down vagabond. You have schemed and schemed until you have succeeded in stealing her heart from her home, and disgracing me."

"Adam Goodrich, you lie," said Dick, pale with mingled anxiety for the girl, and angry that her father should thus accuse him. "Do you understand me? I say that you lie. That you are the most contemptible liar that I have ever known. Your whole life is a lie." He spoke in a low tone, but there was something underlying the quiet of his voice and manner that contrasted strangely with the loud bluster of the older man, and made the latter tremble. This was a new experience for him, and something in the manly face of the one who uttered these hard words startled and frightened him.

"You have forced your daughter to drop her church work, and have goaded her into the society of people whose only claim to respectability is their wealth. You value your position in the world more than your daughter's character, and you yourself are to blame for this. I tell you again, sir, that you are a liar. I do not know where your daughter is, but if she is on earth I will find her and bring her back to your home; not for your sake, but for hers. Now go. Get out. The very atmosphere is foul with your rotten hypocrisy."

"Whew!" whistled George a moment later, as he Stepped into the room, having passed Adam on the stairway. "What's the matter with his Royal Highness, Dickie? He looks like he had been in a boiler explosion." But his expression changed when Dick told him of the interview and apologized for driving a good customer from the office. "Good customer!" he shouted; "good customer! A mighty bad customer. I say you'd better apologize for not throwing him into the street. I'll never set up another line for him unless it's an invitation to his funeral."

For many days Dick searched for the missing girl, bringing to bear all his painfully acquired knowledge of life, and the crooked ways of the world. Though unknown to Mr. Goodrich, the detective from Chicago, whom he employed, was an old companion of Dick's, and to the officer only, he confided the full story of Amy's visit to the park. But they, only learned that she had boarded the twelve-forty Kansas City Southern, for Jonesville, and that a woman answering to her description had stopped there until nearly noon the next day, when she was seen in conversation with a man whose face was badly bruised on the under left side of the chin. The two had taken the same train east on the "Frisco." They found also that her companion of that night at the park, James Whitley, had hurriedly left Boyd City on the morning train, over the "Frisco," to Jonesville, and had not returned, nor could his whereabouts be discovered. It was given out in public, among the society items of the Whistler, that he had been called suddenly to the bedside of a sick friend; but Dick and the detective knew better.

Gradually the interest on the part of the citizens subsided, and the detective returned to Chicago to other mysteries, demanding his attention. Adam Goodrich refused to talk of the matter, and gave no sign of his sorrow, save an added sternness in his manner. But the mother's health was broken; while Frank, declaring that he could not stand the disgrace, went for a long visit to a friend in a neighboring city. Finally Dick himself was forced to give up the search; but though baffled for a time, he declared to Udell and his pastor, that he would yet bring Amy home as he had promised her father. And while he went about his work as usual, it was with a heavy heart, and a look on his face that caused his friends who knew him best to pity.

CHAPTER XVIII

The summer passed and again the catalpa trees shed their broad leaves, while the prairie grass took on the reddish brown of early fall. Jim Whitley suddenly returned to Boyd City and Dick met him in the post-office. "Not a word passed between them, but an hour later a note was put into Jim's hand by a ragged boot-black.

"George," said Dick, that afternoon as they were locking up, "if you don't mind I believe I'll sleep in my old bed in the office to-night."

Udell looked at his helper in astonishment. "What in the world?" he began; then stopped.

"I can't explain now, but please let me have my way and say nothing about it to anyone; not even Clara."

"Why sure, old man," said the other heartily; "only I don't know why." He paused again; then in an anxious tone, "Dickie, I know it's hard, and you've been putting up a great fight, but you're not going to let go now?"

"No, no, it's not that, old man: I'll explain some day." And something in his face assured his friend that whatever it was that prompted his strange request, Dick was still master of himself.

Late that night as Udell passed the office on his way home, after spending the evening with Miss Wilson, he was astonished to see Jim Whitley entering the building. He stood watching for a moment; then fearing possible danger for Dick, he ran lightly up the stairs. But as he reached out to lay his hand on the door latch, he heard a key turn in the lock and his friend's voice saying, "I thought you would come." George paused, and then with a shrug of his shoulder, and a queer smile on his rugged face, turned and went softly down to the street again.

Dick and his visitor faced each other in the dimly lighted office.

"Well," said Whitley, with an oath, "what do you want?"

"I want you to take your hand out of your pocket first," flashed Dick; "that gun won't help you any tonight," and a heavy revolver in his own hand covered Whitley's heart.

His request was granted instantly.

"Now walk into the other room."

They passed into the stock room, which was well lighted. The windows were covered with heavy paper; the long table was cleared and moved out from its place near the wall.

Dick closed the door and pointed to the table. "Lay your gun there. Be careful," as Whitley drew his revolver. Jim glanced once at the determined eyes and steady hand of his master and sullenly obeyed.

"Now sit down."

Crossing the room, he seated himself in the chair indicated, which placed him in the full glare of the light. Dick took the other chair facing him, with the long table between them. Placing his weapon beside the other, within easy reach of his hand, he rested his elbows on the table and looked long and steadily at the man before him.

Whitley was uneasy. "Well," he said at last, when he could bear the silence no longer. "I hope you like my looks."

"Your figure is somewhat heavier, but shaving off your beard has made you look some years younger," replied Dick, dryly.

The other started to his feet.

"Don't be uneasy," said Dick, softly resting his hand on one of the revolvers; "keep your seat please."

"I never wore a beard," said the other, as he dropped back on his chair. "You are mistaken."

"Then how did you know the meaning of my note, and why did you answer it in person. You should have sent the right man."

Whitley saw that he had betrayed himself but made one more effort.

"I came out of curiosity," he muttered.

Dick laughed—a laugh that was not good to hear. "I can easily satisfy you," he said; "permit me to tell you a little story."

"The story begins in a little manufacturing town a few miles from Liverpool, England, just three years ago today." Beneath the unwavering eyes of the man leaning on the table Whitley's face grew ghastly and he writhed in his chair.

"An old man and his wife, with their two orphaned grand-sons, lived in a little cottage on the outskirts of the town. The older of the boys was a strong man of twenty; the other a sickly lad of eight. The old people earned a slender income by cultivating small fruits. This was helped out by the wages of the older brother, who was a machinist in one of the big factories. They were a quiet and unpretentious little family, devout Christians, and very much attached to each other.

"One afternoon a wealthy American, who was stopping at a large resort a few miles from the village, went for a drive along the road leading past their home. As his carriage was passing, the little boy, who was playing just outside the yard, unintentionally frightened the horses and they shied quickly. At the same moment, the American's silk hat fell in the dust. The driver stopped the team and the lad, frightened, picked up the hat and ran with it toward the carriage, stammering an apology for what he had done.

"Instead of accepting the boy's excuse, the man, beside himself with anger, and slightly under the influence of wine, sprang from the carriage, and seizing the lad, kicked him brutally.

"The grandfather, who was working in his garden, saw the incident, and hurried as fast as he could to the rescue. At the same time, the driver jumped from his seat to protect the child, but before they could reach the spot, the boy was lying bruised and senseless in the dust.

"The old man rushed at the American in impotent rage, and the driver, fearing for his safety, caught him by the arm and tried to separate them, saying, 'You look after the boy. Let me settle with him.' But the old man was deaf and could not understand, and thought that the driver, also an American, was assisting his employer. In the struggle, the American suddenly drew a knife, and in spite of the driver's efforts, struck twice at his feeble opponent, who fell back in the arms of his would-be protector, just as the older brother rushed upon the scene. The American leaped into the carriage and snatched up the lines. The mechanic sprang after him, and as he caught hold of the seat in his attempt to climb in, the knife flashed again, cutting a long gash in his arm and hand, severing the little finger. With the other hand, he caught the wrist of the American, but a heavy blow in the face knocked him beneath the wheels, and the horses dashed away down the road.

"The driver was bending over the old man trying to staunch the flow of blood, when several workmen, attracted by the cries of the helpless grandmother, who had witnessed the scene from the porch, came running up. "E's one on 'em—'e's one on 'em,' cried the old lady. "E 'eld my man while 'tother 'it 'im.'

"The driver saw her mistake instantly, and realizing his danger as the man passed into the house with the body of the old man, he ran down the street and escaped. Two days later, he read in a Liverpool paper that the grandfather and boy were both dead, and that the dying statement of the old man, the testimony of the grandmother and the brother, was that both the strangers were guilty.

"How the wealthy American made his escape from the country you know best. The driver shipped aboard a vessel bound for Australia, and later, made his way home."

When Dick had finished his story, Whitley's face was drawn and haggard. He leaped to his feet again, but the revolver motioned him back. "What fiend told you all this?" he gasped hoarsely. "Who are you?"

"I am the driver."

Whitley sank back in his chair; then suddenly broke into a harsh laugh. "You are a crazy fool. Who would believe you? You have no proof."

"Wait a bit," replied Dick, calmly. "There is another chapter to my story. Less than a year after the tragedy, the invalid grandmother died and the young machinist was free to enter upon the great work of his life, the bringing to justice of his brother's murderer, or as *he* believed, murderers. He could find no clue as to the identity of the obscure driver of the carriage, but with the wealthy American it was different, and he succeeded at last in tracing him to his home in this city. Unfortunately though, the long search had left the young mechanic without means, and he arrived in Boyd City in a penniless and starving condition, the night of the great storm winter before last. You are familiar with the finding of his body by George Udell."

Again Whitley sprang to his feet, and with an awful oath exclaimed, "How do you know this?"

Dick drew forth a long leather pocket-book, and opening it, took out a package of papers, which he laid on the table between the two revolvers.

"There is the story, written by his own hand, together with the testimony of his grandfather and grandmother, his own sworn statement, and all the evidence he had so carefully gathered."

Whitley sprang forward; but before he could cross the room, both revolvers covered his breast.

"Stop!"

The voice was calm and steady, but full of deadly menace.

Whitley crouched like an animal at bay. The hands that held the weapons never trembled; the gray eyes that looked along the shining barrels never wavered. Slowly he drew back. "Name your price," he said sullenly.

"You have not money enough to buy."

"I am a wealthy man."

"I know it."

He went back to his seat. "For God's sake, put down those guns and tell me what you want."

"I want to know where you left Miss Goodrich."

"What if I refuse to tell?"

Dick laid a pair of handcuffs upon the table.

A cunning gleam crept into Whitley's eyes. "You'll put them on yourself at the same time. The evidence is just as strong against you."

"If it were not, I would have turned you over to the law long ago."

"But you fool, they'll hang you."

"That won't save you, and you'll answer to God for another murder."

"You would not dare."

"I am innocent; you are the coward."

Then Whitley gave up and told how he had met Amy in Jonesville, and had taken her east to Buffalo, New York, where he had left her just before returning to Boyd City.

"Did you marry her?" asked Dick.

Whitley shrugged his shoulders. "I am not looking for a wife," he said.

"But was there no form of a ceremony?" persisted Dick.

Again Jim shrugged his shoulders. "It was not necessary."

It was Dick's turn to be agitated now; his hand played nervously on the handle of his revolver. But the other did not notice.

"Why did you leave her so soon?"

"I had business of importance at home," with a sneer.

Slowly the man behind the table rose to his feet, his form trembling violently, his strong hands clinching and unclinching in his agitation. Slowly he reached out and lifted the weapons of death from the table; slowly he raised them. The criminal sat as though fascinated; his face livid with fear. For a full minute the revolver covered the cowering victim; then suddenly Dick's hand fell.

"Jim Whitley," he said, in a voice that was strangely quiet. "If I were not a Christian, you could not live a moment. Now go!" He followed him from the room and watched him down the stairs; then returning, locked the door again, and throwing himself on the floor, wept as only a strong man can weep, with great shuddering sobs, until utterly exhausted, he fell into a stupor, where George found him in the morning.

Dick told his employer the whole story, and took the first train east. The same day, Whitley left the city.

CHAPTER XIX

Whitley's sudden return to Boyd City, and his departure so soon after, revived some whispering gossip about Amy's strange disappearance. And of course the matter was mentioned at the Ministerial Association, which still held its regular Monday morning meetings. Then, as was natural, the talk drifted to the much discussed topic, the low standard of morality in Boyd City. Old Father Beason said, "Brethren, I tell you the condition of things in this town is just awful. I walked down Broadway last Saturday night, and I declare I could hardly get along. I actually had to walk out in the street, there was such a crowd, and nearly all of them young men and young women. I never saw anything like it; and there are all of these dives always open, and always full. Candidly, Brethren, what are we doing? I just tell you we are not doing one thing. We are not beginning to touch the problem. It costs just all we can scrape and dig to keep the churches, running, and so far as I know, only Brother Cameron here has even attempted any aggressive work. Brethren, I wish we could put our heads together and formulate some plan that would stir this town and save our boys and girls, who are growing up in utter disrespect for Christianity and the teaching of Christ."

"What we want here is a Young Men's Christian Association," exclaimed Rev. Hugh Cockrell. "An Association is the very thing for a town like this. You all know how it operates. It don't conflict with the work of the churches in the least. It furnishes parlor, sitting room, libraries, gymnasium, bath rooms, and all such things, at a very nominal cost to young men. As I have said in our meetings before, I think we ought to write to the State Secretary and get him to come here and look over the situation."

"That's all right, Brother Cockrell," said the big Brother Howell, rising to his feet and pushing his hands deep into his pockets; for the big minister was lots more of a man than he was a preacher, and put his hands into his pockets when he chose, without any closely buttoned, clerical cut coat to prevent him. "That's all right about the Young Men's Christian Association. It's a good thing; a splendid thing; and I'd like to see one started here in Boyd City, but a dozen Associations won't meet the needs of this place. Those who could afford to pay the fee would enjoy the parlors and baths;

those who could read might enjoy the books; and those who had worked in the mines digging coal all day, might exercise in the gymnasium, but what about the hundreds of young men who can't afford the fees, and don't want a parlor so much as a bite to eat, or a gymnasium so much as a bed, or a reading room so much as a job of work? We need something in this town that will reach out for the ignorant, fallen, hard-up, debauched, degraded men and women."

Father Beason nodded emphatic approval.

"I don't know, I'm sure," said the Rev. Jeremiah Wilks, "what you Brethren are going to do. If you hit on any plan to raise the money for all this, I'd like to know what it is. I'm going night and day now, trying to raise the debt on our new organ, and I've got to raise our benevolences yet; and besides this, my own salary is behind. I'm doing more work than any three preachers in the city. I tell you, the men who have got the money are going to hang on to it. There's Mr. Richman; I met him on the street yesterday; he was talking with a friend; and I stopped and said: Good morning, Brother Richman—he's not a member of any church you know. I only called him Brother to make him feel good you know. He said: Good morning, Reverend; kind of short; and then deliberately turned his back on me and went on talking with his friend. I didn't like to leave him like that, you know, for he's got a lot of money, I'm told. And you know we preachers never would get anything if we always quit like that; so I said, Brother Richman, I don't like to interrupt you, but can't you give me a little something this morning? I'm behind on our new organ, and on our benevolences and some other things, and my own salary is not all paid yet. I thought maybe you would help me a little. He looked at me a minute, then said with a sneer: 'I always like to know what returns I may expect for the money I invest. I'm no church member, that I have money to throw away. What do I get for it if I give you five dollars?' Why, I said, you might be a Christian some day. Brother Richman, I'd like mighty well to have you join my church. We'll all pray for you if you'd like to have us. And do you believe it, he just stood there and laughed and laughed; and the other fellow, he laughed too. Yes, he did. Well, I didn't know what to do you know, but I wanted that five dollars, so I said: But won't you help us a little, Brother Richman? It will be very acceptable. 'I tell you, Mr. Wilks,' he said; 'when you can show me that my money is doing some actual good among the poor people in this city, or that it's saving the young folks from the degrading influences here, I'll invest; and until then, I'll keep my money, and you can keep your prayers.' And do you know, he wouldn't give me a cent." The Rev. Jeremiah sat down with an air of mingled triumph and suffering, as much as to say, "See how gladly I bear persecution for the Lord."

"I understand that Mr. Richman gave to Cameron's institution though," the big preacher remarked. "How is it Brother Cameron?"

"Yes," replied Cameron, "he gave a hundred dollars unsolicited, and promised more if it were needed."

There was silence for a moment; then the president said, "Brother Cameron, would you mind telling the Association just how your work is conducted? I for one, would like to know more about it, and perhaps we could all adopt a similar plan. What would you suggest as a remedy for the existing conditions in this city?"

"As far as our work goes, we have hardly touched the matter yet," replied Cameron. "There is room for every church In the place; but what we need, I feel sure, is a united effort, and—"

"Brethren," interrupted the Rev. Dr. Frederick Hartzel, "I must beg that this useless discussion be stopped. So far as I can see, all of this is of no profit whatever. My time is altogether too valuable to waste in such foolish talk as this. I endeavor to put some thought into *my* sermons, and I cannot take this valuable time from my studies. If the Association persists in taking up the meetings with such subjects, instead of discussing some of the recent theological themes that are attracting the attention of the clergy everywhere, I must beg that I be given optional attendance. These new-fangled notions of uneducated young men may be all right for some, but you can't expect such men as myself to listen to them. I move that we adjourn."

"Brother Cameron has the floor and I think the Brethren would like to hear him," suggested the president.

"Brother President," said Cameron, calmly, before the others could speak, for he saw the light of righteous indignation creeping into the eye of the big Rev. Howells; "if the Brethren wish to talk with me of our work, they know that they are always welcome at my home; and I will be glad to discuss any plan for reaching those for whom our Saviour died. I second Rev. Hartzell's motion to adjourn." And the meeting dismissed with prayer as usual, that God would fill their hearts with love, and help them to do their Master's work, as He would have it done, and that many souls might be added to their number.

That evening, lost in troubled thought, the young pastor of the Jerusalem Church sat alone before the fire, in his little study. Once his wife knocked timidly and opening the door, said, "James, dear, it's time you're going to bed."

"Not now, Fanny," he answered; and she, knowing well what that tone of voice meant, retired to her room, after seeing everything snug for the night.

The cocks were crowing midnight; the fire burned lower and lower. Once he impatiently hitched his chair a little closer, but made no other move, until, just as the clock chimed three, he arose stiffly to his feet and stood shivering with cold, looking at the blackened embers. Then he made his way to his chamber, where he fell asleep like a man tired out with a hard day's work.

All the next day he said nothing, but was silent and moody, and the following night sat once more alone in his study, thinking, thinking, thinking, until again the fire went out and he was cold.

"Fanny," he said, the following afternoon, entering the kitchen and putting his arm about his wife, as she stood at the table busy with her baking. "Fanny, what can we do for the young people of Boyd City? Amy is only one of many. It is all the result of the do-nothing policy of the church, and of the Goodrich type of Christians, who think more of their social position than they do of the souls of their children, or the purity of their characters."

"Oh, James, you oughtn't to say that. Mr. Goodrich may not look at those things as you do perhaps, but we ought to remember his early training."

"Early training, bosh," answered the minister, losing his patience as even ministers will sometimes do. "You'd better say his lack of early training. I tell you, Fanny, the true gentleman, whether he be Christian or not, values character more than position, while the sham aristocrat is a sham in everything, and doesn't even know the real article when he sees it."

"Oh, here, here," cried Mrs. Cameron, "that's not the way for a preacher to talk."

"Preacher or no preacher, it's the truth," he replied excitedly. "Let me forget that I belong to the class that has produced such a thing as this kind of religion, and remember that I am only a man. If the ministers in this city cared half as much for the salvation of souls and the teaching of Christ, as they do for their own little theories and doctrines, the world could not hold such a churchified hypocrite as Adam Goodrich, and girls would not go wrong as that poor child did. The Rev. Hartzell, D. D., is the cause; and if you go down on Fourth Street, or East Third you can see the effect; egotism, bigotry, selfishness, man-made doctrines and creeds in the pulpit; saloons and brothels on the street; church doors closed over a mawkish sentimentality, and men and women dying without shelter and without God. Truly we need a preacher, with a wilderness training like John the Baptist who will show us the way of the Lord, rather than a thousand theological, hot-house posies, who will show us only the opinions of the authorities." And the Rev. James tramped up and down the kitchen, speaking with all the vehemence of a political spellbinder, until his wife caught him by the coat and insisted that she wanted to be kissed. When that operation was successfully performed, she said, "Now run away to your study, dear, and don't bother about this just now. You're excited." And the preacher went, of course.

Though expressing themselves as very much alarmed over the situation, and the condition of the churches, the members of the Ministerial Association went no farther in the matter than the discussions at their regular meetings and private talks from time to time. It would be hard to give a reason why this was so if Cameron's criticism were not true; but so it certainly was. Cameron, however, was much wrought up. He did not in the least mind the Rev. Hartzell's opinion of himself or his work, and cared not one whit that he had been prevented from expressing himself to his brethren. He did care, however, for the work itself, regardless of the preachers, and the train of thought which he had so often followed was stirred afresh in his mind by the incident. With his heart so full of the matter it was not at all strange that he should preach another of his characteristic sermons on what he called "Applied Christianity." His house was crowded, as it always was on Sunday evenings, largely with young men and women, though many business men were in attendance.

He introduced his subject by showing the purpose and duty of the church: that it was not a social club, not simply a place to see and be seen, not a musical organization, and not an intellectual battlefield; but that it was a place to build Christ-like characters, and that the church had no excuse for living, save as it preached Christ's gospel and did His work. Then he asked, "Is the church doing this?" and called attention to the magnificent buildings, expensive organs, paid choirs, large-salaried preachers, and in the same city hundreds and thousands of men and women who were going to eternal ruin. "Did Christ make a mistake when he said, 'And I, if I be lifted up, will draw all men unto myself?' Or was it that men were lifting up themselves instead of the Master?"

He showed that the reason why more laborers and business men were not Christians was because Christianity had become, not a work, but a belief; that it had grown to be, not a life, but a sentiment; and that laborers and business men had not much place for beliefs and sentiments. "The church," said Cameron, "must prove herself by her works as did Christ, and her work must be the same as Christ's."

It caused a great deal of talk, of course. No preacher can branch out from the old, well-beaten paths, without creating talk. He was roundly scored by his Brethren in the ministry, and accused of all sorts of sensationalism, but bore it all without a word, except to say, "I am glad if I can even stir you up enough that you will condemn me; though I cannot help but think that if you would spend the same energy in remedying the evils you well know exist, you would do more for Christ and your fellow men." But to his wife he said, "Fanny, I am convinced that if we ever have a practical working plan for helping the poor and needy, and for the protection of the boys and girls in this city, on a scale sufficient to at all meet the needs, it will come from the citizens and not from the preachers. The world really believes in Christ, but has lost confidence in the church. And if some plan could be started, independent of the churches, but on a Christian basis, I believe it would succeed."

"Well," said his wife, with a smile, "I think I know one preacher who will have a hand in it anyway, and I know you do not include the Young People's Society with the church."

Cameron jumped to his feet and walked rapidly up and down the room. "Fanny," he said at last, facing his companion. And as he stood, with both hands in the side pockets of his short coat, and his feet braced wide apart, he looked so much a boy that the good wife laughed before she answered, "Yes sir, please, what have I done?"

"Do you know that I am to speak at the regular union meeting of the Young People next Sunday night?"

"Yes sir," meekly.

"And you know that the subject of the evening is 'Beaching the Masses.'"

She nodded.

"And do you know what I am going to do?"

"No sir."

"Well, just wait and see," and planting a kiss on the upturned lips, he ran off to shut himself up in his study.

The practical Christian work of the home established by the young people of the Jerusalem Church, and the remarkable success of the reading rooms, was proving a great educational factor in the life of Boyd City. The people were beginning to realize the value of such work, and the time was ripe for larger things. As has been said, Cameron's sermon caused no little talk, while the preachers did not hesitate to help the matter along, and to keep the pot boiling by the fire of their criticism.

It was a custom of the Young People's Societies in the city, to meet for union services once each month, at which time one of the pastors would speak on some topic of particular interest to young Christians, dealing with social, civil, or political questions, from the standpoint of Christianity, and this happened to be Cameron's turn to deliver the address. The young pastor was a favorite generally, in spite of his somewhat questionable standing with the theologians; so when it was announced that he would speak, and that the subject was one upon which he was known to have strong ideas, the public looked forward to the meeting with more than usual interest. When the time came, the Zion Church, which was the largest in the city, was crowded to its utmost capacity.

> Cameron began by reading from the twenty-fifth chapter of Matthew, "Inasmuch as ye have done it unto one of the least of these, my Brethren, ye have lone it unto me."

Then he said that as his talk was in no way to be a sermon, he felt free to give himself more liberty perhaps, than if he were in the pulpit; and that he would discuss the question not simply from the standpoint of Christianity, but of good citizenship, and the best interests of the people as well.

The audience settled itself at these words and waited breathlessly.

The speaker then laid down the proposition, that the question of reaching the masses, did not have to do simply with those who called themselves Christians, but with all society, all business, all government; in fact, with all that touched mankind. He showed how the conditions of the least of these gave rise to bad conditions everywhere, and bred crime, anarchy and animalism; and how that the physical, moral and intellectual life of all men is concerned. Then he took his hearers from street to street in their own city, bidding them to look at the young men and women on the corners, in the saloons and wine rooms, and asked, without any reference to Christianity in any way, "What will be the legitimate fruit of such sowing? What influence are we throwing about our boys and girls, and upon what foundation are we building our social, business and municipal life?"

Then turning to Christians, he reviewed the grand work that the church had done in the past, in moulding the lives of men and nations; and plead that she prove true to the past by rising to the present and meeting the problems of to-day. He called upon them in the name of their common Master, to put their minds to this question and to rest not from their study until a practical solution had been found. He urged, too, that those standing outside the church with idle hands, content to criticize and condemn, were not doing even so much as the institution with which they refused to stand identified. "I can see no difference," he said, "and before God, I believe there is none, between an idle church member and a do-nothing man of the world. They both stand on the same plane, and that plane is the plane of death."

Then, after an earnest appeal that the teaching of Jesus be applied, that the worth of souls be judged by the price paid on Calvary, and that all men, within and without the church, unite for the common cause, humanity; he turned suddenly to the chairman and said: "Mr. President, because of these things regarding the church, which all men know to be true; because of these things regarding our city, which all men know to be true; for the sake of Christ and His gospel, for the sake of our country and our laws, for the love of our boys and girls, I suggest that each society in this union appoint a committee of three from their membership, each of these committees to add to itself one good business man who believes in the teaching of Christ, but who is not connected with any church; the joint committee to meet in council for the purpose of formulating some plan to meet the needs of this city along the lines of our subject this evening."

At this strange and unexpected ending of Cameron's address, the audience sat astonished. Then, from all over the house, voices were heard murmuring approval of the plan.

Rev. Jeremiah Wilks was the first to speak. "I'm heartily in favor of the suggestion," he said. "I think it's a good thing. It will get some of our moneyed men interested in the church and it will do them good. I've often told our people that something like this ought to be done, and I know the preachers of the city will be glad to take hold of the matter and help to push it along. I'll bring it before our Ministerial Association. You can count on me every time."

"But, Mr. President," said a strange gentleman, when Rev. Wilks had resumed his seat, "Is it the idea of the gentleman who suggests this plan, that the movement be under the control of or managed by the ministers?"

A painful hush fell over the audience. The president turned to Cameron, who answered, "It is certainly *not* my idea that this matter be placed in the hands of the ministers; whatever part they have in the movement must be simply as Christian citizens of this community, without regard to their profession."

The audience smiled. Rev. Frederick Hartzel was on his feet instantly: "Ladies and gentlemen, I must protest. I do not doubt but that your young brother here means well, but perhaps some of us, with more experience, and with more mature thought, are better able to handle this great question. Such a plan as he has proposed is preposterous. A committee without an ordained minister on it, thinking to start any movement in harmony with the teaching of Christ is utter folly. It is a direct insult to the clergy, who, as you know, compose the finest body of men, intellectually and morally, in the country. I must insist that the regularly ordained ministers of the city be recognized on this committee."

Rev. Hugh Cockrell agreed with Hartzel, in a short speech, and then Uncle Bobbie Wicks obtained a hearing.

"I don't reckon that there's much danger of Brother Hartzel's amendment goin' through, but I just want a word anyhow. To-be-sure, you all know me, and that I'm a pretty good friend to preachers." The audience laughed. "I aint got a thing in the world agin 'em. To-be-sure, I reckon a preacher is as good as any other feller, so long as he behaves himself; but seein' as they've been tryin' fer 'bout two thousand years to fix this business, an' aint done nothin' yet, I think it's a mighty good ide' to give the poor fellers a rest, and let the Christians try it fer a spell."

"You've got to recognize the church, sir," cried Hartzel; and Uncle Bobbie retorted: "Well, if we recognize Christ, the church will come in all right, I reckon;" which sentiment so pleased the people that Cameron's suggestion was acted upon.

And thus began the movement that revolutionized Boyd City and made it an example to all the world, for honest manhood, civic pride and municipal virtue.

CHAPTER XX

When Amy Goodrich went to her room after the scene with her brutal father, wounded pride, anger at his injustice, and reckless defiance filled her heart. Mrs. Goodrich had heard the harsh words and quietly followed her daughter, but the door was locked. When she called softly for admittance, Amy only answered between her sobs, "No, no, mamma; please go away. I want to be alone." But the girl did not spend much time in weeping. With a look of determination upon her tear-stained face, she caught up a daily paper that was lying where she had dropped it that morning, and carefully studied time-cards. Then removing as far as possible the evidence of her grief, she changed her dress for a more simple and serviceable gown, and gathering together a few necessary articles, packed them, with her jewelry, in a small satchel. She had finished her simple preparations and was just writing the last word of her brief farewell message, when Mrs. Goodrich came quietly to the door again.

Amy started to her feet in alarm when she heard the low knock, and then as she listened to her mother's voice softly calling her name, the hot tears filled her eyes once more, and she moved as though to destroy the note in her hand. But as she hesitated, her father's words came back: "You may have your tramp, but don't call me father. You are no daughter of mine," and a cruel something seemed to arrest her better impulse and force her to remain silent.

Mrs. Goodrich, when she received no answer to her call, thought that her daughter was sleeping, and with a sigh of relief, went to her own room. A little later, the father came upstairs and retired. Then Frank returned home, and the trembling listener heard the servants locking up the house. When all was still, and her watch told her that it was a few minutes past midnight, she carefully opened the door, and with her satchel in her hand, stole cautiously down the stairs and out of the house. Hurrying as fast as she could to Broadway, she found a cab, and was driven to the depot on the east side.

As Amy stepped from the vehicle beneath the electric light and paused a moment to give the driver his fare, a man came out of a saloon on the corner near by. It was Mr. Whitley. He recognized the girl instantly, and springing to one side, drew back into the shadow of the building, where he waited until she went to the ticket office. Then going quickly to the open window of the waiting room, he heard her ask for a ticket to Jonesville. After the train had pulled in and he had watched her aboard, he entered the cab that had brought her to the station, and was driven to his hotel.

The next morning Whitley was the first to learn from Frank Goodrich, of Amy's quarrel with her father, and the reason. Without a word of what he had seen, he made hurried preparation and followed her on the next train.

At Jonesville, he easily made the rounds of the hotels and carefully examined the registers, but Amy's name was on none of them. Concluding that she must be at the home of some friend, he had placed his own name on the last book he examined, and seated himself to think over the situation, when he heard a bell-boy say: "That girl in number sixteen wants a 'Frisco' time-table."

Whitley lounged carelessly up to the counter and again glanced over the register. Number sixteen was occupied by a Miss Anderson. Catching the eye of the clerk, he placed his finger on the name and winked. "When did she get in?" he asked, in a low tone, at the same time slipping a gold-piece beneath the open page.

"On the one-thirty from the west, last night," the fellow replied, in the same cautious manner, as he whirled the book toward him and deftly transferred the coin to his own pocket, without attracting the attention of the landlord who stood near by.

"I believe I'll go to my room and clean up," said Whitley, a moment later.

"Show this gentleman to number fifteen," promptly called the clerk, and Whitley followed the boy who had answered Miss Anderson's call upstairs.

When he had placed the heavy grip on the floor, the boy turned to see Whitley holding out a dollar bill.

"Did you get a look at the lady in number sixteen, when you went up with that time-card?"

"Course I did."

"Can you describe her?"

"You bet, mister; she's a daisy too." And as he folded the bill and carefully placed it in his vest pocket, he gave an accurate description of Amy.

Whitley, dismissed the boy and seated himself to watch through the half-closed door, the room across the hall. He had not long to wait. Amy stepped out into the corridor and started toward the stairway. In an instant Whitley was by her side. The girl gave a start of surprise and uttered a frightened exclamation.

"Don't be frightened, Miss Goodrich, I have very important news for you from home. Step into the parlor please."

Too bewildered to do other than obey, she followed him.

"I have been searching for you all day," he said, as he conducted her to a seat in the far corner of the empty room.

Amy tried to look indignant and started to reply when he interrupted her.

"Wait a moment, please, Miss Goodrich, and hear me, before you condemn. When your father discovered this morning, that you had left home, he came at once to me and told me the whole story. I tried to explain to him that it was I, and not Falkner, who had been with you, but he would not listen; and in spite of my pleading, declared that you should never enter his home again. I am sorry, but he is very angry and I fear will keep his word, for a time at least. He even accused me of telling falsehoods to shield you, and insisted that I should forget you forever and never mention your name in his hearing again. I learned at the depot that you had purchased a ticket to this city, and took the first train, hoping to find and offer you any assistance that might be in my power to give. A girl in your position needs a friend, for you cannot go home just now."

In spite of herself, Amy was touched by the words spoken with such seeming truth and earnestness, but her heart was filled with anger at her father, and her face was hard and set as she replied coldly: "I thank you, but you might have saved yourself the trouble. I have no wish to go home."

"Indeed, I do not see how you can feel differently under the circumstances," admitted the other with apparent reluctance; "but have you thought of the future? What can you do? You have never been dependent upon yourself. You know nothing of the world."

Amy's face grew white. Seeing his advantage, Whitley continued, drawing a dark picture of a young woman without friends or means of support. At last, as he talked, Amy began to cry. Then his voice grew tender. "Miss Goodrich—Amy—come to me. Be my wife. I have long loved you. I will teach you to love me. Let me comfort and protect you."

The girl lifted her head. "You dare ask that after what happened the other night?"

"God knows how I regret that awful mistake," he replied earnestly. "But you know I was not myself. I am no worse than other men, and—" He hesitated—"you must remember that it was through you that I drank too much. I could not refuse when you gave me the glass. I never was intoxicated before. Won't you forgive me this once and let me devote my life to righting the wrong?"

Amy's eyes fell. The seeming justice and truth of his words impressed her.

Again the man saw his advantage and talked to her of the life his wealth would help her to live. She would be free from every care. They would travel abroad until her father had forgotten his wrath, and could she doubt that all would be well when she returned as his wife?

Amy hesitated, and again he pointed out the awful danger of her trying to live alone. As he talked, the girl's utter helplessness overcame her, and rising to her feet she faltered, "Give me time to think; I will come to you here in an hour."

When she returned she said: "Mr. Whitley, I will marry you; but my people must not know until later."

Whitley started toward her eagerly, but she stepped back. "Not now. Wait. We will go east on the evening train and will take every precaution to hide our course. We will travel in separate cars as strangers, and while stopping at hotels will register under assumed names, and will not even recognize each other. When we reach New York, I will become your wife."

Whitley could scarcely conceal his triumph; that she should so fully play into his hand was to him the greatest good luck. With every expression of love he agreed to everything; but when he would embrace her she put him away—"Not until we are married;" and lie was compelled to be satisfied.

For a while longer they talked, completing their plans. Then drawing out his pocket-book he said: "By-the-way, you will need money." But she shook her head: "Not until I have the right. Here are my jewels; sell them for me."

He protested and laughed at her scruples. But she insisted. And at last, he took the valuables and left the hotel. Going to a bank where he was known, he drew a large sum of money, and returning, placed a roll of bills in her hand. Thinking that it was the price of her rings, she accepted it without the slightest question.

That night, he bought a ticket for Chicago, over the Wabash from St. Louis, taking a chair car, while she purchased one for a little town on the Alton, and traveled in a sleeper. But at St. Louis, they remained two days, stopping at a hotel agreed upon, but as strangers. Then they again took tickets for different stations, over another road, but stopped at Detroit. It was here that Amy's suspicions were aroused.

She was sitting at dinner, when Whitley entered the dining room with two traveling men who seemed to be well acquainted with him. The trio, laughing and talking boisterously, seated themselves at a table behind her. Recognizing Whitley's voice, she lifted her eyes to a mirror opposite, and to her horror, distinctly saw him point her out to his friends.

Amy's dinner remained untasted, and hiding her confusion as best she could, she rose to leave the room. As she passed the table where Whitley and the men were eating, the two drummers looked at her in such a way that the color rushed to her pale cheeks in a crimson flame. Later, at the depot, she saw them again, and was sure, from Whitley's manner, that he had been drinking.

Once more aboard the train, the girl gave herself up to troubled thought. Worn out by the long journey under such trying circumstances, and the lonely hours among strangers at the hotels, and now thoroughly frightened at the possible outcome when they reached New York, the poor child worried herself into such a state that when they left the cars at Buffalo, Whitley became frightened, and in spite of her. protests, registered at the hotel as her brother and called in a physician.

The doctor at once insisted that she be removed to a boarding place, where she could have perfect rest and quiet, and with his help, such a place was found; Whitley, as her brother, making all arrangements.

For three weeks the poor girl lay between life and death, and strangely enough, in her delirium, called not once for father or mother or brother, but always for Dick, and always begged him to save her from some great danger. Whitley was at the house every day, and procured her every attention that money could buy. But when at last she began to mend, something in her eyes as she looked at him, made him curse beneath his breath.

Day after day she put him off when he urged marriage, saying "When we get to New York." But at last the time came when she could offer no excuse for longer delay, and in a few firm words she told him that she could not keep her promise, telling him why and begging his forgiveness if she wronged him.

Then the man's true nature showed itself and he cursed her for being a fool; taunted her with using his money, and swore that he would force her to come to him.

That afternoon, the landlady came to her room, and placing a letter in her hand, asked, "Will you please be kind enough to explain that?"

Amy read the note, which informed the lady of the house that her boarder was a woman of questionable character, and that the man who was paying her bills was not her brother. With a sinking heart, Amy saw that the writing was Jim Whitley's. Her face flushed painfully. "I did not know that he was paying my bills," she said, slowly.

"Then it is true," exclaimed the woman. "He is not your brother?"

Amy was silent. She could find no words to explain.

"You must leave this house instantly. If it were not for the publicity I would hand you over to the police."

She went to a cheap, but respectable hotel, and the next morning, Whitley, who had not lost sight of her, managed to force an interview.

"Will you come to me now?" he asked. "You see what you may expect from the world."

Her only reply was, "I will take my own life before I would trust it in your hands." And he, knowing that she spoke the truth, left her to return to Boyd City.

A few days later, when Dick Falkner stepped from the cars at Buffalo, and hurried through the depot toward the hack that bore the name of the hotel where Whitley had left Amy, he did not notice that the girl he had come so far to find, was standing at the window of the ticket office, and while the proprietor of the hotel was explaining why Miss Wheeler had left his house, the west-bound train was carrying Amy toward Cleveland.

Whitley had written a letter to the landlord, explaining the character of the woman calling herself Miss Wheeler, and had just dropped it in the box, when Dick met him in the post office on the day of Jim's arrival home.

With the aid of the Buffalo police, Dick searched long and carefully for the missing girl, but with no results, and at last, his small savings nearly exhausted, he was forced to return to Boyd City, where he arrived just in time to take an active part in the new movement inaugurated by Rev. Cameron and the Young People's Union.

In Cleveland, Amy sought out a cheap lodging house, for she realized that her means were limited, and began a weary search for employment.

Day after day she went from place to place answering advertisements for positions which she thought she could fill. Walking all she could she took a car only when her strength failed, but always met with the same result; a cold dismissal because she could give no references; not a kind look; not an encouraging word; not a helpful smile. As the days went by, her face grew hard and her eyes had a hopeless, defiant look, that still lessened her chances of success, and gave some cause for the suspicious glances she encountered on every hand, though her features showed that under better circumstances she would be beautiful.

One evening as she stood on the street corner, tired out, shivering in the sharp wind, confused by the rush and roar of the city, and in doubt as to the car she should take, a tall, beautifully dressed woman stopped by her side, waiting also for a car.

Amy, trembling, asked if she would direct her. The lady looked at her keenly as she gave the needed information, and then added kindly, "You are evidently not acquainted in Cleveland."

Amy admitted that she was a stranger.

"And where is your home?"

"I have none," was the sad reply.

"You are stopping with friends, I suppose?"

Amy shook her head and faltered, "No, I know no one in the city."

The woman grew very kind. "You poor child," she said, "you look as though you were in distress. Can't I help you?"

Tears filled the brown eyes that were lifted pleadingly to the face of the questioner, and a dry sob was the only answer.

"Come with me, dear," said the woman, taking her kindly by the arm. "This is my car. Come and let me help you."

They boarded the car, and after a long ride, entered a finely furnished house in a part of the city far from Amy's boarding place. The woman took Amy to her own apartments, and after giving her a clean bath and a warm supper, sat with her before the fire, while the girl poured out her story to the only sympathetic listener she had met.

When she had finished, the woman said, "You have not told me your name."

"You may call me Amy. I have no other name."

Again the woman spoke slowly: "You cannot find work. No one will receive you. But why should you care? You are beautiful."

Amy looked at her in wonder, and the woman explained how she had many girls in her home, who with fine dresses and jewels, lived a life of ease and luxury.

At last the girl understood and with a shudder, rose to her feet. "Madam, I thank you for your kindness; for you *have* been kind; but I cannot stop here." She started toward the door, but the woman stopped sher.

"My dear child; you cannot go out at this time of night again, and you could never find your way back to your lodging place. Stay here. You need not leave this room, and you may bolt the door on this side. Tomorrow you may go if you will."

Amy could do nothing but stay. As she laid her tired head on the clean pillow that night, and nestling in the warm blankets watched the firelight as the flames leaped and played, she heard the sound of music and merry voices, and thought of the cold, poorly-furnished bed-room, with coarse sheets and soiled pillows, at her lodging place, and of the weary tramp about the streets, and the unkind faces that refused her a chance for life. What would the end be when her money was gone, she wondered; and after all, why not this?

The next morning, when she awoke, she could not for a moment, remember where she was; then it all came back, just as a knock sounded on the door.

"Who is it?" she called.

"Your coffee, miss," came the answer, and she unlocked the door, admitting an old negro woman with a neat tray, on which was set a dainty breakfast.

Later, when she was dressed, Madam came. "And do you still feel that you must go?" she asked.

"Yes, yes, I must. Don't tempt me."

The woman handed her a card with her name and address. "Well, go, my dear; and when you are driven to the street, because you have no money and are cold and hungry, come to me if you will, and earn food and clothing, warmth and ease, by the only means open to you." Then she went with her to the street and saw that she took the right car.

As Amy said good-bye, the tears filled her eyes again, and oh, how lonely and desolate the poor girl felt, as she shivered in the sharp air, and how hopelessly she again took up her fight against the awful odds.

But the end came at last as Madam had said it would. Without money, Amy was turned from her boarding place. One awful night she spent on the street, and the next day she found her way, half frozen, and weak from hunger, to Madam's place.

CHAPTER XXI

That Frank Goodrich had managed to keep himself free from all appearance of evil since the night he so nearly became a thief, was not because of any real change in his character. He gambled no more. Not from a matter of principle, but because he feared the results, and he accepted Whitley's sarcastic advice about religious services, not because there was any desire in his heart for a right life, but because he felt it was good policy. Like many others, he was as bad as he dared to be; and while using the church as a cloak to hide his real nature, was satisfied if he could keep the appearance of respectability. In short, he was a splendid example of what that old Satanic copy-book proverb, "Honesty is the best policy" will do for a life if it be lived up to in earnest.

He was not a little alarmed over his sister's conduct, because he feared that Whitley, in a spirit of revenge, would demand payment of the notes; which could only mean his open disgrace and ruin. And his feelings reached a climax two weeks after Dick's return when he received a curt note from Jim saying:

"You will remember that I promised to surrender those notes of yours upon certain conditions. Those conditions now can never be met, and it becomes necessary for us to make other arrangements. You will meet me with a horse and buggy at Freeman Station tomorrow night, ten-thirty. Wait for me at the crossroads south of the depot. If anyone learns of our meeting it will be all up with you."

Freeman Station was a little cluster of houses near the great hay farms twelve miles from Boyd City, and the drive was not one to be made with pleasure; but there was no help for it, and about dusk Frank set out. It had been raining steadily for several days and the mud was hub deep, while in many places the road was under water. Once he was obliged to get out, and by the flickering light of his lantern, to pick his way around a dangerous washout. Several times he was on the point of giving up and turning back, but thoughts of Whitley's anger drove him on, and he at last reached the place, several minutes after the train had passed on its way across the dark prairie. As he stopped at the corner, Whitley appeared by the side of the buggy, and clambered in without a word. Taking the lines from Frank, he lashed the tired horse with the whip and they plunged forward into the night.

Once or twice Frank tried to open a conversation with his companion, but received such short replies that he gave up and shrank back in the corner of the seat in miserable silence.

After nearly an hour, Whitley brought the horse to a standstill, and jumping out of the buggy, began to unhitch. Against the dark sky, Frank could see the shadowy outlines of a house and barn.

"Where are we?" he asked.

"At my place, nine miles south of town," Whitley answered. "Help me put up the horse, can't you?"

Frank obeyed.

"No, don't take the harness off," said Jim again; "you'll want him before long." And then he led the way to the house.

Taking a key from its hiding place beneath one corner of the step, he unlocked the door and entered; and while Frank stood shivering with the cold and wet, found a lamp and made a light. The room where they stood was well carpeted and furnished, and upon the table were the remains of a meal, together with empty bottles and glasses, and lying on the chair was a woman's glove.

Frank looked around curiously. He had heard rumors of Whitley's place in the country, but this was his first visit.

"Well," said Jim shortly, "sit down while I build a fire and get something to drink; things are not very gay here to-night, but we'll do the best we can."

When the room was warm and they had removed their wraps and outer clothing, and Jim had partaken freely from a supply of liquor on the sideboard, he stretched himself in an easy chair and spoke more pleasantly. "Well, I suppose you are ready to pay those notes, with the interest."

Frank moved uneasily. "You know I can't," he muttered. "I thought from your letter, that we might make other arrangements. Amy, you know, might come.—"

"Oh, cut that out," interrupted Whitley, with an oath; "your esteemed sister is out of this deal for good." Then, as he lit his cigar, "We might fix things in another way though, if you only had the nerve."

"How?" asked Frank, eagerly.

"That printer of Udell's has some papers in his possession that I want. Get them for me and I'll turn over your notes and call it square."

Frank looked at his companion in wonder. "What do you mean?" he said at last.

"Just what I say. Can't you hear?"

"But how does that tramp happen to have any papers of value to you?"

"That is, most emphatically, none of your business, my friend. All you have to do is to get them, or—" he paused significantly.

"But will he give them up?"

Whitley looked at him a few minutes in amused contempt, then said, mockingly, "Oh yes; of course he will be glad to favor us. All you need to do is to put on your best Sunday School manners and say sweetly: 'Mr. Falkner, Mr. Whitley would like those papers that you have in the long leather pocket-book tied with a shoe-string.' He'll hand them over instantly. The only reason I have taken all this trouble to meet you out here to-night is because I am naturally easily embarrassed and don't like to ask him for them myself."

Frank was confused and made no reply, until Whitley asked: "Where does the fellow live now?"

"I don't know, but he's in old man Wicks' office every evening; has a desk there, and works on some fool Association work."

Whitley nodded. "Then you will find the papers in Uncle Bobbie's safe."

"But how am I to get them?"

"I don't know; you can't buy them. You can't bluff him. And he won't scare. There's only one other way I know."

"You mean that I must steal them?" gasped Frank.

Whitley looked at him with an evil smile. "That's rather a hard word for a good Christian, isn't it? Let's say, obtain possession of the documents without Mr. Falkner's knowledge. It sounds better."

"I'm no thief," snapped Frank.

Jim lifted his eyebrows as he skillfully flipped the ashes from his cigar. "Oh, I see; you did not rob the old gentleman's safe that night. I saved you from committing murder. You only negotiated a trifling loan with your loving parent. You'll be telling me next that you didn't gamble, but only whiled away a leisure hour or two in a social game of cards. But, joking aside, I honestly believe, Frank Goodrich, that you are more kinds of a fool than any man I have ever had the pleasure to know. The case in a nutshell is this: I must have those papers. I can't go after them myself. You've got to get them for me."

"I won't," said Frank, sullenly. "I can't."

"You can, and you will," retorted the other, firmly; "or I'll turn those notes over to my lawyer for collection, inside of twenty-four hours, and the little story of your life will be told to all the world. My young Christian friend, you can't afford to tell *me* that you won't."

For another hour they sat before the fire, talking and planning, and then Frank drove alone, through the mud and rain, back to the city, reaching his home just before day.

A few nights later, as Dick sat at his work in Mr. Wicks' office, a rubber-tired buggy drove slowly past close to the curbing. Through the big front window, Dick could be seen plainly as he bent over his desk, just inside an inner room, his back toward the door, which stood open. A burly negro leaped to the sidewalk without stopping the carriage. So absorbed was Dick with the task before him, that he did not hear the outer door of the office open and close again; and so quickly did the negro move that he stood within the room where Dick sat before the latter was aware of his presence.

When Dick did raise his head, he looked straight into the muzzle of a big revolver.

"Don't move er ye'r a goner," growled the black giant; and reaching out with his free hand he swung to the door between the rooms, thus cutting off the view from the street.

Dick smiled pleasantly as though his visitor had called in the ordinary way. "What can I do for you?" he asked, politely.

"Yo jest move 'way from dat 'ar desk fust; den we kin talk. I don' 'spect you's got a gun handy, an' we don' want no foolin'."

Dick laughed aloud as though the other had made a good joke. "All right, boss; just as you say." And leaving his chair he seated himself on the edge of a table in the center of the room. But the negro did not notice that he had placed himself so that a heavy glass paper-weight was just hidden by his right leg.

"Better take a seat yourself," continued Dick cordially. "Might as well be comfortable. How are the wife and babies?"

The negro showed his teeth in a broad grin as he dropped into the revolving chair Dick had just vacated. "Dey's well, tank yo' kindly sah." Then as he looked at the young man's careless attitude and smiling face, he burst forth, admiringly: "Dey done tole me as how yo' wor' a cool cuss an' mighty bad to han'le; but fo' God I nebber seed nothin' like hit. Aint yo' skeered'?"

Dick threw up his head and laughed heartily. "Sure I'm scared," he said. "Don't you see how I'm shaking? I expect I'll faint in a minute if you don't put up that gun."

The negro scowled fiercely. "No yo' don't. Yo' kan't come dat on dis chile. Dat gun stay pinted jus' lak she is; an' hit goes off too ef yo' don' do what I says, mighty sudden."

"Just as you say," replied Dick, cheerfully. "But what do you want me to do?"

"I wants yo' to unlock dat air safe."

"Can't do it. I don't know the combination."

"Huh," the negro grunted. "Yo' kan't gib me no such guff es dat. Move sudden now."

"You're making a mistake," said Dick, earnestly. "I have only desk room here. I don't work for Mr. Wicks, and have no business with the safe. Besides, they don't keep money there anyway."

"Taint money I'm after dis trip, mistah; hit's papers. Dey's in a big leather pocket-book, tied with er sho' string."

Like a flash, Dick understood. The papers were in the safe, but as he said, he did not know the combination. "Papers?" he said, in a tone of surprise, in order to gain time.

"Yes sah, papers; dat yo' keeps in dar." He nodded toward the safe. "I wants em quick." The hand that held the revolver came slowly to a level with the dark face.

"Shoot if you want to," said Dick, easily, "but I'm telling you the truth. I don't know how to open the safe."

The negro looked puzzled, and Dick, seeing his advantage instantly, let his hand fall easily on his leg, close to the paper weight. "Besides," he said carelessly, "if its my papers you want, that's my desk behind—" He checked himself suddenly as though he had said more than he intended.

The negro's face lighted at what he thought was Dick's mistake, and forgetting himself, half turned in the revolving chair, while the muzzle of the revolver was shifted for just the fraction of a second. It was enough. With the quickness of a serpent, Dick's hand shot out, and the heavy weight caught the negro above the right ear, and with a groan he slid from the chair to the floor.

When the black ruffian regained consciousness, Dick was still sitting on the edge of the table, calmly swinging his feet, but in his hand was his visitor's weapon.

"Well," he said, quietly, "you've had quite a nap. Do you feel better? Or do you think one of these pills would help you?" He slowly cocked and raised the revolver.

"Don't shoot. Don't shoot, sah."

"Why not?" said Dick, coldly, but with the smile still on his face.

That smile did the business. Oaths and threats the black man could understand; but a man who looked deliberately along a cocked revolver, with a smile on his face, was too much for him. He begged and pleaded for his life.

"Tell me who sent you here?"

"Mistah Goodrich."

Dick was startled, though his face showed no surprise.

"The old gentleman?"

"'No sah, Mistah Frank."

"How did he know that I had any papers?"

"I don' know sah; he only said as how he wanted dem; an' he's er waitin' 'round de cornah in de kerrige."

This was a new feature in the situation. Dick was puzzled. At last he stepped to the phone and, still covering the negro with the revolver, he rang up central and called for Mr. Wicks' residence. When the answer came, he said easily, "Excuse me for disturbing you, Mr. Wicks, but I have a man here in the office who wants to get into your safe, and I need you badly. You had better come in the back way."

"I'll be with you in a shake," was the reply; "hold him down till I get there." And a few minutes later the old gentleman knocked at the door. Dick admitted him and then burst into a hearty laugh at his strange appearance; for in his haste, Uncle Bobbie had simply pulled on a pair of rubber boots and donned an overcoat. With the exception of these articles, he was in his nightshirt and cap. In his hand, he carried a pistol half as long as his arm; but he was as calm as Dick himself, though breathing hard. "To-be-sure," he puffed, "I'm—so—plagey—fat—can't hurry—worth cent—wind's no good—have to take—to smokin' agin—sure."

Dick explained the situation in a few words; "I wouldn't have called you sir, if young Goodrich were not in it. But—but—you see—I don't know what to do," he finished, lamely.

"To-be-sure," said Uncle Bobbie, "I know. To-be-sure. Sometimes a bad feller like him gets tangled up with good people in such a way you jist got t'er let 'em alone; tares an' wheat you know; tares and wheat. To-be-sure Christianity aint 'rithmetic, and you can't save souls like you'd do problems in long division, ner count results like you'd figger interest. What'd ye say?—Suppose you skip down to the corner and fetch him up here."

Dick glanced at the negro. "Never you mind him," said the old gentleman, with a fierce scowl. "Your uncle'll shoot the blamed head off him if he so much as bats an eye; he knows it too." And he trained the long gun on the trembling black.

Dick slipped out of the back door and soon returned holding Frank firmly by the collar. As they entered, Uncle Bobbie said to the negro, "Now's yer chance, Bill; git out quick 'fore we change our minds." And the astonished darkey bolted.

"Now Frank," said the old gentleman kindly, when Dick had placed his prisoner in a chair, "tell us all about it." And young Goodrich, too frightened almost to speak above a whisper, told the whole miserable story.

"Too bad; too bad," muttered Uncle Bobbie, when Frank had finished. "To-be-sure, taint no more'n I expected; gamblin' church members ain't got no call to kick if their children play cards fer money. What'll we do, Dick?"

Dick was silent, but unseen by Frank, he motioned toward the door.

Uncle Bobbie understood. "I reckon yer right," he said, slowly, "tares an' wheat—tares an' wheat. But what about them notes?"

"I'll fix Whitley," replied Dick.

Frank looked at him in wonder.

"Air you sure you can do it?" asked Uncle Bobbie; "'cause if you can't—"

"Sure," replied Dick; "I'll write him a line tonight." Then to Frank: "You can go now, sir, and don't worry about Jim Whitley; he will never trouble you by collecting the notes."

Frank, stammering some unintelligible reply, rose to his feet.

"Wait a bit young man," said Uncle Bobbie, "I want to tell ye somethin' before ye go. To-be-sure, I don't think ye'll ever be a very *bad* citizen, but you've shown pretty clearly that ye can be a mighty mean one. An' I'm afraid ye'll never be much credit to the church, 'cause a feller's got to be a *man* before he can be much of a Christian. Pieces of men like you don't count much on either side; they just sort o' fill in. But what ye want to do is to quit tryin' so blamed hard to be respectable and be *decent*. Now run on home to yer maw and don't tell nobody where ye've been to-night. Mr. Falkner he will look after yer friend Whitley."

CHAPTER XXII

The sun was nearly three hours high above the western hilltops in the mountain district of Arkansas, as a solitary horseman stopped in the shadow of the timber that fringed the edge of a deep ravine. It was evident from the man's dress, that he was not a native of that region; and from the puzzled expression on his face, as he looked anxiously about, it was clear that he had lost his way. Standing in the stirrups he turned and glanced back over the bridle path along which he had come, and then peered carefully through the trees to the right and left; then with an impatient oath, he dropped to the saddle and sat staring straight ahead at a lone pine upon the top of a high hill a few miles away.

"There's the hill with the signal tree beyond Simpson's all right," he said, "but how in thunder am I to get there; this path don't go any farther, that's sure," and from the distant mountain he turned his gaze to the deep gulch that lay at his feet.

Suddenly he leaned forward with another exclamation. He had caught sight of a log cabin in the bottom of the ravine, half hidden by the bushes and low trees that grew upon the steep banks. Turning his horse, he rode slowly up and down for some distance, searching for an easy place to descend, coming back at last to the spot where he had first halted. "It's no go, Salem," he said; "we've got to slide for it," and dismounting, he took the bridle rein in his hand and began to pick his way as best he could, down the steep incline, while his four-footed companion reluctantly followed. After some twenty minutes of stumbling and swearing on the part of the man, and slipping and groaning on the part of the horse, they stood panting at the bottom. After a short rest, the man clambered into the saddle again, and fording a little mountain brook that laughed and sang and roared among the boulders, rode up to the clearing in which the cabin stood.

"Hello!" he shouted.

There was no answer, and but for the thread of smoke that curled lazily from the mud and stick chimney, the place seemed deserted.

"Hello!" he called again.

A gaunt hound came rushing from the underbrush beyond the house, and with hair bristling in anger, howled his defiance and threats.

Again the horseman shouted, and this time the cabin door opened cautiously and a dirty-faced urchin thrust forth a tousled head.

"Where's your father?"

The head was withdrawn, and a moment later put forth again. "He's done gone ter th' corners."

"Well, can you tell me the way to Simpson's? I don't know how to get out of this infernal hole."

Again the head disappeared for a few seconds, and then the door was thrown wide open and a slovenly woman, with a snuff stick in one corner of her mouth, came out, followed by four children. The youngest three clung to her skirts and stared, with fearful eyes, at the man on the horse, while he of the tousled head threw stones at the dog and commanded him, in a shrill voice, to "shet up, dad burn ye Kinney, shet up. He's all right."

"Wanter go ter Simpson's at the corners, do ye?" said the woman. "Wal, yer right smart offen yer road."

"I know that," replied the stranger, impatiently; "I've been hunting turkeys and lost my way. But can't I get to the corners from here?"

"Sure ye kin. Jes' foller on down the branch 'bout three mile till ye come out on the big road; hit'll take ye straight ter th' ford below ol' Ball whar' the lone tree is. Simpson's is 'bout half a quarter on yon side the creek."

The man thanked her gruffly, and turning his horse, started away.

"Be you'ns the feller what's stoppin' at Sim's ter hunt?" she called after him.

"Yes, I'm the man," he answered, "Good-evening." And he rode into the bushes.

Catching the oldest urchin by the arm, the woman gave him a vigorous cuff on the side of the head and then whispered a few words in his attentive ear. The lad started off down the opposite side of the ravine at a run, bending low and dodging here and there, unseen by the stranger.

The hunter pushed on his way down the narrow valley as fast as he could go, for he had no time to spare if he would reach his stopping-place before night, and he knew that there was small chance of finding the way back after dark; but his course was so rough and obstructed by heavy undergrowth, fallen trees and boulders, that his progress was slow and the shadow of the mountain was over the trail while he was still a mile from the road at the end of the ravine. As he looked anxiously ahead, hoping every moment to see the broader valley where the road lay, he caught a glimpse of two men coming toward him, one behind the other, winding in and out through the low timber. While still some distance away, they turned sharply to the left, and as it seemed to him, rode straight into the side of the mountain and were lost to sight.

Checking his horse, he watched for them to come into view again, and while he waited, wondering at their strange disappearance, the men urged their mules up a narrow gulley that was so hidden by the undergrowth and fallen timber as to escape an eye untrained to the woods and hills. After riding a short distance, they dismounted, and leaving the animals, quickly scaled the steep sides of the little cut and came out in an open space about two hundred yards above the trail along which the solitary horseman must pass. Dropping behind the trunk of a big tree that lay on the mountain side, uprooted by some gale and blackened by forest fires, they searched the valley below with the keen glance of those whose eyes are never dimmed by printed page or city lights. Dressed in the rude garb of those to whom clothes are a necessity, not a means of display, tall and lean with hard muscles, tough sinews and cruel stony faces, they seemed a part of the wild life about them; and yet withal, there was a touch of the mountain grandeur in their manner, and in the unconscious air of freedom and self-reliance, as there always is about everything that remains untouched by the conventionality of the weaker world of men.

"'Bout time he showed up, aint it, Jake?" said one as he carefully rested his rifle against the log and bit off a big piece of long green twist tobacco.

"Hit's a right smart piece ter ol' Josh's shack an' th' kid done come in a whoop," returned the other, following his companion's example. "He can't make much time down that branch on hoss back an' with them fine clothes of his, but he orten ter be fur off."

"D'ye reckon he's a durned revenoo sure, Jake?"

"Dunno, best be safe," with an ugly scowl. "Simpson 'lows he's jes' layin' low hisself, but ye can't tell."

"What'd Sim say his name war?"

"Jim Whitley," returned the other, taking a long careful look up the valley.

"An' whar' from?"

"Sim say St. Louie, or some place like that. Sh—thar' he comes."

They half rose and crouching behind the log, pushed the cocked rifles through the leaves of a little bush, covering the horseman below.

"If he's a revenoo he'll sure see th' path ter th' still," whispered the one called Jake; "an' if he turns ter foller hit into th' cut drap him. If he goes on down th' branch, all right."

All unconscious of the rifles that wanted only the touch of an outlaw's finger to speak his death, the stranger pushed on his way past the unseen danger point toward the end of the valley where lay the road.

The lean mountaineers looked at each other. "Never seed hit," said one, showing his yellow teeth in a mirthless grin; "an' I done tole Cap las' night, hit was es plain es er main traveled road an' orter be kivered."

"Mebbe so," replied the other; "an' then agin he mighter ketched on an' 'lows ter fool us."

The other sprang up with an oath. "We uns aint got no call ter take chances," he growled; "best make sure." And with his rifle half raised, he looked anxiously along the trail, but the stranger had passed from view.

A few minutes longer they waited and watched, discussing the situation; then returning to the mules, they rode out of the little gully and on down the branch in the direction the object of their suspicion had taken.

Just across the road from the mouth of the ravine down which the hunter had come, was a little log cabin, and in the low doorway an old woman sat smoking a cob pipe. "Howdy Liz," said one of the men, "Seed anythin'?"

"Yep," returned the woman. "He done ast th' way ter Simpson's. 'Low'd he'd been huntin' turkey an' lost hisself. I done tole him he orter git someone ter tromp 'roun' with him er he might git killed."

She laughed shrilly and the two men joined in with low guffaws. "Reckon yer right, Liz," said one. "Jake, why don't ye hire out ter him."

Jake slapped his leg. "By gum," he exclaimed, "that thar's a good ide'. I shor' do hit. An' I'll see that he don't find nothin' bigger'n turkey too; less'n he's too durned inquisitive; then I'll be—." He finished with an evil grin. "You all tell Cap I've done gone ter hunt with Mistah Whitley ef I don't show up." And beating his mule's ribs vigorously with his heels, he jogged away down the road, while his companion turned and rode back up the little valley.

Jim Whitley, enraged at Frank's failure to rescue the papers held by Dick, and alarmed by the latter's letter telling him of young Goodrich's confession, had come into the wild backwoods district to await developments. He was more determined now than ever, to gain possession of the evidence of his crime, and in his heart was a fast-growing desire to silence, once for all, the man whose steady purpose and integrity was such an obstacle in his life. But he could see no way to accomplish his purpose without great danger to himself; and with the memory of the gray eyes that had looked so calmly along the shining revolvers that night in the printing office, was a wholesome respect for the determined character of the man who had coolly proposed to die with him if he did not grant his demands. He feared that should Dick find Amy and learn the truth, he would risk his own life rather than permit him to go unpunished, and so he resolved to bury himself in the mountains until chance should reveal a safe way out of the difficulty, or time change the situation.

The afternoon of the day following his adventure in the little valley, Whitley sat on the porch of the post office and store kept by his host, telling his experience to a group of loafers, when the long mountaineer called Jake, rode up to the blacksmith shop across the street. Leaving his mule to be shod, the native joined the circle just in time to hear the latter part of Whitley's story.

"Lookin' fer turkey, war ye Mister?" asked Jake, with a wink at the bystanders.

"Yes, have you seen any?" replied Jim.

"Sure, the bresh's full of 'em ef ye know whar' ter hunt."

The company grinned and he continued: "I seed signs this mo'nin' in th' holler on yon side ol' Ball, when I war' huntin' my mule. An' thar's a big roost down by th' spring back of my place in th' bottoms."

Whitley was interested. "Will you show me where they are?" he asked.

"Might ef I could spar' th' time," replied Jake slowly; "but I've got my craps ter tend."

Another grin went the rounds. "Jake's sure pushed with his craps," remarked one; "Raises mo' corn, 'n 'ary three men in Arkansaw," remarked another, and with this they all fired a volley of tobacco juice at a tumble bug rolling his ball in the dust near by.

Needless to say, the conversation resulted in Whitley's engaging the moonshiner for seventy-five cents a day, to hunt with him; and for the next two weeks they were always together.

All day long the native led the way over the hills and through the deep ravines and valleys, taking a different course each day, but always the chase led them away from the little ravine that opened on the big road. When Whitley suggested that they try the country where he had lost his way, his guide only laughed contemptuously, "Ain't ye killin' turkey every trip. Ye jist foller me an' I'll sure find 'em fer ye. Ain't nothin' over in that holler. I done tromped all over thar' huntin' that dad burned ol' mule o'mine, an' didn't see nary sign. Thay's usen' 'round th' south side th' ridge. Ye jist lemme take ye 'round." And Jim was forced to admit that he was having good luck and no cause to complain of lack of sport. But he was growing tired of the hills and impatient to return to the city, while his hatred of the man whom he feared, grew hourly.

Jake, seeing that his employer was fast growing tired of the hunt, and guessing shrewdly, from his preoccupied manner, that hunting was not the real object of his stay in the mountains, became more and more suspicious. His careless, good-natured ways and talk changed to a sullen silence and he watched Whitley constantly.

One morning, just at daybreak, as they were walking briskly along the big road on their way to a place where the guide said the game was to be found, Take stopped suddenly, and motioning Jim to be silent, stood in a listening attitude.

Whitley followed his companion's example, but for a minute could hear nothing but the faint rustle of the dead leaves as a gray lizard darted to his hiding place, and the shrill scream of a blue-jay calling his sleepy mates to breakfast. Then the faint thud, thud, thud, of a galloping horse came louder and louder through the morning mist. Evidently someone was riding rapidly toward them.

"Whitley was about to speak, when the other, with a fierce oath and a threatening gesture, stopped him.

"Git inter th' bresh thar' quick an' do's I tell ye. Don't stop t' plaver. Git! An' gimme yer gun."

Too astonished to do anything else, Jim obeyed, and hastily thrusting the rifle under a pile of leaves by a log near by, the moonshiner forced his companion before him through the underbrush to a big rock some distance from the road. The sound of the galloping horse came louder and louder.

"Stand thar' behin' that rock 'n if ye stir I'll kill ye," whispered Jake; and taking a position behind a tree where he could watch Jim as well as the road, he waited with rifle cocked and murder written in every line of his hard face.

Nearer and nearer came the galloping horse. Whitley was fascinated and moved slightly so that he could peep over the rock. A low hiss from Jake fell upon his ear like the warning hiss of a serpent, and half turning, he saw the rifle pointing full at him. He nodded his head, and placing his finger upon his lips to indicate that he understood, turned his face toward the road again, just as the horse and his rider came into view.

The animal, though going freely, was covered with dust and dripping with sweat, which showed a creamy lather on his flanks, and where the bridle reins touched his neck. The rider wore a blue flannel shirt, open at the throat, corduroy trousers, tucked in long boots, and a black slouch hat, with the brim turned up in front. At his belt hung two heavy revolvers, and across the saddle he held a Winchester ready for instant use. He sat his horse easily as one accustomed to much riding, but like the animal, he showed the strain of a hard race.

Whitley was so wrought up that all these details impressed themselves upon his mind in an instant, and it seemed hours from the moment the horseman appeared until he was opposite the rock, though it could have been but a few seconds.

The watcher caught one glimpse of the rider's face, square jawed, keen eyed, determined, alert, stained by wind and weather.

"Crack!" went the rifle behind Whitley.

Like a flash the weapon of the rider flew to his shoulder. "Crack!" and the bark flew from the tree within an inch of Jake's face.

Whitley saw the spurs strike and the rider lean forward in his saddle to meet the spring of his horse. "Crack!" Jake's rifle spoke again. A mocking laugh came back from the road as the flying horseman passed from sight. Then, "I'll see you later," came in ringing tones, and the thud, thud, thud, of the galloping horse died away in the distance.

The mountaineer delivered himself of a volley of oaths, while Whitley stood quietly looking at him, his mind filled with strange thoughts. The man who could deliberately fire from ambush with intent to kill was the man for his purpose.

"Who is he?" Jim asked at last, when the other stopped swearing long enough to fill his mouth with fresh tobacco.

"A revenoo, an' I done missed him clean." He began to curse again.

"He came near getting you though," said the other, pointing to the mark of the horseman's bullet.

"Yas, hit war' Bill Davis. Aint nary other man in the hull dad burned outfit could er done hit." He looked with admiration at the fresh scar on the tree.

"But what is he doing?" asked Whitley.

Jake looked at him with that ugly, mirthless grin. "Mebbe he's huntin' turkey too."

Whitley laughed, "I guess he was goin' too fast for that," he said; but his companion's reply changed his laughter to fear.

"Thar's them that better be a follerin' of him mighty sudden."

"What do you mean?"

"I mean you, Mister. The boys has had ther' eye on ye fer sometime. We know yer huntin's all a blind, an' now Bill Davis he's come in. I aint right shor' myself er I'd a kep' mum an' he'pped 'em take ye."

Whitley turned pale. "Do you mean that the people here think I'm a revenue agent looking for moonshiners?"

"That's about hit, Mister, an' they'll be fer takin' ye out ter night shor'."

The fellow's meaning was too clear to be mistaken, and for some time Whitley remained silent. He was thinking hard. At last he said: "Jake, I'll tell you something. The boys are mistaken. I'm not here to get anybody into trouble, but because I'm in a hole myself."

"As how?" asked Jake, moving nearer and speaking in a lower tone.

"I won't tell you how unless you'll help me; and if you will, I'll pay you more money than you can make in this business in a thousand years."

The moonshiner's eyes gleamed. "Bill Davis is sure after us an' that thar' means trouble every time," he said slowly. "Ye heard him say as how he'd see me agin, an' I never knowed him ter miss befo'." He looked at the bullet mark on the tree again. "Tell ye what, Mister Whitley, I'll chance her; but we ain't got no time ter talk now. We gotter git away from here, fer some er the boys 'll be along purty quick. We'll just mosey 'round fer a spell an' then go back ter th' corners. I'll send th' boys off on er hot chase en' fix Sim so's ye kin git erway t'-night, an' ye come ter my shack; hit's on th' river below that hill with the lone tree on top, jes' seven mile from th' corners. Ye can't miss hit. I'll be thar an' have things fixed so's we kin light out befo' th' boys git back."

They reached Simpson's in time for dinner and Jake held a long whispered conversation with that worthy, while Jim sat on the porch after the meal.

As Jake passed him on his way to the mule that stood hitched in front of the blacksmith shop as usual, he said, in the hearing of those near: "Hit's all right fer to-morrow, is hit, Mister Whitley? An' we'll go over tother side Sandy Ridge?"

The words "all right" were accompanied by a wink that Whitley understood.

"Yes," he answered carelessly, "I'll be ready. I want to rest this afternoon and get a good sleep tonight. I'll be with you in the morning."

Jake rode off, and all the rest of the day Whitley felt that he was the mark for many scowling glances, while many whispered words were passed between the gaunt natives as they slouched in and out of the post office. Later, when the loafers had seemingly disappeared, Simpson came, and leaning carelessly against the door post within a few feet of Whitley, said, in a low voice: "They's a watchin' ye from th' shop yonder; be keerful an' don't let on. Yer hoss is tied in th' bresh down th' road a piece. Ride easy fer th' first mile."

Jim rose slowly to his feet, and stretching his arms above his head, yawned noisily. "Guess I'll turn in," he said. And then as he passed Simpson, he put a roll of bills into his hand. The landlord stepped out on the porch and took the chair Whitley had just left, while that gentleman slipped quietly out by the back door and crept away to his horse.

An hour later, Whitley knocked at the door of the cabin on the river bank and was admitted by Jake.

"Did ye make hit all right?" the mountaineer asked, as Jim entered.

The other nodded. "Simpson is sitting on the front porch and I'm supposed to be in bed."

Jake chuckled. "Cap an' th' boys air way up th' holler after Bill Davis, an' I'm in the bresh er watchin' you. Now let's git down ter biz right sharp."

Whitley soon told enough of his story, omitting names and places, to let his companion understand the situation.

When he had finished, Jake took a long pull from a bottle, and then said slowly: "An' ye want me ter put that feller what holds th' papers out o' yer' way?"

Whitley nodded. "It'll pay you a lot better than shooting government agents, and not half the risk."

"What'll ye give me?"

"You can name your own price?"

The outlaw's face glittered and he answered in a hoarse whisper, "I'll do hit. What's his name, an' whar'll I find him?"

"Richard Falkner. He lives in Boyd City—"

Slowly the man who had just agreed to commit a murder for money rose to his feet and stepped backward until half the width of the room was between them.

The other, alarmed at the expression in his companion's face, rose also, and for several minutes the silence was only broken by the crackling of the burning wood in the fireplace, the shrill chirp of a cricket and the plaintive call of a whip-poor-will from without. Then with a look of superstitious awe and terror upon his thin face, the moonshiner gasped, in a choking voice, "Boyd City—Richard Falkner—Mister, aint yo' mistaken? Say, ar' ye right shor'?"

Whitley replied, with an oath, "What's the matter with you? You look as though you had seen a ghost."

The ignorant villain started and glanced over his shoulder to the dark corner of the cabin; "Thar' might be a ha'nt here, shor' 'nough," he whispered hoarsely. "Do yo' know whar' ye air, Mister?"

Then as Whitley remained silent, he continued: "This here's th' house whar' Dickie Falkner war' borned; an' whar' his mammy died; an'—an' I'm Jake Tompkins; me 'n his daddy war' pards."

Whitley was dazed. He looked around the room as though in a dream; then slowly he realized his situation and a desperate resolve crept into his heart. Carefully his hand moved beneath his coat until he felt the handle of a long knife, while he edged closer to his companion.

The other seemed not to notice, and continued, as though talking to himself: "Little Dickie Falkner. Him what fed me when I war' starvin', an' gimme his last nickel when he war' hungry hisself; an' yo' want me ter kill him."—He drew a long shuddering breath. "Mister, yo' shor' made 'er bad mistake this time."

"I'll fix it though," cried Whitley; and with an awful oath he leaped forward, the knife uplifted.

But the keen eye of the man used to danger, had seen his stealthy preparation, and his wrist was caught in a grasp of iron.

The city-bred villain was no match for his mountain-trained companion and the struggle was short.

Keeping his hold upon Whitley's wrist, Jake threw his long right arm around his antagonist and drew him close, in a crushing embrace. Then, while he looked straight into his victim's fear-lighted eyes, he slowly forced the uplifted hand down and back.

Whitley struggled desperately, but his left arm was pinned to his side and he was held as in a circle of steel. In vain he writhed and twisted; he was helpless in the powerful grasp of the mountaineer. Slowly the hand that held the knife was forced behind him. He screamed in pain. The glittering eyes that looked into his never wavered. Jake's right hand behind his back, touched the knife, and Whitley saw that evil, mirthless grin come on the cruel face, so close to his own. The grip on his wrist tightened. Slowly his arm was twisted until his fingers loosened the hold of the weapon, and the handle of the knife was transferred to the grasp of the man who held him. Then there were two quick, strong thrusts, a shuddering, choking cry, and the arms were loosed as the stricken man fell in a heap on the cabin floor, on the very spot where years before, the dying mother had prayed: "Oh Lord, take ker' o' Dick."

"You—have—killed—me—"

"I reckon that's about hit, Mister."

"Tell—Falkner—I—lied—Amy—is—pure—and tell—"

But the sentence was never finished.

CHAPTER XXIII

After several weeks of careful investigation and study of the conditions and needs of Boyd City, along the lines suggested by Rev. Cameron in his address before the Young People's Union, a plan to meet these conditions was at last fixed upon, the main points of which were as follows: That a society or company be organized and incorporated to furnish places of recreation and education for young men and women; the place to be fitted with gymnasium, library, reading rooms, social parlors, a large auditorium and smaller class-rooms for work along special lines. There should also be a department where men out of employment might earn something to eat and a place to sleep, by working in wood-yards, coal mines, factories, or farms connected with the institution; and a similar place for women. It also provided for a medical dispensary and hospital for the care of the sick. The whole institution was to be under the charge of some Christian man who should deliver an address on the teachings of Christ every Sunday afternoon in the large auditorium.

Besides this, Bible classes could be organized by different workers as they chose, with this restriction, that no teaching of any particular sect or denomination should be allowed, and only the life and laws of Jesus Christ should be studied. Classes in other studies, such as pertain to the welfare or the government of the people, could be organized for those who wished, all educational work being under the supervision of directors elected by the society.

Every department of the institution was to be free to the public at all hours. To make this possible, the funds of the Society would be raised from the sale of shares, for which the holder was to pay annually twenty-five dollars. Members of the Association were entitled to one vote in the society for every four shares. It was expected that the department for the needy would be self-supporting.

The purpose and plans of the society were to be fully set forth in a little pamphlet, and placed in the hands of every citizen. The people were to be urged to co-operate with the institution by refusing absolutely to give any man, able to work, either food, clothing or lodging, on the ground that he could obtain the needed help by paying for it in labor at the institution; and that they further assist the work by contributing clothing, by employing laborers, and using the products of the institution as far as possible.

The office of the Superintendent was to be in direct communication with the police station, and anyone applying for help and refusing to work, when it was offered, would be turned over to the authorities to be dealt with for vagrancy. The hope was expressed that the city would co-operate with the institution by contributing liberally for the building fund, and by using the workers in their street-cleaning department.

When the time came to hear the committee's report, the opera house was crowded as it seldom was for any political speech or theatrical display. The young people from the various societies occupied the front seats on the floor of the house; and back of them, in the dress circles and galleries, were the general public, while on the rostrum were the leading business men, bankers, merchants, and the city officials, together with the committee.

"Look there, Bill," said a saloon keeper, who had come to watch his interest, "look at that. Blast me if there aint Banker Lindsley; and see them reporters. And there's the editor of the Whistler. Say, this aint no bloody church meeting; there aint a preacher on the stage. Them fellers mean business. We've got to watch out if they keep on this tack. And would you look at the people?"

"Come on out of here," growled his companion, a gambler; "we don't want any truck with this outfit."

"I'm going to stay and see what they propose doing," said the other. "Get a grip on yourself and wait."

Just then the assembly was called to order, and the two men dropped into seats near the rear entrance.

The president stated the object of the meeting and reviewed the action of the previous one at the Zion Church, where Cameron had spoken, strongly emphasizing the fact that this was not a meeting of the young people's societies only, but that every one present was to have a share in it, and all should feel free to express themselves either by voice or ballot. "Mr. Richard Falkner, the chairman of the committee, will make the report, and at their request, will speak for a few moments on the subject."

As Dick arose from his place in the rear of the stage and stepped forward, the saloon keeper turned to his companion, and in a loud whisper said, "Say, aint he that bum printer of Udell's?"

The other nodded and then replied, as his companion began to speak again, "Shut up, let's hear what he is going to say."

As Dick came slowly forward to the front of the rostrum, and stood for a moment as though collecting himself, the audience, to a man almost, echoed the thought that the saloon keeper had so roughly expressed. "Could it be possible that this was the poor tramp who had once gone from door to door seeking a chance to earn a crust of bread?" And then as they looked at the calm, clear-cut, determined features, and the tall, well-built figure, neatly clothed in a business suit of brown, they burst into involuntary applause. A smile crept over Dick's face as he bowed his handsome head in grateful acknowledgment. And then he held up his hand for silence.

Instantly a hush fell over the audience, and in a moment they were listening, with intense interest, to the voice of the once tramp printer.

"Our president has already detailed to you an account of the meeting preceding this. You understand that I am but the mouthpiece of the council appointed at that time, and that I do but speak their will, their thoughts, their aims, as they have voiced them in our meetings."

He then told of the methods adopted by the committee, of the help they had received, and how they had at last decided upon the report which he was about to submit; then carefully detailed the plan, enlarging upon the outlines as he proceeded. Drawing upon the mass of information gathered in the few weeks, he painted the city in its true colors, as shown in the light of their investigation; and then held out the wonderful promises of the plan for the future.

As he talked, Dick forgot himself, and forgot his audience. He saw only the figure of the Christ, and heard Him say, "Inasmuch as ye did it unto one of the least of these, my Brethren, ye did it unto me." While his hearers sat lost to the surroundings under the magic spell of his eloquence; an eloquence that even his most intimate friends never dreamed that he possessed.

Charlie Bowen was enraptured. Clara Wilson wept and laughed and wept again. Uncle Bobbie could only say, "I jing," and "To-be-sure," while George Udell sat in wonder. Could this splendid man who, with his flashing eye and glowing face, with burning words and graceful gestures, was holding that immense audience subject to his will, could this be the wretched creature who once fell at his feet fainting with hunger? "Truly," he thought, "the possibilities of life are infinite. The power of the human soul cannot be measured, and no man guesses the real strength of his closest friend."

As Dick finished and turned to resume his seat by the side of Mr. Wicks, a perfect furor of applause came from the people. In vain the chairman rapped for order; they would not stop; while on the rostrum men were crowding about the young orator, standing on chairs and reaching over each other's shoulders to grasp his hand. At last, the president turned to Dick. "Mr. Falkner, can you stop them?"

Dick, with face now as pale as death, and lips trembling with emotion, came back to the front of the stage. "I thank you again and again, for your kindness and the honor you show me, but may I further trespass upon that kindness by reminding you that this matter will never be met by clapping hands or applauding voices. Too long in the past have we applauded when our hearts were touched, and allowed the sentiment to die away with the echo of our enthusiasm. Shall it be so this time? Men and women, in the name of Jesus of Nazareth, the Christ who died on Calvary, what will you do for the least of these, His Brethren?"

As he again took his seat, the gambler, who with his friend had been sitting drinking in every word of Dick's speech, sprang to his feet and cried, in a loud, clear voice, "Mr. President."

Upon being recognized by the chair, who knew him and called him by name, every head turned, for all knew of Chris Chambers, the most notorious gambler in the city.

Said Chambers, "I came here to-night out of curiosity, to see if this movement in any way threatened my business as a professional gambler. I have, as most of you know, for the last five years, been conducting my place in your city, in open violation of your laws. To-night, for the first time, I see myself in the true light, and as a testimony of my good faith, and as evidence of the truth of my statement, when I say that I will never again take money from my fellow men but in honest business, I wish to make the motion that the report of this committee be accepted, that the plan be approved, and that the committee be discharged with the hearty thanks of the citizens of Boyd City."

The motion was seconded and carried. Then came the critical moment. For a full minute there was a pause. "What is the will of the meeting?" said the chairman, calmly, but with a silent prayer. There was a buzz of conversation all over the house. Every man was asking his neighbor, "What next?"

For a short time it looked as if things were at a standstill, but upon the stage men were putting their heads together, and soon Banker Lindsley shouted: "Mr. Chairman."

Instantly the people became quiet and all turned toward Boyd City's leading financier.

"I am requested to ask all those who wish to become charter members of an association as suggested in the report of the council, to meet here on the stage at once, and I move that we adjourn."

The president, after calling attention of the audience to the importance of answering Mr. Lindsley's request, immediately put the question, and the assembly was dismissed.

Among the first to push his way to the front was the stalwart form of the gambler, Chambers, and the stage was soon crowded with business men and not a few women. Mr. Lindsley looked around. "Where's Falkner?" he said. No one knew. And when Dick could not be found, Mr. Lindsley called the company to order.

The editor of the Whistler was chosen to preside, with Mr. Conklin the express agent, for secretary. Then a committee on constitution and by-laws was appointed, and the company adjourned to meet in the Commercial Club rooms the next Wednesday night.

But where was Dick? Unnoticed by the audience while their attention was diverted toward Mr. Lindsley, he had slipped from the rear of the stage and had made his way by the back stairs to the street. A half hour later, some of the people, on their way home from the meeting, noticed a tall figure, dressed in a business suit of brown, standing in the shadow of the catalpa trees on the avenue, looking upward at a church spire, built in the form of a giant hand, and at the darkened stained-glass window, in which was wrought the figure of the Christ holding a lamb in his arms. Later, they might have seen the same figure walking slowly past a beautiful residence a few blocks farther up the street, and when opposite a corner window, pausing a moment to stand with bared head, while the lips moved softly as though whispering a benediction upon one whose memory filled the place with pleasure and with pain.

About one o'clock on the following Wednesday, Uncle Bobbie Wicks dropped into the printing office. Udell had not returned from dinner. "Good afternoon, Mr. Wicks," said Dick, looking up from his work, "take a seat. You want to see a proof of those letter-heads, I suppose. Jack, take a proof of that stuff of Mr. Wicks'."

> Uncle Bobbie sank, puffing, into a chair. "I jing. Wish't I didn't get so fat. Quit smokin' about a month ago. Wife, she wanted me to. To-be-sure, I don't care nothin' fer it nohow. Mighty mean habit too. Where's your pipe?"

Dick smiled. "Oh, I haven't any now."

"Uh! took to smokin' segars, I reckon."

"No," said Dick, "I don't smoke at all."

"Oh." Uncle Bobbie looked long and thoughtfully at his young friend. "To-be-sure, I don't, *much*.—But I told wife this mornin' I'd have to begin agin if I don't quit gettin' so plaguey fat. D' ye reckon it'd make me sick?"

Dick laughed. "You look rather fleshy," he said, encouragingly.

"Well, you're a good deal fatter yourself, than you were when I first seen you," said Uncle Bobbie, looking him over with a critical eye.

"Yes," admitted Dick, "I guess I am; these are my fat years you know. I'm getting to look at those lean ones as a very bad dream."

Dick's young helper handed them a proof-sheet, and after looking over the work for a few moments, Mr. Wicks said: "That new Association meets t'-night, don't it?" Dick nodded; and the old gentleman continued carelessly, as he arose to go, "Stop fer me when you go by, will you? An' we'll go down t'gether."

"But I'm not going," said Dick, quickly. Uncle Bobbie dropped back in his seat with a jar and grasped the arms of his chair, as though about to be thrown bodily to the ceiling. "Not goin'," he gasped; "Why, what's the matter with you?" And he glared wildly at the young man.

"Nothing particularly new is the matter," said Dick, smiling at the old gentleman's astonishment. "My reason is that I cannot become a member of the Association when it is organized, and so have no right to attend the meeting to-night. I may go in after a time, but I cannot now."

"Why not?" said Mr. Wicks, still glaring.

"Because I haven't the money."

Uncle Bobbie settled back in his chair with a sigh of relief. "Oh, is that all? To-be-sure, I thought mebbe you'd got your back up 'bout somthin'."

"Yes, that's all," said Dick quietly, and did not explain how he had spent everything in his search for the wealthy hardware merchant's daughter. But perhaps Uncle Bobbie needed no explanation.

"Well, let me tell you, you're goin' anyhow; and you're goin' t' have votin' power too. Be a pretty kettle o' fish if after that speech of your'n, you weren't in the company. Be like tryin' to make a cheese 'thout any milk."

"But I haven't the money and that's all there is about it. I will go in as soon as I can."

"Well, ye can borrow it, can't you?"

"Borrow. What security can I give?"

"Aint ye'r Christianity security enough?"

Dick laughed at him. "Is that the way men do business in Boyd City?"

"Well, ye kin laugh if you want to, but that's 'bout th' best security a feller can have in th' long run. Anyhow, it's good 'nough fer me. I'll lend you a hundred fer a year. To-be-sure," he added hastily, as he saw Dick's face, "You'll have to pay me th' same interest I can git from the other fellers. I've got th' money to loan, and its all th' same to me whether I loan it to you or some other man."

"Suppose I die, then what?" asked Dick.

"Well, if Christ goes on yer note I reckon it'll be good sometime," muttered Uncle Bobbie, half to himself, as he took a check-book from his pocket and filled it out. "I'll fix up th' papers this afternoon. Don't forget t' stop fer me."

When Dick and Uncle Bobbie reached the rooms of the Commercial Club that evening, they found them filled with a large company of interested citizens, and when the opportunity was given, over two hundred enrolled as members of the Association.

Mr. Lindsley, the banker, was elected president, with Mr. Wallace, a merchant, for vice president. Then, with great enthusiasm, the unanimous ballot of the Association was cast for Mr. Richard Falkner as secretary, while to Dick's great delight, Uncle Bobbie was given the place of treasurer.

The papers of the city gave a full and enthusiastic account of the new movement, and when the citizens saw that the Association was really a fact, with men at its head who were so well qualified to fill their respective positions, they had confidence in the plan, and began straightway to express that confidence by becoming members.

A prospectus setting forth the object of the Association, together with its plans and constitution, was gotten out by the secretary, and sent to the citizens. The papers continued to speak well of the plan, and finally, through the influence of the strong business men interested, the Commercial Club endorsed the movement, and through the influence of that body, the city appropriated five thousand dollars to the building fund, and one thousand a year, for five years.

With such backing as it now had, the Association began preparation for active work. A fine building site was purchased and Dick was sent to study different plans and institutions that were in operation for similar work in several of the large cities.

"Well, good-bye old man," said Udell, when Dick ran into the office on his way to the depot. "I can see right now that I'll lose a mighty good printer one of these days."

Dick shook his head as he grasped his employer's hand, and with hope shining in his eyes, replied: "You know why I am glad for this chance to go east again, George."

And his friend answered, "Right as usual, Dickie; God bless you. If Clara was somewhere way out there in the big world without a friend, I-I reckon I'd go too."

CHAPTER XXIV

Amy was kindly received by Madam when she reached her house after that terrible night on the streets of Cleveland, and under the woman's skillful treatment, rapidly regained her strength and beauty. Never doubting that Whitley had made it impossible for her ever to return to Boyd City, she felt that she was dead to the kindly world she had once known, and looked upon the life she was entering as her only refuge from the cruel world she had learned to know. Several of the girls proved very pleasant and sympathetic companions. Little by little she grew accustomed to her surroundings and learned to look upon the life they led from their point of view; and when the time came for her to join the company in the parlor she accepted her lot with calm resignation.

When she had carefully dressed in a silken evening gown provided by Madam, she made her way alone down to the wine rooms. The scene that met her eye was beautiful and fascinating. The apartment was large and brilliantly lighted; the furniture, appointments and pictures were of the finest, with rare bits of statuary half-hidden in banks of choicest flowers. Upon the floor were carpets and rugs, in which the foot sank as in beds of moss; and luxurious chairs and couches invited the visitor to ease and indolence. From behind silken curtains came soft strains of music, and deft waiters glided here and there, bearing trays of expensive wines and liquors.

Seated at the card tables, drinking, laughing and playing, were the wealthy patrons of the place, and mingling with them, the girls, all of exceptional grace and beauty, dressed in glittering evening costume; but not one eclipsed the radiant creature who stood with flushed cheeks and shining eyes hesitating on the threshold.

Madam, moving here and there among her guests, saw Amy as she stood in the doorway, and went to her at once. Leading the girl to a little alcove at one end of the room, she presented her to a middle-aged man who was seated by himself and seemed to be waiting for someone. Amy did not know that he was waiting for her. As the three stood there chatting, a servant came quietly to Madam's side and whispered in her jeweled ear.

"Certainly," she answered, "Tell them to come in." Then turning, she stepped to a table and rapping with her fan to attract attention, cried, "The Salvation Army people want to hold a prayer meeting here, what do you say?"

There was a babble of voices, shrieks of feminine laughter, and an oath or two from the men. Some shouted, "Let them come." Others protested until Madam stopped the clamor by saying sharply: "Of course they shall come in. You know it is my custom never to refuse these people. I respect and admire them. They believe in their own teaching and live what they preach; and I want it understood that they shall not be insulted in this house. Jake—" A huge ex-prize fighter stepped into the room from a side door. "You all know Jake, gentlemen," continued Madam, with a smile; "and if you are not acquainted with him you can easily obtain an introduction by making some slighting remark, or offering an insult to these Salvation Soldiers. Here they come; remember."

As the little band of men and women filed slowly in, everybody rose at a sign from Madam, and gathered about the soldiers, who took their position in the center of the room; all except the girl in the alcove, who turned her back to the group and stood partly screened by the lace drapery of the archway.

The visitors opened their service with a song, rendered with much good taste and feeling. Not loud and martial as on the street, but soft, low and pleading. Many eyes glistened and many lips trembled when the song came to a close; and as the singers dropped to their knees, not a few heads involuntarily bowed.

One after another, the little band prayed, pleading with God to be kind and merciful to the erring; asking the Father, in the name of Jesus, to pity and forgive. Truly it was a picture of great contrasts—of brightest lights and deepest shadows—almost as when the Son of God prayed for his enemies, and wept because they were his enemies.

Three out of the six had offered their prayers and the fourth began to speak: "Our Father and our God,"—At the first word, uttered in a clear, manly, but subdued tone, the girl behind the curtain started violently; and as the prayer continued slowly, in that voice so full of manly truth and vigor, she raised her head and the rich blood colored neck and cheek. Little by little the hard look in her eyes gave way to mingled wonder, doubt and awe; then the blood fled back to the trembling heart again, leaving her face as white as the marble figure near which she stood; and then, as though compelled by a power superior to her own will, she turned slowly, and stepped from her hiding place into full view. As if stricken dumb, she stood until the prayer was finished. The captain gave the signal and the little company rose to their feet.

"O God!" The young soldier who had prayed last, sprang forward; but he was not quick enough, for before he could cross the room, with a moan of unutterable anguish, the girl sank to the floor.

"God help us, she's dead," cried Dick. And dropping on one knee, he supported the senseless girl in his arms.

All was confusion in an instant. Men and women crowded about their companion, and the Salvationists looked at one another in pity, surprise and wonder. Then Madam spoke: "Girls be quiet. Gentlemen make way. Amy is not dead. Bring her in here." The stalwart prize-fighter touched Dick on the shoulder and the latter, with the lovely form still in his arms, followed as in a dream, to Madam's own private apartments. A doctor came, in answer to a hurried call, and after no little effort the color slowly returned to the cheeks and the long, dark lashes began to tremble.

The physician turned to Dick. "Leave us now; she must not see you at first."

Dick looked at Madam. "May I have a few words privately with you?"

The woman nodded; and with the Army captain, they retired to another room, leaving Amy in charge of the doctor and one of the Salvation lassies.

Then Dick told Madam and the captain the whole story of Amy's life and home, how she had gone away because of her father's mistake, how Whitley had deceived her, and how they had searched for her in vain. Then as he told of the mother's broken health, and the sorrowing friends, though he made no mention of himself, they could not but read as he spoke of others, something of his own trouble.

Tears gathered in Madam's eyes, and when the tale was finished, she said: "Somehow I have always felt that Amy would never remain with us." And then she told of the poor girl's bitter experience alone in the great city, and how as a last resort, she had accepted her present situation. "She is more refined and gentle than the others," continued Madam, "and in my heart, I have always hoped that she would leave here. But what could she do? She had no friends; and we can't afford to have any feelings in this wretched business. Oh sir, this life is a very Hell on earth, and bad as I am, I would never lay a straw in any girl's way who wanted to get out of it. I am glad, glad, that you came in time. You know, captain, that I have never opposed your work; and have seen you take several girls from my place without protest. But I can't be expected to look after them myself."

They discussed the situation for some time, and finally Madam said again, "Mr.—; I don't know your name, and I don't want to; you wear that uniform and that's enough for me—just let Amy remain here for a day or two. One of the Salvation girls will stay with her, and can do more for her than you. She shall have my own room and no one shall see her. Then when she is strong enough, you may come and take her if she will go; and I am sure she will. She will be as safe here as in her father's home."

The captain nodded. "Madam has passed her word, sir," he said. "You come with me and arrange for the future while your friend is getting strong again. Our Sarah will remain with her and keep us posted."

Dick yielded; and after hearing from the doctor that Amy was resting easier, they bade Madam goodnight and passed out into the room where again the music played, jewels sparkled, wine flowed, and the careless laugh and jest were heard.

With a shudder of horror Dick muttered, "My God, Amy in such a place." And yet—another thought flashed through his mind, that brought a flush of shame to his cheek. "But Amy—" And again the strong man trembled, weeping like a child.

Never, though he lived to be an old man, could Dick look back upon that night and the days following, without turning pale. How he lived through it he never knew. Perhaps it was because he had suffered so much in his checkered career that he was enabled to bear that which otherwise would have been impossible. And the consciousness of the great change in his own life led him to hope for Amy, when others would have given up in despair.

On his tour of study and investigation for the Association, he had presented his letters to the Salvation Army people, and had been warmly welcomed by them, as is everyone who manifests a desire to help humanity. Every kindness and courtesy was shown him, and at the invitation of the captain, he had gone with them on one of their regular rescue trips. He had donned the uniform of the Army, for greater convenience and safety; for the blue and red of these soldiers of the cross is received and honored in places where no ordinary church member, whatever be his professed purpose, would be admitted.

While Dick and his friends planned for Amy's future, Sarah, the Salvation girl, remained by her bedside caring for her as a sister. Not one hint of reproach or censure fell from her lips; only words of loving kindness, of hope and courage. At first the poor girl refused to listen, but sobbing wildly, cried that her life was ruined, that she could only go on as she had started, and begged that they leave her alone in her disgrace and sin.

But Sarah herself could say, "I know sister, I have been through it all; and if Jesus could save me he can save you too." So at last love and hope conquered; and as soon as she was strong enough, she left the place and went with Sarah to the latter's humble home. There Dick called to see her.

"Mr. Falkner," she said, sadly, after the pain and embarrassment of the first meeting had passed off a little. "I do not understand; what makes you do these things?"

And Dick answered, "Did I not tell you once that nothing could make me change; that nothing you could do would make me less your friend? You might, for the time being, make it impossible for me to help you, but the desire, the wish, was there just the same, and sought only an opportunity to express itself. And besides this," he added gently, "you know I'm a Christian now."

Amy hung her head. "Yes," she said slowly, "you are a Christian. These Salvation soldiers are Christians too; and I—I—am—oh, Mr. Falkner, help me now. Be indeed my friend. Tell me what to do. I cannot go back home like this. I do believe in Christ and that He sent you to me. I'm so tired of this world, for I know the awfulness of it now; and these good people have taught me that one can live close to Christ, even in the most unfavorable circumstances."

Dick told her of their plan; how his friend, the captain, had arranged for her to live with his brother on a farm in northern Missouri, and that they only wanted her consent to start at once. Would she go?

"But how can I? I have no money, and I have never been taught to work."

"Miss Goodrich," answered Dick, "can you not trust me?"

Amy was silent.

"You must let me help you in this. Thank God, I can do it now. Prove to me that you are still my friend, by letting me make this investment for Christ. Will you?"

The next day they bade good-bye to the sturdy soldiers of the cross who had been so true to them, and started on their westward journey.

Dick saw Amy safe in her new home, and then with a promise that she would write to him regularly, and an agreement that he would send her letters and papers addressed to the people with whom she lived, he left her; satisfied that she was in kind hands, and that a new life was open before her.

But when Dick was once more aboard the train, alone with his thoughts, without the anxiety for Amy's immediate welfare upon his mind, the struggle of his life began. He loved Amy dearly; had loved her almost from the moment she came into George Udell's printing office three years ago; loved her in spite of the difference in their position, when he was only a tramp and she was the favored daughter of wealth; when he was an unbeliever and she was a worker in the church; loved her when he saw her losing her hold on the higher life and drifting with the current; loved her when she left home, and as he thought, honor behind. And he was forced to confess, in his own heart, that he loved her yet, in spite of the fact that their positions were reversed; that he was an honored gentleman, respected and trusted by all, while she, in the eyes of the world, was a fallen woman with no friend but himself.

But what of the future? Dick's dreams had always been that he would win such a position in the world as would enable him, with confidence, to ask her to share his life. But always there had been the feeling that he never could be worthy. And with the dark picture of his own past before him, he knew he had no right to think of her as his wife. But now there was no question as to his position. But what of hers? Could he think of taking for a wife, one whom he had seen in that house at Cleveland? On the one hand, his love plead for her; on the other, the horror of her life argued against it. Again his sense of justice plead, and his own life came before him like a horrid vision as it had done that morning when he learned of his father's death. He saw his childhood home, smelt the odor of the fragrant pines upon the hills, and heard the murmur of the river running past the cabin. Again he heard his drunken father cursing in his sleep, and caught the whisper of his mother's dying prayer; and again he crept stealthily out of the cabin into the glory of the morning, with a lean hound his only companion.

Slowly and painfully he traced his way along the road of memory, recalling every place where he had advanced; every place where he had fallen; going step by step from the innocence of boyhood to the awful knowledge of the man of the world. He had fought, had fallen, had conquered and risen again; always advancing toward the light, but always bearing on his garment the smell of the fire, and upon his hands the stain of the pitch. And now, because he was safe at last and could look back upon those things, should he condemn another? Would not Amy also conquer, and when she *had* conquered, by what right could he demand in her that which he had not in himself? Christ would as freely welcome her as He had welcomed him. Christianity held out as many glorious hopes for her as for him. Her past might be past as well as his. Why should he not shut the door upon it forever, and live only in the present and future? And then his mind fell to picturing what that future, with Amy by his side, might be. They were equals now, before God and their own consciences. What should he care for the world?

And so the fight went on in the battle-ground of his inner life, until the whistle blew a long blast for the station, and looking from the window of the car, he saw the smelter smoke and dust of Boyd City.

CHAPTER XXV

John Barton and his wife, Anna, with whom Amy was to make her home for a while, could fully sympathize with the girl in her sad position, though one would never dream that the quiet, reserved John knew more of life than of his pigs and cattle, or that his jolly-faced, motherly companion had ever been beyond the quiet fields that surrounded her simple dwelling. Years before, they had been rescued from the world in which Amy had so nearly perished, by the same kind hand that had been stretched out to her, the Salvation Army; and now well on in middle life, happy and prosperous, they showed scarce a trace of the trouble that had driven them to labor on a farm. As hired help, they had gained their experience, and by ceaseless industry and careful economy, had at last come to own the place where they now lived. With no child of her own, Mrs. Barton took a mother's place in Amy's life from the first, and was very patient with the girl who had never been taught to do the simplest household task. Amy returned the loving kindness full measure, and, determined to be a help to those who so much helped her, advanced rapidly in the knowledge of her homely duties. Dressed in the plain working garb of a farm girl, with arms bare and face flushed by the heat of the kitchen, one would scarcely have recognized in her the beautiful young woman who moved with Boyd City's society leaders, or the brilliant novice who stood hesitating at the entrance to a life of sin in Madam's wine-rooms; and certainly, one would never have classed the bright eyes, plump cheeks, and well-rounded figure, with the frightened, starving, haggard thing that roamed about the streets of Cleveland a few short months before.

But great as was the change in Amy's outward appearance, the change within was even greater. She was no longer the thoughtless, proud, pleasure-loving belle that her parents had trained; nor was she the hard, reckless, hopeless creature that the world had made. But she was a woman now, with a true woman's interest and purpose in life. The shallow brilliance of the society girl had given place to thoughtful earnestness, and the dreary sadness of the outcast had changed to bright hopefulness.

One warm day in June, Mrs. Barton laid the last neatly ironed garment on the big pile of clothes nearby, and noisily pushing her irons to the back of the stove, cried, "Thank goodness, that's the last of that for this week." And "Thank goodness, that's the last of that," exclaimed Amy, mimicking the voice of her friend as she threw out the dishwater and hung the empty pan in its place.

Anna wiped the perspiration from her steaming face. "Come on; let's get out of this Inferno for a while and do our patching in the shade. I shall melt if I stay here a minute longer." And the two were soon seated in their low chairs on the cool porch, with a big basket of mending between them.

"Hello, there's our man back from town already," suddenly exclaimed Anna a few minutes later, as her husband drove into the barnyard; then with a mischievous twinkle in her blue eyes, she called, "Hurry up, John, Amy wants her letter." John smiled in his quiet way as he came up to the porch and handed the girl an envelope with the Boyd City postmark. Then the old people both laughed at the other's pretty confusion when Anna, rising, said in her teasing voice, "Come on hubby, I'll fix your dinner. We've kept it warm. Can't you see the selfish thing wants to be alone with her treasure?"

But when Mrs. Barton returned to her mending, after a long talk with her husband, her jolly face wore an expression of seriousness that was unusual, and she failed to notice that Amy's hands were idle and her work was lying untouched in her lap as she sat looking wistfully far away across the sunlit meadows and pastures.

Both took up their tasks in silence and plied their needles with energy, while their thoughts were far away; but one thought of a great city in the far-away east; the other of a bustling mining town in the nearer west.

At last Anna spoke with a little sigh: "Amy dear, I suppose you will be leaving us one of these days before long."

The girl answered with a loving smile: "Are you so tired of me that you are going to send me out into the world again?"

"No, no, dear. You have a home with John and me as long as you live. Surely you know that, don't you, Amy dear?" There was a wistful note in the kind voice, and dropping the stocking she was darning, Anna leaned forward and placed her hand on the arm of Amy's chair.

A rush of tears was her answer, as the girl caught the toil-stained hand and carried it passionately to her lips. "Of course I know. Mother forgive me; I was only 'funnin' as little Jimmie Clark says."

"But I am not 'funnin,'" replied the other. "I'm awfully in earnest."

There seemed to be a hidden meaning in her words and Amy looked at her anxiously. "I do not understand why you think that I should leave you," she said earnestly.

"Because—because—I—this life must be so degrading to you. You could live so differently at home. You must feel this keenly."

Amy looked at her steadily. "That is not your reason, Mother," she said gently. "You know that a woman degrades herself when she does nothing useful, and that I count my present place and work, far above my old life at home. Why just think"—with a quiet smile—"John said last night that he couldn't tell my biscuits from yours. And wasn't the dinner all right to-day? And isn't that a beautiful patch?" She held up her work for inspection.

The other shook her head, while she smiled in answer. "I know, dear girl, you do beautifully; but that's not it. There is your father and mother and brother; you know you can't stay away from them always."

Amy's face grew troubled, while her hand nervously sought the letter hidden in her bosom. "You do not understand, mother," she replied slowly; "My people do not want me to come home. My father said I should not, until—until—" she hesitated.

"But your father has surely forgotten his anger by this time, and when he sees you he will be glad to forgive and take you back."

The brown eyes looked at her in startled surprise. "When he sees me?" But the other continued hurriedly, "And there are the letters you know."

Amy's face grew rosy. "Why the letters?" she murmured in a low voice.

"Because he loves you, dear, don't you see?"

"He has never told me so."

"Not in words perhaps."

Amy was silent.

"He will come for you one of these days and then you will go with him."

The girl sadly shook her head, and turning her face, looked away across the fields again, where silent, patient John sturdily followed his team.

The shadow of the big sycamore was stretching across the barn lot almost to the gate, where the cows stood watching for the boy to come and let them in; a troop of droning bees were paying their last visit for the day to the peach-tree, that flung its wealth of passionate blossoms almost within reach of the porch, and over the blue distant woods the last of the feathery banks of mist hung lazily, as though tangled in the budding branches, reluctant to say good-night.

Suddenly leaving her chair, Amy threw herself on the floor and burying her face in the older woman's lap, burst into tears. Anna's own eyes were wet as she softly smoothed the brown hair of the girl she had taken to her mother's heart. "You do love him, don't you dear?"

And Amy answered, between her sobs, "Because I love him so, I must never see him again. He—he—is so strong and good and true—he must not care for one who would only bring reproach upon his name."

"I know, dear girl, and that is why you must go home; take your own place in the world again and then the way is clear."

Amy lifted her head. "Oh, if I only could—but you do not know—my going home would only widen the distance between us. My father—" She paused again, her quivering lips could not form the words.

"Amy, I am sure you are mistaken; you must be. When you meet your father it will all come right, I know."

Again there seemed to be a hidden meaning in her words. "When I meet my father?" Amy repeated slowly.

Anna grew confused. "Yes—I—we—you know John has been trying to sell for a long time; we want to go back to Cleveland; and to-day he learned that a buyer was coming from Boyd City to—"

Amy's face grew white as she rose, trembling, to her feet. "My father," she gasped—"coming here?"

Anna took the frightened girl in her arms—"There, there, dear, don't be afraid. All will be for the best, I am sure. John and I will stand by you and you shall go with us if you wish. But I am sure your father will be glad to take you home with him; and you ought to go; you know you ought; not for your family's sake alone, but for his, you know."

And so they talked as the shadows grew, until in the twilight John came from the field with his tired team, when they went into the house to prepare the evening meal.

Adam Goodrich had by no means forgiven his beautiful daughter for the blow dealt his pride, though one would not easily detect from his manner that there was anything but supreme self-satisfaction in the life of this worthy member of the Jerusalem Church. Mrs. Goodrich's health was broken, but she still remained the same society-loving, fashion-worshipping woman, who by her influence and teaching had ruined her child. It never occurred to the mother that Amy's conduct was the legitimate outcome of her training or associates, but she looked at it always as a weakness in the girl; and Frank, true son of his father, never mentioned his sister but with a curl of his lip, and lived his life as though she had never existed. The family still attended church once each week, still contributed the same amount to the cause, and still found fault with Cameron for his low tastes and new-fangled methods; while they laughed at the new Association as a dream of fools and misguided enthusiasts.

Adam had long wanted to add a good farm to his possessions, and after some correspondence with the agent who had advertised the Barton property, he boarded the train one bright day, to pay a visit of inspection to his contemplated purchase. Reaching the little city of Zanesville in the evening, he spent the night at a hotel. In the morning he called upon the agent, and the two were soon whirling along the road behind a pair of wiry little ponies.

The drive of eight or ten miles passed very pleasantly between the real estate man and his prospective customer in such conversation as gentlemen whose lives are spent in the whirl of the money world indulge in between moments of activity.

At last they neared the farm, and bringing the ponies to a walk, the agent began pointing out the most desirable features of the property: the big barn, the fine timber land in the distance, the rich soil of a field near by, the magnificent crop of corn, the stream of water where cattle stood knee-deep lazily fighting the flies, and the fine young orchard just across the road from the house.

"Yes, the building is old"—as they drove up in front of the big gate; "but it is good yet, and with just a little expense, can be converted into a model of modern convenience and beauty."

As they drove into the yard and got out to hitch the ponies, Mrs. Barton came to the door.

"Just come right in, Mr. Richards, John is over in the north field; I'll go for him."

"Oh No, Mrs. Barton, I'll go. This is Mr. Goodrich, who wishes to look at the farm. Mr. Goodrich, just wait here in the shade and I'll go after Mr. Barton."

"I believe," said Adam, "if you don't mind, I'll walk through the orchard until you return."

"Certainly, certainly," said both the agent and the farmer's wife; and the woman added, nervously, "just make yourself at home, Mr. Goodrich; you'll find the girl out there somewhere. Dinner will be ready in about an hour."

Leisurely crossing the road, Adam paused at the orchard gate, to watch some fine young shoats that were running about with their mother nearby.

From the pigs, his gaze wandered about the farm buildings, the fields, and the garden. Turning at last to enter the orchard, he saw a young woman, clad in the homely every-day dress of a country girl; her face hidden beneath a large sun-bonnet of blue gingham. She was gathering apple blossoms. Something in her manner or figure struck him as being familiar, and with his hand on the gate, he paused again. As he stood watching her all unconscious of his presence, she sprang lightly from the ground in an effort to reach a tempting spray of blossoms, and at her violent movement the sun-bonnet dropped from her head, while a wealth of brown hair fell in a rippling mass to her waist. Then as she half turned, he saw her face distinctly, and with a start of surprise and astonishment, knew her as his daughter.

Under the first impulse of a father's love at seeing his child again, Adam stepped forward; but with the gate half open, he checked himself and then drew back, while the old haughty pride, that dominant key in his character, hardened his heart again; and when he at last pushed open the gate once more, his love was fairly hidden.

When Amy first caught sight of her father advancing slowly toward her beneath the blossom-laden trees she forgot everything and started quickly toward him, her face lighted with eager welcome, ready to throw herself in his arms and there pour out her whole tearful story and beg his love and forgiveness. But when she saw his face, she dared not, and stood with downcast eyes, trembling and afraid.

"So this is where you hide yourself, while your family faces your shame at home," began Adam, coldly. "Tell me who brought you here and who pays these people to keep you."

The girl lifted her head proudly. "No one pays them sir; I am supporting myself."

The man looked at her in amazement. "Do you mean that your position here is that of a common servant?"

"There are worse positions," she replied sadly. "The people here are very kind to me."

"But think of your family; you are a disgrace to us all. What can I tell them when I go back and say that I have seen you?"

"Tell them that I am well, and as happy as I ever expect to be."
She pressed her hand to her bosom where a letter was hidden.

"But what will people say when they know that my daughter is working on a farm for a living?"

"They need never know unless you tell them."

Then the man lost all control of himself; that this girl who had always yielded to his every wish, without so much as daring to have a thought of her own, should so calmly, but firmly, face him in this manner, enraged him beyond measure. He could not understand. He knew nothing of her life since that night he had refused to listen to her explanation, and in his anger taunted her with being the plaything of Dick Falkner, and then, because her face flushed, thought that he had hit on the truth and grew almost abusive in his language.

But Amy only answered, "Sir, you are mistaken now, as you were when you drove me from home; Mr. Falkner had nothing to do with my leaving Boyd City."

"You are my daughter still," stormed Adam, "and I will force you to leave this low position and come home to us. You cannot deceive me with your clever lie about supporting yourself. What do you know about a servant's work? That cursed tramp printer is at the bottom of all this, and I'll make him suffer for it as I live. I will force you to come home."

Amy's face grew pale, but she replied quietly, "Oh no, father, you will not do that, because that would make public my position you know. I have no fear of your proclaiming from the housetops that your daughter is a hired girl on a farm."

"But father," she said, in softer voice, as Adam stood speechless with rage; "Father, forgive me for this, for I know that I am right. Let me stay here and prove that I am not useless to the world, and then perhaps I will go to you. In the meantime, keep my secret and no one shall know that your claim on society has teen lessened because your daughter is learning to do a woman's work."

Just a shade of bitter sarcasm crept into her voice, but Adam did not notice, for he saw the agent and the farmer coming. "Very well," he said hurriedly, "you have chosen your path and must walk in it. But you cannot expect me to acknowledge a servant as my daughter." And turning his back, he went to meet the men, while Amy slipped off to the house with her blossoms.

Mrs. Barton needed no word to tell her of the result of the interview from which she had expected so much, and with a kiss and a loving word, permitted the girl to go upstairs, where she remained until Mr. Goodrich had left the place.

After completing the purchase of the farm, Adam wrote his daughter from the office of the agent in Zanesville: "The place where you are living now belongs to me, and the Bartons must give possession at once. If you will promise never to speak to that man Falkner again, you may come home and be received into your old place, but on no other terms will I acknowledge you as my daughter. Refuse and you are thrown on the charity of the world, for you cannot remain where you are."

Amy carried the letter to her friends, together with her reply, and they, by every argument of love, tried to induce her to go with them back to Cleveland; but she refused in tears. And when she would not be persuaded, they were compelled to leave her. With many expressions of love, they said good-bye, and departed for their old home in the eastern city; but before going, they arranged with a kind neighbor to give her a place in their already crowded home until she could find means of support.

Upon Dick's return from his Cleveland trip, he had thrown himself into his work with feverish energy, while in his heart the struggle between love and prejudice continued. But as the weeks went by and Amy's letters had come, telling of her life on the farm, and how she was learning to be of use in the world; and as he had read between the lines, of her new ideas and changed views of life, his love had grown stronger and had almost won the fight. Then a letter came, bidding him good-bye, and telling him that she was going away again, and that for her sake, he must not try to find her; that she was deeply grateful for all that he had done, but it was best that he forget that he had ever known her.

Dick was hurt and dismayed. It seemed to him that she had given up, and the devil, Doubt, ever ready to place a wrong construction upon the words and deeds of mortals, sent him into the black depths of despair again.

"I never saw such a man," declared George Udell to Clara Wilson, one evening, as they caught a glimpse of him bending over a desk in Mr. Wicks' office, "he works like a fiend."

"Like an angel, you'd better say," replied Clara. "Didn't I tell you that he was no common tramp?"

"Yes, dear, of course; and you never made a mistake in your life; that is, never but once."

"When was that?" asked Clara curiously.

"When you said 'No' to me night before last. Won't you reconsider it, and—"

"Where do you suppose Amy Goodrich is now?" interrupted the young lady. "Do you know, I have fancied at times, that Mr. Falkner learned something on his trip last fall, that he has not told us?"

George opened his eyes. "What makes you think that?"

"Oh, because; somehow he seems so different since he returned."

But George shook his head. "I thought so too for a while," he replied; "but I talked with him just the other day, and I'm afraid he's given up all hope. He works to hide the hurt. But I'll tell you one thing, girlie, if anything could make a Christian of me, it would be Dick's life. There's something more than human in the way he stands up against this thing."

Then Dick received another letter, from a post office in Texas.

"Dere Dikkie: I take my pen in hand to let u no that Ime wel an hoape u ar the same. Jim Whitly is ded he don tried to nife me an i fixed him. he wanted to hire me to kil u fer some papers an we was in you ol caben kross the river from the still. He said ter tel u thet he lied to u an that Amy is pure. I don't no what he means but thot u ort ter no. I skipped—burn this. your daddys pard.

"JAKE THOMPSON."

The Association building was finished at last, and the pastor of the Jerusalem Church sat in his little den looking over the morning mail. There were the usual number of magazines, papers, and sample copies of religious periodicals, with catalogues and circulars from publishing houses; an appeal to help a poor church in Nebraska whose place of worship had been struck by lightning; a letter from a sister in Missouri, asking for advice about a divorce case; one from a tinware man in Arkansas, who inquired about the town with a view of locating; and one that bore the mark of the Association, which informed him, over the signature of the Secretary, that he had been unanimously called to take charge of the new work. Cameron carried the letter, in triumph, to the kitchen.

"Well," said the little woman; "didn't I tell you that one preacher would have a hand in whatever work was started here? Of course you'll accept?"

"I don't know," Cameron answered. "We must think about it."

A day later he called for a consultation with Elder Wicks, and Uncle Bobbie said:

"To-be-sure, it's mighty hard for me to advise you in a thing like this; for as a member of the church, I'm bound to say stay; and as a member of the Association, I say, accept. I jing! I don't know what to do." And for a few moments, the old gentleman thoughtfully stroked his face; then suddenly grasping the arms of the chair fiercely, he shouted: "As a Christian, I say, accept, an' I reckon that settles it."

And so Cameron became the manager of the new work; and his first recommendation to the directors was that they send their Secretary away for a vacation. And indeed Dick, poor fellow, needed it, though at first he flatly refused to go. But Dr. Jordan came down on him with the cheerful information that he would die if he didn't, and Uncle Bobbie finished matters by declaring that he had no more right to kill himself by over work, than he had to take Rough on Eats, or blow his head off with a gun; "and besides," added the old gentleman, "you aint paid me that hundred dollars yet. To-be-sure, the note aint due for sometime; but a fellow has got to look after his own interest, aint he?"

The first address delivered by Cameron in the auditorium of the Association building, was from the text, "Ye shall know the truth, and the truth shall make you free." The audience room was crowded, and the young minister had never appeared to better advantage, or declared the teaching of his Master with greater freedom, earnestness and vigor; and to the astonishment of the people, who should come forward at the close of the service, to declare his belief in, and acceptance of Christ as the Son of God, but the so-called infidel printer, George Udell.

CHAPTER XXVI

In Southwestern Missouri, in the White Oak district, there are many beautiful glens and sheltered valleys, where a sturdy people have tamed the wildness of nature and made it obedient to their will. The fields lie fertile and fruitful on either bank of murmuring streams, clear to the foot of the hills where the timber grows. Always a road winds down the valley, generally skirting the forest, and the farmhouses are nearly all built of logs, though more modern and finished dwellings are fast taking the place of the primitive mansions. Every few miles, one may see little school-houses, most often made of good lumber and painted white, with heavy shutters and a high platform in front. For the Ozark settler takes great pride in his school-house, which is also a church and a political rallying point, and meeting-place for the backwoods "Literary;" and though he may live in a rude log hovel himself, his hall of education must be made of boards and carefully painted.

To this romantic region Dick Falkner went to spend his vacation, during the latter part of October, the loveliest season of the year in that section of the country. Mr. Cushman, who was a successful farmer living in the White Oak district, and an old friend of Uncle Bobbie's, gladly welcomed the young man, of whom his old partner, Wicks, had written so highly. When Dick left the train at Armourdale, a little village in the lead and zinc field, he was greeted at once by his host, a bluff, pleasant-faced, elderly gentleman, whom he liked at first sight, and who was completely captivated by his guest before they had been together half an hour.

Oak Springs Farm, which was to be Dick's home for the next month, took in the whole of a beautiful little glen, and many acres of timber-land on either side. Crane Creek had its source, or rather one of its sources, within a hundred feet of the house, where a big spring bubbled from beneath the roots of a giant oak, and the water went chattering and laughing away to the south and east.

Three-quarters of a mile from Oak Springs, just over the ridge in another hollow, another stream gushed bright and clear, from beneath another ancient oak and went rushing away to join its fellow brook a mile distant, where the little glens broadened into a large valley, through which the creek hurried onward to the great river, miles away in the heart of the wilderness.

It was all very beautiful and restful to the young man, wearied and worn by the rush and whirl of the city, and stifled with the dust and smoke from factory and furnace. The low hills, clothed with foliage, richly stained by October's brush; the little valley lying warm in the sunlight, was a welcome change to the dead monotony of the prairie, where the sky shut down close to the dull brown earth, with no support of leafy pillars. And the mother quail, with her full-grown family scurrying to cover in the corner of the fence; the squirrel scolding to his mate in the tree-tops, or leaping over the rustling leaves, and all the rest of the forest life, was full of interest when compared to the life of busy men or chattering sparrows in the bustling mining town.

Though Mr. Cushman and his wife had raised a large family of boys and girls, only one, a daughter, remained with them on the farm. The others had, one by one, taken their flight from the home nest, to build home nests of their own in different parts of the great world wilderness.

Kate was a hearty, robust, rosy-cheeked country lass of eighteen, the youngest of the flock; her father's chum, with all his frank, open ways; and her mother's companion, with all her loving thoughtfulness. And, best of all, she possessed the charming freshness, innocence and purity of one who had never come in touch with those who, taught by the world she had never known, were content to sham her virtues as they tried to imitate the color of her cheek.

Dick sank to rest that night with a long sigh of relief, after meeting the mother and daughter and enjoying such a supper as one only finds on a prosperous farm. And strangely enough, the last picture on his mind before he fell asleep, was of a little school-house which he had seen just at sunset, scarcely a quarter of a mile up the valley; and he drowsily wondered who taught the children there; while a great owl, perched in an old apple-tree back of the chicken house, echoed his sleepy thoughts with its "Whoo! Whoo!"

With a whoop and hallo and whistle, the noisy troop of boys and girls came tumbling out of the doorway of the White Oak School, their dinner pails and baskets on their arms, homeward bound from the irksome duties of the day. The young teacher, after standing a few moments in the doorway, watching her charges down the road and out of sight in the timber across the valley, turned wearily back, and seating herself at a rude desk in the rear of the room, began her task of looking over the copybooks left by the rollicking youngsters. Had she remained a moment longer in the door-way she would have seen a tall, well-dressed gentleman coming leisurely up the hill. It was Dick. He had been roaming all the afternoon over the fields and through the brown woods.

He came slowly up the road, and crossing the yard, stood hesitating at the threshold of the building. The teacher, bending low, did not see him for a moment; but when she raised her head, she looked straight into his eyes.

Dick would have been dull indeed had he failed to interpret that look; and Amy would have been more than dull had she failed to see the love that shone in his glance of astonishment and pleasure.

For an instant, neither spoke; then, "I have found you again," said Dick, simply. "I hope you will forgive me, Miss Goodrich; I assure you the meeting is entirely by accident. I stopped for a drink of water."

"Please help yourself, Mr. Falkner," said the girl, with a little choke in her voice. "There it is." And she pointed to a wooden pail and tin dipper near the door.

"I am spending my vacation in the Ozarks; or rather, I came here to rest." He paused awkwardly. "I—I did not dream of your being here, or of course I should not have come, after your letter. Forgive me and I will go away again."

He turned to leave the room, but with his foot on the threshold, paused, and then walked back to the desk where the girl sat, leaning forward with her face buried in her arms.

"There's just one thing though, that I must say before I go. Are you in need of any help? If so, let me be of use to you; I am still your friend."

The brown head was raised and two glistening eyes proudly pleading looked at Dick.

Through a mist in his own eyes he saw two hands outstretched and heard a voice say, "I do need your help. Don't go. That is—I mean—leave me here now and to-morrow call, and I will tell you all. Only trust me this once."

Dick took the outstretched hands in his and stood for a moment with bowed head; then whispered softly, "Of course I will stay. Shall I come at this hour to-morrow?" Amy nodded, and he passed out of the building.

Had Dick looked back as he strode swiftly toward the timber, he would have seen a girlish form in the door holding out her hands; and had he listened as he climbed the fence, he might have heard a sweet voice falter, "Oh Dick, I love you. I love you." And just as he vanished at the edge of the woods, the girl who was more than all the world to him, fell for the second time in her life, fainting on the floor.

All the forenoon of the next day, Dick wandered aimlessly about the farm, but somehow he never got beyond sight of the little white school-house. He spent an hour watching the colts that frolicked in the upper pasture, beyond which lay the children's playground; then going through the field, he climbed the little hill beyond and saw the white building through the screen of leaves and branches. Once Amy came to the door, but only for a moment, when she called the shouting youngsters from their short recess. Then recrossing the valley half a mile above, he walked slowly home to dinner along the road leading past the building. How he envied the boys and girls whose droning voices reached his ears through the open windows.

While Dick was chatting with his kind host after dinner, as they sat on the porch facing the great oak, the latter talked about the spring and the history of the place; how it used to be a favorite camping ground for the Indians in winter; and pointed out the field below the barn, where they had found arrowheads by the hundreds. Then he told of the other spring just over the ridge, and how the two streams came together and flowed on, larger and larger, to the river. And then with a farmer's fondness for a harmless jest, he suggested that Dick might find it worth his while to visit the other spring; "for," said he "the school-marm lives there; and she's a right pretty girl. Sensible too, I reckon, though she aint been here only since the first of September."

When the farmer had gone to his work, Dick walked down to the spring-house, and sitting on the twisted roots of the old oak, looked into the crystal water.

"And so Amy lives by a spring just like this," he thought, "and often sits beneath that other oak, perhaps, looking into the water as I am looking now."

A blue-jay, perched on a bough above, screamed in mocking laughter at the dreamer beneath; an old drake, leading his family in a waddling row to the open stream below the little house, solemnly quacked his protest against such a willful waste of time; and a spotted calf thrust its head through the barn-yard fence to gaze at him in mild reproach.

In his revery, Dick compared the little stream of water to his life, running fretted and troubled, from the very edge of its birthplace; and he followed it with his eye down through the pasture lot, until it was lost in the distance; then looking into the blue vista of the hills, he followed on, in his mind, where the stream grew deeper and broader. Suddenly, he sprang to his feet and walked hastily away along the bank of the creek. In a little while, he stood at the point of land where the two valleys became one, and the two streams were united, and with a long breath of relief, found that the course of the larger stream, as far as he could see, was smooth and untroubled, while the valley through which it flowed was broad and beautiful.

At the appointed time, Dick went to the school-house, and with Amy, walked through the woods toward the farm where she lived, while she told him of her life since last they met; of her father's visit and his threats, and of her fear that he would force her to go home. The farm had been sold the day after Adam was there, and how through her friends, she had obtained her present position in the school. She told of her pride and desire to wipe out alone, the disgrace, as alone she had fallen. She longed to be of use in the world.

As she talked, Dick's face grew bright. "This is good news indeed," he said. "I'm so glad for your sake." Then, with a smile, "I see you do not need my help now that you can be of so much help to others."

"But won't you help me plan for the future?" said Amy, trying to hide the slight tremble in her voice. "Won't you tell me what is best to do? I have thought and thought, but can get no farther than I am now."

"Let us say nothing about that for a time," replied Dick. "We will talk that over later."

And so it came about that the farmer's advice, spoken in jest, was received in earnest; and for four happy weeks the two lived, unrestrained by false pride or foolish prejudice; walking home together through the woods, or wandering beside the little brooks, talking of the beauties they saw on every hand, or silently listening to the voices of nature, But at last the time came when they must part, and Dick gave his answer to her question.

"You must go home," he said.

"But you know what that means," answered Amy. "I will be forced to give up my church work and be a useless butterfly again; and besides, the conditions father insists upon—." She blushed and hesitated.

"Yes," said Dick, "I know what it means for me, your going home. But you need not again be a useless butterfly as you say. Write your father and tell him of your desire; that you cannot be content as a useless woman of society. He will ask you to come home, I am sure. And when your present term of school is finished, you can take your old place in the world again. You will find many ways to be of use to others, and I know that your father will learn to give you more liberty."

"And the past?" asked Amy, with a blush of shame.

"Is past," said Dick, emphatically. "No one in Boyd City knows your story, nor need they ever know."

"One man there can tell them," answered the girl, with averted face.

"You are mistaken," said Dick, quietly. And then, as gently as he could, he told her of Whitley's death. But of his connection with him and the real cause of the fight in the cabin, he said nothing.

It was hard for Dick to advise Amy to go home, for as she was then, they were equals. If she went back to Boyd City, all would be changed. But he had fought over the question in his own mind and the right had conquered.

Amy agreed with him that it was best, and added, "I have felt all along that I ought to do this after a while, but I wished to see you again first, and had you not happened to find me, I should have written to you later."

And so it was settled. No word of love was spoken between them. Dick would not permit himself to speak then, because he felt that she ought not to be influenced by her present surroundings; and even had he spoken, Amy would not have listened, because she felt her work could only be complete when she had returned to her old position and had proved herself by her life there.

And so they parted, with only a silent clasping of hands, as they stood beside the brook that chattered on its way to join the other; though there was a world of love in both the gray eyes and the brown; a love none the less strong because unspoken.

Upon Dick's return to the city, he took up his work again with so light a heart that his many friends declared that he had entirely recovered his health, and their congratulations were numerous and hearty.

During the holidays, there was some gossip among the citizens when it was announced in the Daily Whistler, that Miss Goodrich would soon return to her home. The article stated that she had been living with some friends in the east, finishing her education, and the public accepted the polite lie with a nod and a wink.

Mrs. Goodrich, though her mother heart was glad at the return of her child, received the girl with many tearful reproaches; and while Amy was hungering for a parent's loving sympathy and encouragement, she could not open her heart to the woman who mourned only the blow dealt her family pride and social ambition.

Adam was formal, cold and uncompromising, while Frank paid no more attention to his sister than if she were a hired servant in the house. Only the girl's firm determination, awakened womanhood, patience and Christian fortitude enabled her to accept her lot. But in spite of the daily reproaches, stern coldness and studied contempt, she went steadily forward in her purpose to regain the place she had lost; and somehow, as the weeks went by, all noticed a change in Amy. Her father dared not check her in her work, for something in the clear eyes, that looked at him so sadly, but withal so fearlessly, made him hesitate. It was as though she had spoken, "I have been through the fire and have come out pure gold. It is not for you to question me." And though she attended to her social duties, her influence was always for the good, and no one dared to speak slightingly of religious things in her presence; while the poor people at the Mission learned to love the beautiful young woman who visited their homes and talked to them of a better life, and never failed to greet them with a kindly word when they met her on the street.

Of course Dick could not call at her home. He knew well that it would only provoke a storm; nor did Amy ask him to. They met only at church or at the Mission; and nothing but the common greetings passed between them. No one ever dreamed that they were more than mere acquaintances. But they each felt that the other understood, and so were happy; content to wait until God, in his own way, should unite the streams of their lives.

CHAPTER XXVII

It was about nine o'clock in the evening, and Dick was in his office at the Association building, writing some letters pertaining to the work, when the door opened, and to his great astonishment, Amy entered hurriedly, out of breath and very much excited.

"I beg your pardon for interrupting you, Mr. Falkner," she began, as soon as she could speak; "but I must tell you." And then she broke down, sinking into a chair and crying bitterly.

Dick's face was very grave, and stepping to the window he drew the curtain, then turned the key in the door.

"Now what is it, Miss Goodrich? Please be calm. You know you have nothing to fear from me."

Amy brushed away her tears, and looking up into his face, "I'm not afraid of you," she said. "But—but—, our secret is out."

Dick nodded that he understood, and she continued: "You know that Frank has been at Armourdale the last few weeks, looking after papa's interests in the mines there, and—and he came home this afternoon?"

"Yes, I know," said Dick calmly.

"I was in the sitting-room and he and father were in the library. I—I did not mean to listen, but the door was open and I heard them speak your name."

"Yes," said Dick again.

"Frank met Mr. Cushman and spent several days at the farm where they are prospecting, and—and of course learned that we were together there. Father believes the awfullest things and threatens to kill you; he is so angry. I—I'm afraid for you—and—and I slipped away because I—I thought you ought to know." The poor girl finished with a sob and buried her face in her hands.

Dick thought rapidly for a few moments. He remembered that he had never told Amy how her father had accused him of taking her away at first, and he saw now how that belief would be strengthened by her brother's story. Then as his heart bitterly rebelled at the thought of such a misunderstanding, and of the danger to Amy, his mind was made up instantly.

"Miss Goodrich," he said; "can you let me talk to you plainly?"

She nodded and grew quiet.

"I have known all along that these things would come out sooner or later. I have foreseen that the whole story must be told, and have prayed that the time might be put off until your life could give the lie to the thought that the past was not passed forever, and now I thank God that my prayers have been answered. No harm can come to you now for your Christianity is no vain trifle, but a living power that will help you to bear the reproach that must come. Had this happened before you were strong, it would have driven you back again. But now you can bear it. But Miss Goodrich—Amy—I don't want you to bear this alone. Won't you let me help you? You know that I love you. I have told you so a thousand times, though no word has been spoken. And I know that you return my love. I have seen it in your eyes, and I have waited and waited until the time should come for me to speak. That time is here now. Amy, dearest, tell me that you love me and will be my wife. Give me the right to protect you. Let us go to your father together and tell him all. He dare not refuse us then."

The beautiful girl trembled with emotion. "You must not. Oh, you must not," she said. "Don't, don't tempt me." She buried her face in her hands again. "You—you cannot take for your wife one who has been what I have."

"Amy dear, listen," said Dick. "You and I are Christians. We each have fallen; but Christ has forgiven and accepted both. God has only one love for each, one Saviour for each, one forgiveness for each. There is only one promise, one help, one Heaven for us both. Darling, don't you see that we are equal? I cannot reproach you for your past, because I too, have been guilty. You, in your heart of hearts, must recognize this great truth. Won't you forget it all with me?"

The girl lifted her face and looked into his eyes long and searchingly, as though reading his very soul.

Had there been anything but love in Dick Falkner's heart then, he would have argued in vain. But he returned the look unflinchingly, then—

"Amy listen. On the soul that has been pardoned in the name of Jesus Christ, there is no spot. Won't you put your past beneath your feet as I put mine in the dust, and come to me upon the common ground of Christ's love and forgiveness? Come, because we love each other, and for the good we can do."

The brown eyes filled with tears again; the sweet lips trembled, as holding out her hand she replied, "Oh Dick, I do love you. Help me to be strong and true and worthy of your love. I—I—have no one in all the world but you."

A few minutes later, Dick said, "I must take you home now."

"No, no," she answered, hurriedly; "the folks will think that I am calling on some of the neighbors, even if they miss me at all. I often run out of an evening that way. It is not late and I'm not afraid."

"Listen to me, dearest," he answered. "You must not see your father alone until I have told him everything. I will go up to the house with you now, and we will settle this matter once for—" A loud knock at the door interrupted him. Amy trembled in alarm. "Don't be frightened dear. No harm can come to you from this visit now. Thank God you have given me the right to speak for you."

The knock was repeated. "Step in here," he said, leading her to a chair in the next room, "and be a brave girl now. It's just some fellow on business. He'll be gone in a moment." And leaving her with the door partly closed, he stepped across the room just as the knock came the third time.

Dick threw open the door, and without waiting for an invitation, Adam Goodrich stepped across the threshold. To say that Dick was astonished but faintly expressed his feelings, though not a muscle of his face quivered, as he said:

"Good evening, sir, what can I do for you?"

"You can do a good deal," said Adam. "But first lock that door; we want no visitors here to-night."

Without a word, Dick turned the key again.

"Now sir, I want to know first, is it true that you were with my daughter in the Ozark Mountains this summer? Don't try to lie to me this time. I'll have the truth or kill you."

"I have never lied to you, sir," answered Dick; "and have no desire to do so now. It is perfectly true I did meet you daughter last summer while on my vacation."

"I knew I was right," raved Adam. "I knew you led her away from home. Oh, why did you ever come to this city? Why did I ever see you? Here." And he frantically tore a check-book from his pocket. "Fill this out for any amount you choose and go away again. Oh, I could kill you if I dared. You have ruined me forever—you—"

"Stop sir," said Dick; and when Adam looked into his face, he saw again that nameless something which compelled him to obey.

"You have said quite enough," continued Dick, calmly, "and you are going to listen to me now. But first, I want to beg your pardon for the language I used when you called on me before." —He heard a slight rustle in the next room—"when you accused me of taking your daughter from her home; I told you that you were a liar. I beg your pardon now. I was excited. I know that you were only mistaken. You would not have listened to me then, nor believed me, had I told you what I knew. But the time has come when you *shall* listen, and be forced to know that I speak the truth."

Adam sat as though fascinated. Once he attempted to answer, but a quick "Silence, sir, you *shall* hear me," kept him still, while Dick detailed the whole story, omitting nothing from the evening when he had rescued Amy from her drunken escort, to the day he had said good-bye in the Ozark Mountains. When he had finished, the old gentleman sat silent for a moment.

"Can it be possible," thought Dick, "that I have misjudged this man, and that he is grateful for the help that I have given Amy?"

But no; Dick had not misjudged him. There was not a thought of gratitude in Adam Goodrich's heart. Thankfulness for his daughter's salvation from a life of sin had no part in his feelings; only blind rage, that his pride should be so humbled. Leaping to his feet, he shouted, "The proof, you miserable scoundrel; the proof, or I'll have your life for this."

Dick remained perfectly calm. "You shall have the proof," he said, quietly, and turning, stepped to the next room, coming back an instant later with his arm encircling Amy's waist.

Adam sprang forward. "You here at this hour alone? Go home at once. Drop her, you ruffian," turning to Dick.

The latter stood without moving a muscle, and Goodrich started toward him.

"Stop," said Dick, still without moving; and again the older man was forced to obey that stronger will.

"Father," said Amy. "I am going to marry Mr. Falkner. I heard you and Frank talking in the library, and when you said that you would kill him I came to warn him, and—and—his story is every word true. Oh papa, don't you see what a friend he has been to me? You forced me to the society that ruined me, and he saved me from an awful life. I love him and will be his wife, but I can't be happy as I ought, without your forgiveness. Won't you forgive us papa?"

Never in his life had it been Dick's lot to see a face express so much, or so many conflicting emotions, love, hate, pride, passion, remorse, gratitude, all followed each other in quick succession. But finally, pride and anger triumphed and the answer came; but in the expression of the man's face rather than in his words, Dick found the clue to his course.

"You are no longer a daughter of mine," said Adam. "I disown you. If you marry that man who came to this town a common tramp, I will never recognize you again. You have disgraced me. You have dragged my honor in the dust." He turned toward the door. But again Dick's voice, clear and cold, forced him to stop. "Sir," he said; "Before God, you and not this poor child, are to blame. By your teaching, you crippled her character and made it too weak to stand temptation, and then drove her from home by your brutal unbelief."

Adam hung his head for a moment, then raised it haughtily. "Are you through?" he said with a sneer.

"Not quite," answered Dick. "Listen; you value most of all in this world, pride and your family position. Can't you see that by the course you are taking, you yourself proclaim your disgrace, and forfeit your place in society. No one now but we three, knows the story I have just related to you; but if you persist in this course the whole world will know it."

He paused, and Adam's face changed; for while his nature could not forgive, pity, or feel gratitude, such reasoning as this forced its way upon his mind, a mind ever ready to cheat the opinions of men. "What would you suggest?" he asked coldly.

"Simply this," answered Dick. "Do you and Amy go home together. No one shall ever know of this incident. Live your life as usual, except that you shall permit me to call at the house occasionally. Gradually the people will become accustomed to my visits, and when the time comes, the marriage will not be thought so strange. But remember, this woman is to be my wife, and you shall answer to me if you make her life hard."

"Very well," answered Adam, after a moment's pause; "I can only submit. I will do anything rather than have this awful disgrace made public. But understand me sir; while you may come to the house occasionally, and while you force me to consent to this marriage by the story of my daughter's disgrace, I do not accept you as my son, or receive the girl as my daughter; for my honor's sake, I will appear to do both, but I shall not forget; and now come home."

"Good-night, dearest, be brave," whispered Dick. And then as he unlocked and opened the door, he could not forbear smiling at Adam and wishing him a good-night, with pleasant dreams.

CHAPTER XXVIII

Mother Gray and her husband were sitting before a cheery fire in their little parlor, at the Institution for Helping the Unemployed. The cold November rain without came beating against the window panes in heavy gusts, and the wind sighed and moaned about the corners of the house and down the chimney.

"Winter's coming, wife," said Mr. Gray, as he aroused himself and stirred the fire. "We'll not be having such an easy time as we did this summer. When cold weather gets here in earnest the poor will begin calling on us."

"Yes, but that's the time people need kindling wood the worst, so there will be enough to feed them," answered the good wife brightly, as she too aroused and began knitting with great vigor.

"I fear we are going to have a hard winter this year, mother; my old bones begin to complain a little now; but thank God, we're sure of a comfortable home and enough to eat. What we'd a done without this place is more than I know, with Joe away and me not able to do heavy work in the mines. If Maggie were only with us." And the old man wiped a tear from his eyes.

"Yes, father, but Maggie is better off than we. It's Joe that hurts my heart. To think that he may be hungry and cold like some of the poor fellows we fed here last spring. Hark. Isn't that someone knocking at the door?" She dropped her knitting to listen.

The old man arose and stepped into the next apartment, which was used as a kind of reception hall and office. A faint rapping sounded more clearly from there; and crossing the room, he opened the door, and in the light streaming out, saw a woman. "Come in," he cried, reaching forth and taking her by the arm. "Come in out of the rain. Why, you're soaked through."

"Oh please sir, can I stay here all night? They told me this was a place for people to stop. I'm so hungry and tired."

And indeed she looked it, poor thing. Her dress, though of good material and nicely made, was soiled with mud and rain. Beneath the sailor hat, from which the water ran in sparkling drops, her hair hung wet and disheveled;

her eyes were wild and pleading; her cheeks sunken and ashy pale; while the delicately turned nostrils and finely curved, trembling lips, were blue with cold. Beyond all doubt, she had once been beautiful.

Mr. Gray, old in experience, noted more than all this, as he said, "We are not allowed to keep women here, but it's a little different in your case, and I'll see my wife. Sit down and wait a minute."

He gave her a chair and went back to the sitting-room, returning a moment later with Mother Gray at his heels.

"My poor dear," said the good woman, "of course you must stay here. I know, I know," as the girl looked at her in a questioning manner. "Anyone can see your condition; but bless your heart, our Master befriended a poor woman, and why should not we?"

And soon the girl was in the other room and Mrs. Gray was removing her hat and loosening her clothing.

"Father," whispered the old lady, "I think you had better go for Dr. Jordan. He'll be needed here before morning."

When the doctor returned with Mr. Gray, the patient, dry and clean, was wrapped in the soft blankets of Mother Gray's own bed, with one of Maggie's old night-dresses on, and hot bricks at her tired feet. But warmth and kindness had come too late. The long, weary tramp about the streets of the city, in the rain; the friendless shutting of doors in her face; the consciousness that she was a mark for all eyes; and the horror of what was to come, with the cold and hunger, had done their work. When the morning sun, which has chased away the storm clouds, peeped in at the little chamber window, Dr. Jordan straightened up with a long breath, "She will suffer no more pain now, mother, until the end."

"And when will that be, Doctor?"

"In a few hours, at most; I cannot tell exactly."

"And there is no hope?" asked Mrs. Gray, smoothing the marble brow on the pillow, as she would have touched her Maggie.

"Absolutely no hope, Mother," said the physician, who knew her well.

"Ah well, tis better so," murmured the old lady. "This world is not the place for such as she. Christ may forgive, but men won't. The man alone can go free. And the little one too—surely God is good to take them both together. Will she come to, do you think, Doctor, before she goes?"

"Yes, it is probable that she will rally for a little while, and you may find out her name perhaps. There was no mark on her clothing, you say?"

"Not the sign of a mark, and she would tell me nothing; and see, there is no wedding ring."

They were silent for some time, and then: "She is awakening," said the doctor.

The blue eyes opened slowly and looked wonderingly about the room. "Mother," she said, in a weak voice, "Mother—who are you?—" looking at the doctor and Mrs. Gray. "Where am I?" and she tried to raise her head.

"There, there, dear; lie still now and rest. You have been sick you know. We are your friends and this is the doctor. Your mother shall come when you tell us where to send for her."

The poor creature looked for a full minute into the kind old face above her, and then slowly the look of wonder in her eyes gave place to one of firmness, pain and sorrow, and the lips closed tightly, as though in fear that her secret would get out.

"Oh honey, don't look like that, don't. Tell us who you are. Have you no mother? I know you have. Let us send for her at once, that she may come to you."

The lips parted in a sweet, sad smile. "I'm going to die then? You would not look so if I were not. Oh, I am so glad, so glad." And in a moment she was sleeping like a child.

"Poor girl," muttered Doctor Jordan, wiping his own eyes. Very sharp professional eyes they were too. "I fear you will have to take her mother's place. I must go now, but I will look in again during the day. Don't have any false hopes; there is nothing to be done, save to make the end easy."

For an hour the stranger slept, with a smile on her lips; and then opened her eyes again. But there was no pain, no fear in them now; only just a shadow of trouble, as she asked in a whisper, "Where is it?"

The woman, with one hand smoothed back the hair from the forehead of her patient, and with the other pointed upward; the troubled shadow passed from the eyes of the young mother, and she slept again. Later in the day, the doctor called, and once more she awoke.

"I thank you, doctor," she said, in a weak voice; but shook her head when he offered her medicine.

"But, dear child, it is only to relieve you from any pain."

She answered, "you said I must go; let me go as I am. Oh, this world is cold and harsh. God knows that I do not fear to die. Christ, who welcomed little children, has my babe, and he knows that in my heart I am innocent."

"But won't you tell us of your friends?"

"No, no," she whispered. "I have no friends but you and God; and I have doubted even his love until you told me that he would take me."

Nor could any argument prevail upon her to change her mind; her only answer was a shake of the head.

That evening, just after dusk, she whispered to her kind nurse, who sat by the bedside, "Won't you tell me your name, please?"

"They call me Mother Gray."

"And may I call you that too?"

"Yes honey, of course you may," answered the old woman. "Of course you may."

"And why do you cry, mother?" as the tears rolled down the wrinkled face. "Are you not glad that God is good to me? Oh, I forgot, you are afraid for me. You don't understand." And she turned her face away.

"Is there anything I can do for you, dear? Brother Cameron is coming to see you just as soon as he gets home. Would you like to talk to him?"

"Brother Cameron—Brother Cameron—I have no brother," she answered, turning to Mother Gray again. "Who is he?"

"Brother Cameron is our pastor; a minister you know."

The lips parted in a scornful smile, and the eyes flashed with a spark of fire that must have once been in them. "Oh, a church member; no, I beg of you, don't let him come here; I want nothing to do with him."

"But, my dear, he is a good man."

"Yes I know," said the girl. "I have met these good church people before."

"But honey, I'm a church member."

"You are a *Christian*, mother; I love Christ and his people; but a man can't prove himself a Christian simply by being a church member. But I am tired. Forgive me if I pain you, mother, but I cannot see the minister. He is a good man, a Christian perhaps, but he can do me no good now; and I would rather die alone with you. The church has driven me from its doors so many, many times. It was always so cold and unfeeling. They bestow their pity on the dead bodies of people, and by their manner, freeze the souls of men."

Exhausted with the effort of so long a speech, she dropped into a stupor again.

Later, after Rev. Cameron had come and gone without seeing her, she suddenly opened her eyes and whispered, "mother, I have been thinking; would you be happier in knowing that I'm not afraid to die?"

The good old woman tightened her grasp on the white hand she held, and made no other answer but to bow her gray head and press her lips to the forehead of the girl.

"I know you would; and I'll tell you."

"I lived—" She was interrupted by a low knock at the door and a sweet voice calling gently: "May I come in, Mother Gray?"

It was Amy, who had come at Cameron's request.

The sufferer half rose in her bed. "Who is it?" she gasped. "I—I—know that voice."

"There, there, dearie," returned the nurse, gently pushing her back on the pillows. "There, there, lie down again; it's only Miss Amy."

"Yes, come in," she called; and Miss Goodrich softly pushed open the door and entered.

"I thought perhaps I could help you, Mother Gray," she said, as she removed her hat and arranged a beautiful bunch of flowers on a little stand in the center of the room. Then turning to the sufferer, she was about to speak again when she paused and her face grew as white as the colorless face upon the pillow.

The wide eyes of the dying girl stared back at her in doubting wonder, while the trembling lips tried to whisper her name.

The next instant, Amy had thrown herself on her knees, her arms about the wasted form upon the bed. "Oh Kate; Kate;" she cried. "How did this happen? How came you here?"

It was Kate Cushman, from Oak Springs Farm.

Mother Gray quickly recovered from her surprise, and with the instinct of a true nurse, calmed Amy and soothed the patient.

"There, there, my dears," she said. "God is good—God is good. Let us thank Him that He has brought you together. You must be brave and strong, Miss Amy. This poor dear needs our help. Yes, yes, dear, be brave and strong."

Amy controlled herself with an effort, and rising from her knees, sat down on the edge of the bed, still holding Kate's hand, while she assisted Mother Gray to soothe her.

When she grew more quiet, Amy said, "We must send for your father and mother at once; they can—"

"No, no, you must not—you shall not—they do not know—in mercy, don't tell them—it would kill them. Promise; oh promise me you will never tell them how I died. In pity for them, promise me."

Mother Gray bowed her gray head, while the tears streamed down her wrinkled cheeks. "Yes, yes, dearie, we'll promise. It's better that they do not know until it's all over; and they need never know all." And whispering to Amy, she added, "The poor child can't last but a little longer."

Reassured, the sufferer sank back again with a long sigh, and closed her eyes wearily, but a moment later, opened them once more to look at Amy.

"I'm so glad you're here," she said feebly; "but I can't bear to have you think that I am all bad." And then in whispered, halting words, with many a break and pause, she told her story; a story all too common. And Amy, listening with white horror-stricken face, guessed that which Mother Gray could not know, and which the sufferer tried to conceal, the name of her betrayer.

"And so we were married in secret, or I thought we were," she concluded. "I know now that it was only a farce. He came to visit me twice after the sham ceremony that betrayed me, and I never saw him again until last night. Oh God, forgive him; forgive him, I—I loved him so."

The poor wronged creature burst into a fit of passionate sobbing that could not be controlled. In vain did Mother Gray try to soothe her. It was of no use. Until at last, exhausted, she sank again into a stupor, from which she roused only once near morning, and then she whispered simply, "Good-bye Mother; Goodbye Miss Amy. Don't let father know." And just as the day dawned in all its glory, her soul, pure and unstained as that of her babe, took its flight, and the smile of innocent girlhood was upon her lips.

When Amy reached home early in the forenoon, she met her brother in the hallway, just going out.

"You look like you'd been making a night of it," he said, with a contemptuous sneer. "Been consoling some wanderer I suppose."

The young woman made no reply, but stood with her back to the door, her eyes fixed on his face.

"Well, get out of my way," he said roughly; "can't you see I want to go out?"

Amy spoke—"I have been at the Institution all night. Kate Cushman and the baby are both dead. Go look at your work."

Frank started as though she had struck him; and then as she stepped aside, he fairly ran from the house as though in fear of his life.

CHAPTER XXIX

In the little country village of Anderson, where the southern branch of the "Memphis" joins the main line, a group of excited citizens were standing in front of the doctor's office. "You're right sure it's small-pox, are you, Doc?"

"There's no doubt of it," answered the physician.

"Who is he?"

"He won't tell his name, but Jack Lane says it's Frank Goodrich. He came in day before yesterday on the 'Memphis,' from Boyd City, where they have just lost a case or two of the worst form."

An angry murmur arose from the little group of men. "What you goin' to do, Doc?" asked the spokesman.

"I've sent to Pleasantville for that nigger who has had the disease, and he'll be in as soon as he can get here. We must find some place out of town for the fellow to stay, and let old Jake take care of him."

Jim Boles spoke up. "Thar's a cabin on my west forty, that's in purty good shape. A couple of us could fix her up in an hour or two; it's way back from the road, a good bit over a mile I reckon—in heavy timber too."

"I know the place," said another. "We run a fox past there last winter, and found him denned in that ledge of rocks 'bout half a quarter on yon side."

"That's it," said another. "It's sure out of the way all right."

"Well," said the doctor, "three or four of you go over there and fix up the cabin as comfortable as possible, and I'll have the negro take him out as soon as he comes."

The cabin, which was built by some early settler, had long ago been abandoned, and was partly fallen into decay. Tall weeds grew up through the ruins where the pole stable had stood; the roof and one side of the smokehouse had fallen in; and the chinking had crumbled from between the logs of the house; while the yard was overgrown with brush and a tangle of last season's dead grass and leaves, now wet and sodden with the late heavy rain. Deep timber hid the place from view, and a hundred yards in front of the hovel a spring bubbled from beneath a ledge of rock, sending a tiny stream trickling away through the forest.

Jim Boles and his helpers had just finished patching up the cabin roof and floor, after first building a huge fire in the long unused fireplace, when they heard the rattle of a wagon, and between the trees, caught a glimpse of a scrawny old horse, harnessed with bits of strap and string, to a rickety wagon, that seemed about to fall to pieces at every turn of the wheel. Upon the board, used for a seat, sat an old negro, urging his steed through the patches of light and shadow with many a jerk of the rope lines, accompanied by an occasional whack from the long slender pole. Behind the negro was a long object wrapped in blankets and comforters.

"Hullo!" shouted the colored man, catching sight of the cabin and the men. "Am dis yar de horspital fer de small-pox diseases? Dey dun tol' me ter foller de road; but fo' Gawd, all de's yar roads look erlike ter me in dis yer place. Nevah seed sich er lonsom ol' hole in all ma' bo'n days. Reckon dars any hants in dat air ol' shack?"

"No, this cabin is all right," shouted one of the men; "but you stay where you are till we get away." And they began gathering up their tools and garments.

"All right, sah; all right, sah," grinned the negro. "You'uns jes clar out ob de way fer de amblance am er comin'. We dun got de right ob way dis trip, shor'."

And so Frank Goodrich was established in the old log house, with the colored man to nurse him. A place was fixed upon where the doctor and citizens would leave such things as were needed, and Jake could go and get them.

Three days passed, and then by bribes and threats and prayers, Frank persuaded the negro to walk to Pleasantville in the night and post a letter to Rev. Cameron, begging the minister to come to him, telling him only that he was in trouble and warning him to keep his journey secret.

What fiend prompted young Goodrich to take such a course cannot be imagined. But let us, in charity, try to think that he was driven to it by the fright and horrors of his condition.

Mrs. Cameron was away in the far east visiting her parents, and when the minister received the letter, he made hurried preparations, and telling Dick that he might be gone several days, left the city that evening. At a little way-station named in the letter, he found the negro, with his poor old horse and rickety wagon waiting him.

"Is you de parson?" asked the colored man.

"Yes, I am a minister," Cameron answered, wondering much at the appearance of the darkey and his strange turn-out. And as he climbed up to the board seat, he questioned his guide rather sharply, but the only answer he could get was: "Mistah Goodrich dun tol' me ter hol' ma tongue er he'd hant me, an' I'm shor goin' t' do hit. Golly, dis yere chile don't want no ghostes chasin' ob him 'roun'. No sah. I'se done fotch yo' t' Mistah Goodrich en he kin tell yo' what he's er mind ter."

Needless to say, all this did not add to Cameron's peace of mind, and the moments seemed hours as the poor old horse stumbled on through the darkness of the night. At last they entered the timber, and how the negro ever guided his crippled steed past the trees and fallen logs and rocks was a mystery; but he did; and at last they saw the light of the cabin.

"Dar's de place, sah. Dis yere's de horspital. We dun got yere at las'." And the colored Jehu brought the horse to a stand-still near the tumbled down smoke-house.

"Go right in, s'ah; go right in. Nobody dar but Mistah Goodrich. I put eway ol' Mose." And he began fumbling at the ropes and strings that made the harness.

Cameron, burning with impatience and curiosity, stepped to the door of the cabin and pushed it open. By the dim light of a dirty kerosene lantern, he could see nothing at first; but a moaning voice from one end of the room, drew his attention in the right direction. "Is that you, Brother Cameron?"

He stepped to the side of the cot. "Why Frank, what are you doing here; and what is the matter?"

"I'm sick," answered the young man, in a feeble voice. "I wanted to see you so bad. I'm awful glad you came."

"But why are you here in this miserable place? I do not understand."

"Small-pox," muttered the sick man. "Folks in town are afraid. The nigger takes care of me. He has had it."

The minister involuntarily started back.

"Oh Brother Cameron, don't leave me here alone," cried Frank. "I can't die like this."

For one brief moment Cameron trembled. He saw his danger and the trap into which he had fallen. He thought of his work and of his wife, and took one step toward the door; then stopped.

"Oh, I can't die alone," said the voice again.

Then with a prayer to his God for help, the minister made up his mind.

"Why of course I'll not leave you, Frank," he said cheerily, resuming his seat. "You know that surely."

And so this man of God wrote his friends in the city that he would be detained a few days, and stayed by the side of the wretched sufferer in the old cabin in the lonely woods.

The disease was not slow in its work, and before many hours had passed, it was clear to Cameron that the end was approaching. Frank also realized that death was not far distant, and his awful fear was pitiful.

"Brother Cameron," he whispered hoarsely, as he held his pastor's hand, while the old negro crouched by the fireplace smoking his cob pipe. "I must tell you—I've lived an awful life—people think that I'm a Christian—but I've lived a lie—"

Then with a look that made Cameron shudder, and in a voice strong with terror, he screamed, "O God, I shall go to Hell. I shall go to Hell. Save me, Brother Cameron, save me. I always said that you were a good fellow. Why do you let me die here like a dog? Don't you know that I want to live? Here you cursed nigger, go fetch a doctor. I'll haunt you if you don't. Do as I say."

The colored man chattering in fright, dropped his pipe in the ashes, and half rose as though to leave the room, but sank back again with his eyes fixed on Rev. Cameron, who was bending forward, his hand on the forehead of the dying man.

"God knows all, Frank," said the minister.

"Yes," muttered the other, "God knows all—all—all." Then in a scream of anguish again, "He has been watching me all the time. He has seen me everywhere I went. He is here now. Look! don't you see his eyes? Look! Brother Cameron; look you nigger!—Look there—" He pointed to one corner of the cabin. "Oh, see those awful eyes, watching—watching—I have fooled men but I couldn't fool God. *Don't. Don't.*—Oh, Christ, I want to live. Save me—save me—" And he prayed and plead for Jesus to heal him. "You know you could if you wanted to," he shouted, profanely; as though the Saviour of men was present in the flesh. Then to Cameron again, "I must get out of here. Don't you hear them coming? Let me go I say," as the minister held him back on the bed. "Let me go. Don't you know that I can't look God in the face? I tell you, I'm afraid."

For a moment he struggled feebly and then sank back exhausted; but soon began to talk again; and the minister heard with horror the dark secrets of his life.

Suddenly he ceased muttering, and with wide-open eyes, stared into the darkness. "Look there, Brother Cameron," he cried, hoarse with emotion. "Amy; don't you see her? She disgraced the family you know; ran away with that low-down printer. But see! Look! Who is that with her? Oh God, it's Kate—Kate—Yes, Kate, I'll marry you. It can't be wrong, you know, for you love me. Only we must not marry now for father would—Look Cameron—" His voice rose in a scream of fear. "She's got smallpox. Drive her out, you nigger; take her away to that cabin in the woods where you kept me. Sh'— Don't tell anyone, Cameron, but she wants me to go with her. She's come to get me. And there's—there's—My God, look—Yes—Yes—Kate, I'm coming—" And he sank back on the bed again.

The negro was on his knees trying to mumble a prayer, while the minister sat with bowed head. The lantern cast flickering shadows in the corners of the room, and the firelight danced and fell. A water bug crawled over the floor; a spider dropped from the rude rafters; and from without came the sound of the wind among the bare branches of the trees, and the old horse feeding on the dead grass and mouldy leaves about the cabin.

Suddenly the sick man spoke once more. "No sir, I will never disgrace you. I am as proud of our family as yourself. I am—home—day—" The sentence trailed off into a few unintelligible words in which only "Mother" and "Amy" could be distinguished. And then, with a last look about the cabin, from eyes in which anguish and awful fear was pictured, he gasped and was gone.

The next day, the old negro dug a grave not far from the house, and at evening, when the sun was casting the last long shadows through the trees, the colored man and the minister lowered the body of the rich man's son, with the help of the rope lines from the old harness, to its last resting place.

A few moments later, the darkey came around to the front of the house.

"Ready to go, sah?"

"Go where?" asked Cameron.

"Why, go home ob course. I reckoned you'd be mighty glad ter get away from dis yer place."

"I'm not going anywhere," the minister answered. "You may unhitch the horse again."

The old man did as he was told; then scratching his woolly head, said to himself, "I golly. Neber thought ob dat. I'll sure hab ter take care ob him next."

In the days which followed, Cameron wrote long letters to his wife, preparing her, with many loving words, for what was, in all probability, sure to come before she could reach home again. He also prepared an article for the Whistler, telling of Frank's death, but omitting all that would tend to injure the young man's character. To Adam Goodrich only, he wrote the awful truth. Other letters containing requests in regard to his business affairs, he addressed to Dick Falkner and Uncle Bobbie Wicks, and one to the President of the Association, in which he made several recommendations in regard to the work. All of these, except the one to his wife, he placed in the hands of the negro to be mailed after his death, if such should be the end.

Then when the symptoms of the dread disease appeared, he calmly and coolly began his fight for life. But his efforts were of no avail; and one night, just before the break of day, he called the old colored man to his bedside and whispered, with a smile, "It's almost over, Uncle Jake; my Master bids me come up higher. Good-bye; you have been very kind to me, and the good Father will not forget you." And so talking calmly of the Master's goodness and love, he fell asleep, and the old negro sat with a look of awe and reverence on his dusky face, as the glorious sunlight filled the cabin and the chorus of the birds greeted the coming of the day.

Much that passed in the weeks following, cannot be written here. Mrs. Cameron's grief and anguish were too keen, too sacred, to be rendered in unsympathetic print. But sustained by that power which had ennobled the life of her husband, and kept by the promises of the faith that had strengthened him, she went on doing her part in the Master's work, waiting in loving patience the call that would unite them again.

A month after the news of Cameron's death reached Boyd City, the president of the Association called on Dick and spent an hour with him talking of the work. Before leaving, he said: "Mr. Falkner, in Rev. Cameron's letter to me, he strongly recommended that you be called to take the place left vacant as director of the Association. With your consent, I will announce that recommendation at our next meeting. But first, I would like to know what answer you would give."

Dick asked for a week to think over the matter, which was granted. And during that time he consulted Elder Wicks.

Uncle Bobbie only said, as he grasped his young friend by the hand, "Behold, I have set before you an open door." And Dick bowed his head in silent assent.

The same day, late in the afternoon, George Udell was bending over some work that he was obliged to finish before going home. His helper had gone to supper, and the boy, a new one in the office, was cleaning up preparatory to closing for the night. "Don't clean that press, Jim," said the printer, suddenly.

"What's the matter; don't you know that it's time to quit?" asked the tired youngster, a note of anxiety in his voice.

"You can quit," replied George, "but I am going to run off some of this stuff before I go." And he proceeded to lock up the form.

With a look of supreme disgust on his ink-stained countenance, the other removed his apron and vanished, as though fearing his employer might change his mind. At the foot of the stairs, the apprentice met Clara Wilson. "He's up there," he said with a grin, and hurried on out of the building, while the young lady passed slowly to the upper floor. The stamping of the press filled the room, and the printer, his eyes on his work, did not hear the door close behind the girl; and only when she stood at his elbow did he look up. The machine made three impressions on one sheet before he came to his senses; then he turned to the young lady inquiringly.

"I—I—thought I'd stop and ask you to come over to the house this evening; Mother wants to see you."

"Hum—m—m, anything important?" asked George, leaning against the press. "You see I'm pretty busy now." He shut off the power and stepped across the room as the phone rang. "Hello—Yes, this is Udell's—I'm sorry, but it will be impossible—We close at six you know. Come over first thing in the morning—Can't do it; it's past six now, and I have an important engagement to-night. All right. Good-bye."

"Oh, if you have an engagement I will go," said Clara, moving toward the door.

"You needn't be in a hurry," said George, with one of his queer smiles. "My engagement has been put off so many times it won't hurt to delay it a few minutes longer. And besides," he added, "the other party has done all the putting off so far, and I rather enjoy the novelty."

The young lady blushed and hung her head, and then—but there—what right have we to look? It is enough for us to know that Udell's engagement was put off no longer, and that he spent the evening at the Wilson home, where the heart of Clara's mother was made glad by the announcement she had long wished to hear.

"Law sakes," snapped the old lady; "I do hope you'll be happy. Goodness knows you ought to be; you've waited long enough." And for just that once, all parties interested were agreed.

Charlie Bowen is in an eastern college fitting himself for the ministry. His expenses are paid by Mr. Wicks. "To-be-sure," said Uncle Bobbie, "I reckon a feller might as well invest in young men as any other kind o' stock, an' the church needs preachers who know a little about the business of this world, as well as the world what's comin'. I don't know how my business will get along without the boy though, but I reckon if we look after Christ's interests he won't let us go broke. To-be-sure, college only puts the trimmins' on, but if you've got a Christian business man, what's all *man* to begin with, they sure do put him in shape; an' I reckon the best 'aint none too good for God. But after all, it's mighty comfortin' for such old, uneducated sticks as me to know that 'taint the trimmings the good Father looks at. Ye can't tell a preacher by the long words in his sermon, no more 'n you can tell a church by the length of its steeple."

Five years later, two traveling men, aboard the incoming "Frisco" passenger, were discussing the business outlook, when one pointed out of the window to the smoke-shrouded city. "That town is a wonder to me," he said.

"Why?" asked his fellow-drummer, who was making his first trip over that part of the road. "What's the matter with it? Isn't it a good business town?"

"Good business town," ejaculated the other, "I should say it was. There's not a better in this section of the country. But it's the change in the character of the place that gets me. Five years ago, there wasn't a tougher city in the whole west. Every other door on Broadway was a joint, and now—"

"Oh yes, I've heard that," interrupted the other, with a half sneer; "struck by a church revival or something, wasn't they? And built some sort of a Salvation Army Rescuing Home or Mission?"

"I'm not sure about the church revival," returned the other slowly, "though they do say there are more church members there now than in any other city of its size in the country. But I'm sure of one thing; they were struck by good, common-sense business Christianity. As for the Rescue Home, I suppose you can call it that if you want to; but it's the finest block in the business portion of the city; and almost every man you meet owns a share in it. But here we are; you can see for yourself; only take my advice, and if you want to do business in Boyd City, don't try to sneer at the churches, or laugh at their Association."

And indeed the traveling man might well wonder at the change a few years had brought to this city in the great coal fields of the middle west. In place of the saloons that once lined the east side of Broadway and the principal streets leading to it, there were substantial buildings and respectable business firms. The gambling dens and brothels had been forced to close their doors, and their occupants driven to seek other fields for their degrading profession. Cheap variety and vulgar burlesque troops had the city listed as no good, and passed it by, while the best of musicians and lecturers were always sure of crowded houses. The churches, of all denominations, had been forced to increase their seating capacity; and the attendance at High School and Business College had enlarged four-fold; the city streets and public buildings, the lawns and fences even, by their clean and well-kept appearance, showed an honest pride, and a purpose above mere existence. But a stranger would notice, first of all, the absence of loafers on the street corners, and the bright, interested expressions and manners of the young men whom he chanced to meet.

And does this all seem strange to you, reader, as to our friend, the traveling man? Believe me, there is no mystery about it. It is just the change that comes to the individual who applies Christ's teaching to his daily life. High purpose, noble activity, virtue, honesty and cleanliness. God has but one law for the corporation and the individual, and the teaching that will transform the life of a citizen will change the life of a city if only it be applied.

The reading-room and institution established by the young people of the Jerusalem Church had accomplished its mission, and was absorbed into the larger one established by the citizens, where boys and girls, men and women, could hear good music, uplifting talk, and helpful entertainment; where good citizenship, good health, good morals, were all taught in the name of Jesus. The institution was free in every department; visitors were restricted only by wholesome rules that in themselves were educational. Co-operating with the city officials, it separated the vicious from the unfortunate, and removed not only the influence of evil, but the last excuse for it, by making virtue a pleasure, and tempting the public to live wholesomely. And as the traveling man testified, it paid from a business standpoint; or as Uncle Bobbie Wicks tells his customers from other towns, "Folks come to Boyd City to live 'cause they 'aint 'fraid to have their boys 'n girls walk down the street alone." And after all, that's about the best recommendation a place can have. And perhaps the happiest couple in all that happy, prosperous city, as well as the best-loved of her citizens, is the young manager of the Association, Mr. Richard Falkner, and his beautiful wife, Amy.

But Dick will soon leave his present position to enter a field of wider usefulness at the National Capitol. For the people declared, at the last election, that their choice for representative was "That Printer of Udell's." And before they leave for their Washington home, Dick and Amy will pay still another visit to a lonely spot near the little village of Anderson. There, where the oaks and hickorys cast their flickering shadows on the fallen leaves and bushes, and the striped ground-squirrel has his home in the rocks; where the redbird whistles to his mate, and at night, the sly fox creeps forth to roam at will; where nature, with vine of the wild grape, has builded a fantastic arbor, and the atmosphere is sweet with woodland flowers and blossoms, not far from the ruins of an old cabin, they will kneel before two rough mounds of earth, each marked with a simple headstone, one bearing no inscription save the name and date; the other this: "Inasmuch as ye have done it unto one of the least of these, my brethren, ye have done it unto Me."